The Lost Promise of Ireland

BOOKS BY SUSANNE O'LEARY

The Road Trip

A Holiday to Remember

SANDY COVE SERIES

Secrets of Willow House

Sisters of Willow House

Dreams of Willow House

Daughters of Wild Rose Bay

Memories of Wild Rose Bay

Miracles in Wild Rose Bay

STARLIGHT COTTAGES SERIES

The Lost Girls of Ireland

The Lost Secret of Ireland

Susanne O'Leary

The Lost Promise of Ireland

bookouture

Published by Bookouture in 2021

An imprint of Storyfire Ltd.
Carmelite House
50 Victoria Embankment
London EC4Y 0DZ

www.bookouture.com

ISBN: 978-1-80314-038-4
eBook ISBN: 978-1-80314-037-7

For Denis

1

The ad popped up while Maggie was scrolling down on her Facebook page on her laptop. She was just idly looking for news and photos of her friends and acquaintances, while chewing on a piece of toast. It was a wet spring morning and she was sitting at the kitchen table about to leave for her job as PE teacher at a girls' school in Dublin, but was, as usual, lingering over her breakfast and her Facebook newsfeed to distract her from the dreary weather and the prospect of a long trip on a crowded bus.

She had been laughing at funny memes and scrolling almost absentmindedly when she saw it. It was a photo of a row of houses perched on a steep incline with stunning sea views. But it wasn't the cloudless sky or the azure sea that made her suddenly freeze, it was the houses and the surrounding landscape. She blinked and looked at it as the setting stirred something deep in her memory. Instead of scrolling past the photo, she enlarged it. Those cottages, that view... *Lovely cottage for rent in old coastguard station in County Kerry,* the ad said.

Maggie's hand stopped on the way to her mouth as she stared at the photo. Yes, it was the house all right: the cottage her family had owned, where they had spent all their summer holidays from when she was eight years old. Maggie remembered that moment when her parents told her they'd bought a holiday cottage at the seaside in Kerry. She had been so excited to spend a whole summer at the seaside with them, her two brothers and her sister. And what wonderful summers they had been.

Maggie looked fondly at the picture, remembering that back bedroom she had shared with her sister, Claire, going to sleep to the sound of the waves. The seagulls would wake her up with their screeching, and she'd jump out of bed looking forward to another fun day on the beach, or climbing the hills above the houses. And that gorgeous village with its tangle of colourful cottages and Victorian houses, the little shops, the ice cream bought in the newsagent's at the end of the main street.

Images went through Maggie's mind like a kaleidoscope: of the sky, the endless ocean, the beach balls and inflatable toys hanging outside the shop, her father carrying a bright green crocodile for them to ride on in the waves, collecting shells and sticking them onto matchboxes. Sausages and chips outside the Harbour Pub, the surf school at the beach and a whole gang of kids playing rounders on the green behind the big shed where they later, as teenagers, had danced at the improvised disco. Happy memories of idyllic summers as she grew up. Until that summer when she was eighteen, when they'd sold the cottage and had all grown up so suddenly.

Maggie stared out of the kitchen window for a moment, thinking about that last summer, the summer of her first real romance and the young man she had met that day on the train. He was American, with wild auburn hair. His bright green eyes betrayed his Irish roots, and she could see his smile in her mind as if she had seen it just yesterday – it was one she knew could break a thousand hearts.

Maggie sighed and was about to close her laptop, when

something occurred to her. That cottage was for rent. Maybe she could take it for the summer – or part of it anyway? She had no plans for the summer just yet and thought she might go to Scotland to stay with Claire and her family. But this... It would be a chance to get away, to have a holiday on her own terms and maybe invite a friend to stay. It would be incredible to go back there after all these years and connect again with the people she had known. The idea made her feel suddenly excited and ready to face the day. She quickly bookmarked the website and turned off her laptop. She'd look up the cottage again that evening.

She couldn't get the photo out of her head as she sat on the packed bus, staring out through the grimy window, the smell of wet wool in her nostrils. If only the rent for the summer wasn't too high, then she could spend the whole season there. It would be just what she needed.

The past year had been awful, trying to cope with the aftermath of her break-up with Dermot. It wasn't a divorce as they hadn't been married, but after twenty-two years together and two grown-up children, it had been a marriage in all but name. He had come home one evening a year ago, announcing that he was leaving her. He had fallen in love with someone else, he'd said. Someone who he had met at a conference. A woman half his age, Maggie had found out later. The shock and bewilderment had felt as if an earthquake had hit, turning her whole existence upside down. It had taken her the best part of a year to come to terms with what had happened.

And now, here she was, in her late forties, a single woman again, living alone after the children had left home. The house that had once felt so cramped was now like a huge mausoleum, where she spent her evenings watching TV or chatting to people she hardly knew online. Even though she was fit and healthy, and with her honey blonde hair and blue eyes, not bad-looking, she felt as if the opportunities for romance were limited. She hadn't felt like going out there into the dating jungle to find someone new to share her life with. The online dating sites her daughter suggested seemed too daunting to even consider. All she had left was a daily routine that was pleasant but increasingly dreary and monotone. Was this all life had to offer at her age? Was she doomed to spend the rest of her years alone? She needed a break and with the summer holidays looming, she knew she had to get away, go somewhere different where she could meet people in real life instead of on social media. But was going back to Sandy Cove after so many years the answer? Was there anyone there who would still remember her? Even if they didn't, was that little village still the friendly place she remembered?

Maggie cast her mind back to those days and all the friends she had made in her teenage years. She remembered a girl called Sorcha, with red hair and freckles who had been great fun. And Brian, who wanted to be a vet when he grew up; what had happened to him? And Maeve and Roisin, who used to spend their summer holidays at Willow House, where their aunt and uncle lived; did they still spend their summers there? Was Dr Pat still working as a GP, curing anything from a scraped knee to tonsillitis? Probably not – he had to be very old by now.

Maggie smiled to herself. The memories of those days were suddenly vivid as the bus stopped in front of the school. She was still smiling when she got off and walked into the schoolyard, deciding there and then that even if it cost an arm and a leg, she would go back to that house and spend the summer there. Even though it wouldn't be life-changing, it might take her down memory lane to places that were a lot happier than here. Why not take a break from her harsh reality? She had absolutely nothing to lose.

And who knows? Maggie thought. *I might create some brand-new happy memories. Going back there might help me go forward again.*

2

Maggie had never understood break-ups. She couldn't get her mind around how anyone can be so intimate with another person for years and then never want to be with them again. All those things couples created together, that everyday familiarity of knowing each other's favourite dish, what music they like, the memories, the cuddles, the personal, unique banter a couple share, all gone overnight. She didn't even understand how all those connections, the family life, the plans and holidays and being part of a gang of friends can all disappear the minute someone says they no longer want to be part of your life. How can anyone let go and leave all that behind and start anew with another person? All that always went through her mind when someone she knew broke up. But when it happened to her, she thought for an instant that it was a joke.

She stared at Dermot, her partner of two decades, as he stood before her in their living room, repeatedly pushing at his hair and looking awkward as he told her that he was leaving her, that there was someone else in his life, someone he had fallen in love with and wanted to be with from now on.

She let out a laugh and said she thought that a very lame

joke. But then the laugh had died on her lips as she noticed his expression and realised that it was true. His eyes were determined and he was sticking out his chin in that way he always did when he had made up his mind and nothing could dissuade him. She knew it would be useless to argue. He was really leaving her.

She stared at him, her body rigid, her hands frozen over the keyboard of her laptop, her mouth open as she tried to say something. 'What?' she finally whispered. 'You're... You... Why?'

'I'm sorry,' he said, rattling his keys in his pocket. 'I really am, Mags. I wish it hadn't happened, I wish I could have stopped myself – or her, but I couldn't.'

She kept staring at him, knowing she was as white as a sheet. She felt cold all over as she was hit by the shockwave of what he had just told her. 'When did it happen?' she asked. 'Who is she? Where are you going? Why are you doing this to me?' she ended in a near whisper.

'I...' he started. Then he sighed. 'Things haven't been the same since the kids left. You know that. It's as if we're not as close anymore, not as connected as we used to be. This house and our life have been feeling so dull and stifling for the past few years.'

'Oh,' she said, not knowing how to respond. But when she thought about it, she realised that there was something in what he said. When they had found themselves free to do what they wanted, they hadn't done things together but separately – Maggie taking up her dancing classes again and meetings with her book club and he with his male friends, going to rugby matches and catching up with them at the pub. But she didn't understand why that meant they had to break up. 'I had no idea you felt like that. Why didn't you say something?'

'I don't know. Didn't see the point,' he said with a shrug. 'I felt we were drifting apart in many ways. I thought you had noticed it too.'

'I did in a way. But I always felt we could be independent and do our own thing and then...' She paused. 'I know we should have tried to get more time together and talk more. But can't we talk about it now?' she tried, even though she knew it was all over. 'Maybe see if we can...'

'No,' he said, his voice dull and tired. 'It's too late. Maybe if I hadn't met Veronica, things would be different. But I did and she's made me feel... alive again.'

'Alive?' she said, her heart contracting. She couldn't believe he had fallen in love with someone else. Someone called Veronica. Him saying the name made it real and even more horrible. She was about to ask who this woman was, where he had met her and how long it had been going on, but he interrupted her.

'There's nothing more to say right now. I packed my bags this morning and now I'll pick them up and leave. We can sort out the rest later. The house is yours anyway, so you'll be fine.'

'Fine?' she said, giving up. 'Yeah, of course I will be. But what on earth am I going to tell the kids?'

'I'll tell them.'

'And then I get to pick up the pieces,' she said bitterly. 'They'll be very upset.'

'They'll cope, I'm sure.' He looked at her for a moment, still rattling his keys. 'I'll just get my bags.'

'How can you?' she asked, wanting to scream at him to stop rattling the keys. 'And now, when we've just lost Sally.'

'Sally was a *dog*, Maggie,' he said, looking exasperated. 'You'd think she was one of our children, the way you carried on.'

'She was part of the family,' Maggie said in a near sob. 'She was my best friend.'

'That's ridiculous.' He sighed. 'Oh, okay, I know you were very fond of her and I'm sorry. But that's beside the point.'

'The point being that you're leaving me?' she asked, as like a drowning woman, their life together flashed before her eyes, right from the moment they met at that party and she had fallen for his charm and his good looks. He said he had fallen for her gorgeous blue eyes and her sexy laugh. But those things had obviously faded for him. They had never married as neither of them had felt it necessary. They loved each other, wasn't that enough? But now love was no more, she realised, as he stood there, avoiding her eyes, trying to explain what had happened to him and how he hadn't been able to stop his feelings for that other woman.

'So that's it then?' she asked, her voice shaking. 'You're moving out right this minute?'

He nodded. 'I'm sure you don't want me around after what I just told you. We might as well tell the kids sooner rather than later so we don't have to lie to them. They're both away and doing their own thing anyway.'

That was true. Their son, Jim, was backpacking with his girlfriend during his gap year and their daughter, Orla, was doing an internship at the European Commission headquarters in Brussels. They kept in touch sporadically but both Jim and Orla were at that stage in their lives when parents aren't that relevant except if they needed money or a place to sleep.

But Maggie had thought that this was her and Dermot's time to do all the things they had planned. She had been happily looking up holiday deals for two people in Spain. But apparently, he had other ideas.

And then it really happened. Dermot moved out of the house that evening. He took on the task of telling their children by calling them, which resulted in a text message on Maggie's phone that said: *Such sad news for us all. Hope you're okay. Will phone soon, love, Jim.*

He phoned her early the following morning, his voice full of anger and disappointment, and Maggie did her best to soothe and explain, trying not to be too hostile against Dermot. She was full of sadness and hurt, but she didn't want Jim to start hating his father, which would poison their relationship for a long time. Dermot and his son were close and that was something she didn't want to ruin. She hung up, having managed to calm him somewhat, but the conversation had exhausted her so much she had to call in sick.

Then there was a phone call from a very upset Orla in Brussels late the following evening.

'Mam,' she said, her voice full of sorrow. 'This is so awful. Mostly for you, of course. How are you coping?'

'I'm okay,' Maggie lied, lying in bed. 'Sad, of course. But I'm coping. You don't have to worry about me. Of course, it was a shock,' she added, fighting to hold back the tears. 'I didn't see it coming, I truly didn't.' *Except*, she said to herself, *maybe I should have? Those evenings working late, the conferences, the long golf sessions...* Had they been all a lie? Had he been with *her* then, that woman he said he now loved? 'I was so stupid,' she said to Orla. 'I thought we were okay.' *Even if things were a little boring lately and Dermot was away so often*, she admitted to herself. 'But...' She paused, trying to think of a way to play down her grief. 'This is between us as a couple. If we're not happy together, the best thing is to separate. But we will still be a family.' She wondered how on earth that was going to work.

'Do you want me to come home?' Orla asked. 'I don't want you to be all alone in that big house.'

'No, please don't,' Maggie begged. 'You have to continue your internship. It was so hard to get and it will lead to a great career eventually. I'll be fine.'

'Yeah, but it's so hard for you right now.'

'It is but there isn't much you can do about it,' Maggie said and blew her nose. She pulled herself together. 'I don't want this to upset your life. You're doing so well and we're both so proud of you. And,' she continued, 'this should not affect your relationship with your father in any way. He loves you and you love him and that's all you should care about.'

'I don't love him very much right now,' Orla remarked.

'You will again in time,' Maggie said, even though Orla's words brought her a tiny bit of comfort. But Maggie meant what she had said. She didn't want the break-up between her and Dermot to ruin their children's relationship with their father. Even though it was hugely tempting to seek revenge by making them take sides, she knew that would cause a lot of misery later on. But she was sure of one thing. She was going to survive and show everyone, especially *him* that she could manage without him and maybe even be happy. One day. 'I'll be fine,' she said to Orla. 'Please don't worry about me.'

'But you're so sad,' Orla said. 'It breaks my heart. I could kill Dad for doing this to you.'

'So could I,' Maggie said. 'But as we can't kill him, we'll just have to accept it and go forward. At least that's what you should do. I have to go through the separation and division of our assets. Not that there's much to divide apart from the furniture and a few other bits.'

'The house belongs to you,' Orla said.

'Yes,' Maggie agreed, feeling a little brighter. The four-bedroom house in the leafy suburb in south Dublin was in her name as she had bought it with the inheritance from her uncle who had died childless and left everything to his four nieces and nephews. Maggie had immediately put an offer on the house that had just been built and they had moved in just after Jim was born, twenty years ago. 'Thank God for my family.'

'Tough luck on Dad,' Orla said cheerfully.

'Yes, though a lifetime of not paying a mortgage has left him in a solid position,' Maggie said with a weak smile. 'He'll be OK. I'm going to tell him to come around and get whatever he wants and pick it up when I'm not here. I'll go away somewhere for a while.'

'Come to Brussels,' Orla suggested. 'It's lovely here in the spring sunshine. Lots of things to see and do. Just for the May bank holiday weekend if nothing else.'

'That's a great idea,' Maggie agreed.

She had done what Orla suggested and gone to Brussels, staying in Orla's little apartment in the middle of town, where they had spent the weekend seeing the sights, eating mussels and fries and met all kinds of people from all over Europe. A fun-filled few days that had cheered Maggie up and further strengthened the bond with her kind, caring daughter. It had given her the strength to go back and deal with the separation and all the little details of ending twenty-two years of family life.

Breaking the news to her family had been the worst part, hearing her brothers and sister telling her what a snake Dermot was and how they had never really trusted him, and her mother sighing on the phone, saying, 'My poor Maggie, how terrible that you've been treated in this way.' On and on it went, her friends pitying her too. Some women had taken Dermot's side, though, and Maggie suspected that their husbands had pressured them into double dates with him and his new girlfriend.

It had all been so painful that Maggie hadn't had the strength to do all that moving on and going forward that she had promised Orla. Life had just continued, one dreary day replacing another, with not much to look forward to. A whole year had passed like this since that terrible day. But now, suddenly she had something to look forward to.

'The whole summer?' the man said on the phone the next day when Maggie called to book the cottage. He had a pleasant voice with an American accent and had introduced himself as Jason O'Callaghan.

'That's right,' Maggie replied, feeling a buzz of excitement. 'I'm a teacher and I have nearly three months off.'

'Of course,' he replied. 'I keep forgetting that Irish summer holidays start at the end of May.'

'That's right. Except if there are exams,' Maggie added. 'But I didn't sign up to help with exams this year so I could leave at the end of term.'

'Which is when?' he asked.

'Next week. So maybe I could start renting the cottage from the following Saturday?'

'Perfect,' he said. 'Do you know how to get here? I put directions and a map on my website, so it should be quite easy.'

Maggie laughed. 'I know the way very well. And I know the cottage too. My family used to own it, you see, way back in the 1980s. They sold it thirty years ago and I haven't been back since.'

'I see,' Jason said. 'Well, I'm sure you'll find it very different. All the houses in the row have been restored and updated. So now they're all very comfortable, you'll find.'

'Oh,' Maggie said, not knowing if this was a good thing or not. She had always felt that the primitive facilities in the cottage had been quite fun and part of living a kind of beachcomber lifestyle in the summertime. But maybe now that she was a little older, a proper bathroom and central heating might be better than lighting the solid fuel cooker in the kitchen every morning and putting up with a tiny shower room where they had to be careful not to use up all the hot water. 'That'll be quite different from what I remember.'

'I'm looking forward to hearing your stories of what it was like then,' Jason said. 'My wife and I live next door, in her cottage and the one you'll be renting is the one I own. We used to be neighbours and got married quite recently, you see.'

'Congratulations,' Maggie said, touched by the smile in his voice. Their love story sounded so romantic.

'Thank you. So it's all decided, then. Once you've transferred the first month's rent to my bank account I'll send you a confirmation email and text you the details for arrival. I can meet you next Saturday when you pick up the keys. Is that all right with you?'

'Perfect,' Maggie said. 'I'll do that straight away.'

They said goodbye and Maggie hung up with a huge smile. There. She had done it. The cottage was booked for the whole summer and she knew it had been a good decision. Three whole months in Kerry, longer than she had ever spent in that part of Ireland. She knew she couldn't go back in time to her childhood or youth, but it felt good to return to a place where she had been so happy. And where she had been so in love for the very first time in her life. It suddenly came back to her so clearly, that feeling of being completely besotted with someone that she forgot everything else, being sure this would change her life forever. So long ago, yet it seemed like only yesterday.

Where was he now, that young man who she had met on the train and spent the summer wandering on the beach with? Paul O'Sullivan... She remembered how they held hands, drew their names in the sand and promised each other to never forget one another and to meet again when they had both finished their studies. She remembered his sweet smile and his green eyes so full of hope and love as he told her how much she meant to him. They had exchanged addresses and written to each other all through the following autumn, talking about meeting again in the spring, but then, just after Christmas, the letters from America had stopped and Maggie had never found out why. She had tried to contact him without success. She had tried to forget about him and concentrated on her studies until she qualified as a PE teacher and got her first job. Then, a few years later, she had met Dermot. Life had continued and her love affair that last summer in Sandy Cove had become but a distant, sweet memory.

Maggie hadn't thought about it for a long time, but now it seemed suddenly so vivid and romantic, even if the memory of her lost love made her feel a little sad. But despite that, it would be wonderful to go back to that place where she had spent so many happy summer days. She would walk on that beach and look out at the ocean, thinking about Paul and how he had loved her and wanted to come back to continue their romance and maybe even make a permanent commitment. Now that Dermot had shown he no longer cared for her, it gave Maggie a tiny bit of comfort to know that once, someone had been in love with her in a very special way.

3

It took a little bit of organising before she could get away, but once Maggie had told her nearest and dearest that she would be spending the summer in Kerry, got her neighbour's teenage son to water her plants and mow the lawn while she was away, she was off. She loaded her car with two suitcases packed with clothes and books, her laptop and other essentials like hiking boots, wellies, a huge golf umbrella, a bodysurfing board, workout weights and a yoga mat, and she drove down the M50 and on to the motorway to the south, her car radio playing a lively Irish melody.

Driving along so happily, she suddenly realised that apart from that weekend in Brussels, she hadn't been out of Dublin for over a year. Dermot had never booked the three weeks in Spain that she had been looking into last year before he left her. And the summer immediately after the separation she had stayed at home, just going to the nearby beach when the weather was nice. And now, leaving for this long holiday felt like stepping out of a prison of loneliness and grief.

Maggie sang along with the cheery tune and pulled the scrunchie out of her hair, shaking it free, suddenly overcome with a feeling of joy and happy anticipation. This would be a summer of discovery, of new beginnings and memories of better days, those days when she had been so happy. How alive she had felt that summer when she was eighteen and so in love...

They had met on the Dublin to Killarney train. Maggie had been on her way to Sandy Cove and her family's holiday home, her mother meeting her at the station. As the train pulled out of Euston station, she had smiled at the young man sitting by the window and asked if the seat next to him was free. He'd nodded and moved his backpack out of the way and rose to help Maggie put her bag on the overhead rack. Then they'd sat down and shook hands, exchanging names. He'd introduced himself as Paul O'Sullivan – apparently, he was from New York and was going on a bike tour of Kerry, heading south to the Beara peninsula in County Cork where his ancestors were from.

'I'm an O'Sullivan Beare,' he said with a laugh. 'But I only just discovered that that has any meaning. It appears the O'Sullivan clan were important people there many years ago and they're still proud of it.'

'You're a Sullivan Beare?' Maggie asked, looking at his auburn hair, green eyes and face full of freckles. 'Well, you certainly look like one.'

'Do you know anything about them?' he asked.

'Not much,' she confessed. 'But we read about them in school. And I think there was a picture of Donal O'Sullivan Beare who had dark red hair like you. The Beara clan fought off the Spanish troops from the Armada or something...' She tried to remember more, but shook her head and laughed. 'Sorry. I mustn't have paid attention then. But you can look it up somewhere, I'm sure. Maybe at the library in Killarney, or at the museum on Beara itself.'

'I'm looking forward to that.' He fixed her with his eyes. 'So you're a Kerry woman, then, Maggie Ryan?'

'No. I'm from Dublin, but my family owns a holiday home

on the Ring of Kerry. In a little village near Waterville. We've spent every summer there since I was eight. I love it,' she said, feeling a dart of sadness as she remembered that the house was going to be sold very soon.

'I might make a detour on my way to Beara,' he said.

'You'll love it too,' she promised. 'It's a little bit in the back of beyond but that's what we love about it. Gorgeous, isolated beaches and mountains to climb if you're into hiking. I've just started learning to surf. It's great fun.'

'Sounds terrific,' he said.

Then, as the train wound its way through the rolling hills of the Midlands, they started to talk about their favourite things, music, movies, books and what they wanted to do in the future. Maggie, who had just spent a month at a ballet course in Dublin, told Paul about her interest in dance and exercise. 'I love dance but it's not a career I'd embark on,' she said, 'It's so hard to make a living, and even if you succeed you have to retire at around forty. Women dancers often do, anyway. So I have applied to a degree course in Physical Education and Biology at UCD. That's one of the main universities in Dublin,' she explained. 'I want to teach teenagers. I know from experience that dance and fitness can give you a lot of self-confidence.'

'You look barely out of your teens yourself,' he remarked.

'I'm nearly nineteen.'

'Which is why you're such a wise old woman,' he teased.

Maggie bristled. 'Well, I can relate to young girls very easily. All that angst about what you look like and if you're pretty enough, if you fit in, if you're one of the cool girls, is quite harrowing.'

'I think you're cool,' he said. 'And very pretty.'

'Thanks, but that's not what I was after,' Maggie said, feeling suddenly self-conscious. 'I was trying to explain what girls go through. I know how hard it is.'

'And how to deal with it?' he asked, looking genuinely interested.

'I think so. I was going through a bad patch when I was around fifteen. I tried too hard to be perfect. I tried all kinds of different diets that were incredibly hard to stick to. But then one of my friends developed an eating disorder and that made me realise what she and I were doing to ourselves. I turned to dance, which helped me a lot.'

'What happened to your friend?'

'She had to have counselling but she eventually recovered.'

'Must have been a good therapist.' He turned sideways to look at her. 'So you managed to pull yourself out of whatever you were going through by turning to dance?'

'I did,' Maggie replied. 'Not only ballet, but modern dance as well. And not to be a professional dancer, but because I love to move to music. And I took a good look at the cool girls and realised they weren't any better than anyone else. So I ignored them and did my own thing. My dance group were a lot more fun, anyway. Who cares about designer clothes and handbags and hanging around shopping malls ogling boys? It seemed so boring to me.'

'How did they take that, then? The fact that you ignored them and didn't join in?'

Maggie shrugged. 'No idea. In any case, this last year was the Leaving Cert year and we all had exams to study for. I shut myself away and studied like mad. I just had to get enough points for that degree course I want to do. But I won't find out if I got it until the end of the summer.'

'Leaving Cert?' he asked. 'Is that like high school exams?'

'I think it's the same.'

'I'm sure you did very well.'

'Hope so,' Maggie said. 'I took that ballet course just to switch off and do something fun. And now I'm looking forward to the rest of the summer in Kerry.'

'You must be very strong mentally,' he said with a touch of admiration. 'To do your own thing and not worry about peer pressure. I find this very interesting. I'm studying psychology at college, you see.'

'Oh,' Maggie said and started to laugh. 'So you were studying me with all your questions?'

He grinned. 'You were a great subject.'

'So you're going to be a psychologist?' Maggie asked, wondering what age he was. Probably only a year or two older than her, even if he seemed wise beyond his years.

Paul shrugged. 'My major is psychology, but my dad wants me to go into the army. Try to get into West Point like him, but I'm not sure I want to do that. I've just finished my college degree and now I'm thinking of going to university to study psychology. But right now, I'm enjoying this break and I won't worry about the future. Go with the flow, you know?'

'Yeah,' Maggie replied. 'I'm just going to have fun until we go back to Dublin. Surfing, swimming, hanging with my friends down there in Sandy Cove. They're a great bunch.'

'I'm sure they are,' Paul said. 'Irish people generally are really fabulous. You just have to go to a pub to find that out. I've met some great guys in Dublin.'

'If you do come to Sandy Cove on your way to Beara,' Maggie said, 'I'll introduce you to my friends. They'd love to meet you.'

'I'm looking forward to my visit already,' he said with a grin. 'But I think I've just met the best of that bunch right here on this train.'

Maggie blushed and laughed, a little embarrassed by his admiring gaze. She had never been able to handle compliments. When she turned sixteen, she had discovered that one of the benefits of her dance training was to make her more attractive to boys, but it was still quite new to her. She changed the subject and they continued talking about their lives, where they lived, and all kinds of other things, arguing about which was the best band around and which TV shows they enjoyed the most until the train arrived in Killarney.

Maggie's mother was waiting in her car outside the station and Maggie pulled Paul along with her and introduced them. 'This is Paul O'Sullivan, Mam,' she said. 'He's an American Sullivan Beare who has come to find his roots.'

'How interesting,' Maggie's mother said. 'Welcome to Ireland, Paul.'

'Thank you. Nice to meet you, Mrs Ryan,' Paul said and shook hands. 'Maggie has told me all about you and your family and the wonderful vacations you have here in Kerry.'

'Oh, yes, we love them,' Breda Ryan said. 'But now the children have grown up and are off to all sorts of places all over the world. So this will be our last summer here.'

'That's a pity,' Paul remarked.

'Yeah,' Maggie said, sad again at the thought of the house being sold. 'It's tough to say goodbye to the house. But we're all going on different holidays from now on. My brothers are spending their holidays abroad and my sister, Claire, is getting married and moving to Scotland. So keeping a house here doesn't really make sense anymore.'

'My husband and I will be going to Portugal to play golf in the summers now,' Breda Ryan said.

'And I thought I might go camping in France with some of my friends next year,' Maggie cut in. 'But we can always come back here individually whenever we want, of course.'

'That was what happened with my family,' Paul said. 'We had a place on Cape Cod when I was a child, but then we all went our different ways, and here I am in Ireland.'

'You must come and visit us in Sandy Cove,' Breda Ryan said. 'If you're passing by, I mean.'

'Oh, yes, I'm definitely coming to Sandy Cove quite soon,'

Paul said, looking at Maggie. 'But now I have to go and collect my bike and be on my way. I'm sure you want to get going too.'

'Yes,' Breda Ryan said. 'We have to do a bit of shopping on the way too.' She held out her hand. 'So I'll say goodbye for now. I hope we'll see you in Sandy Cove during the summer. We're in the coastguard station in a row of houses called Starlight Cottages. You can't miss them. And there is a little hostel on the way to Ballinskelligs where you could stay. We don't have much room, I'm afraid.'

Paul nodded. 'I might see you later on, then,' he said, looking at Maggie.

'That would be great,' Maggie replied, trying her best not to show how much she wanted to see him again.

Then Maggie got into the car with her mother and waved goodbye to Paul, saying a silent prayer he would one day turn up in Sandy Cove.

4

Maggie smiled at the memories as she reached Killarney, where she parked near the church and got out of the car to find a place to have lunch. She walked down the main street, marvelling at the array of elegant shops, cute little cafés and pubs from where traditional Irish music could be heard. Tourists mingled with locals, all chatting to each other and enjoying the mild early summer breeze and warm sunshine. The smell of coffee mingled with garlic and herbs from pizza restaurants and a slight scent of roses came from the many hanging baskets all along the street. It was just as Killarney had always been all those years ago, only more upmarket and swish. But the conviviality of Kerry hadn't changed and Maggie felt right at home as she sat down at a table under an umbrella outside a café and ordered a grilled cheese sandwich and salad from the cheery waitress.

'Are you from around here?' she asked in her sing-song Kerry accent, sticking her pencil behind her ear.

'No, I'm from Dublin,' Maggie replied. 'But my family used to spend all our summer holidays here when I was a child.'

'Where exactly?' the waitress asked.

'Sandy Cove. It's a little village near Waterville.'

The waitress nodded. 'Oh, yes, I know where it is. Great place for surfing. And there's a fabulous restaurant there, too. I went there for Sunday dinner with my boyfriend last week. The Wild Atlantic-something. Gorgeous food. You should try it.'

'I will,' Maggie promised. 'Sounds like Sandy Cove has become quite fashionable since I was here last. Thirty years ago,' she added with a laugh. 'But it seems like yesterday sometimes.'

'Time flies when you're having fun,' the girl said. 'I'll bring your order when it's ready. Nice to meet you.'

Have I had fun? Maggie thought when the girl had left to place her order. *Or has it just been time passing without my paying attention?* There were so many wonderful memories of the children being born, of family life with Dermot that she had cherished but now seemed tarnished by what he had done to her. She had also loved her job at the school, especially teaching young girls with whom she had bonded in a very special way. They had often come to her with their problems and worries and she had become like a confidante and mentor to some who were a little lost and troubled. She hoped she had been some help to those girls and she was looking forward to seeing them all again after her summer break.

But now it was early June and she was looking forward to being in Sandy Cove again and discovering how the village had changed since she had left. Had it lost that cosy old-fashioned feel and become too posh and modern? She hoped not and as she thought of the people she had known there, she felt sure they wouldn't want to lose the soul of that special place.

'Here you go,' the waitress said, putting Maggie's order in front of her. 'Tuck in. You look like you need a little sustenance.'

'It's been a long trip,' Maggie said, looking up at the girl. 'But now I have the whole summer in Kerry to look forward to.'

'In Sandy Cove,' the girl filled in. 'Aren't you the lucky duck?'

'I am,' Maggie agreed, her spirits lifting. 'I'm going to try to find all the people I knew way back then. I'm sure some of them will still be around.'

'Of course they are, only they're older,' the girl remarked. 'I have friend who works at the hairdressing salon there. Her name's Susie. Tell her Sharon said hi.'

'Hairdressing salon?' Maggie asked. 'Sounds really grand. There was no such thing in Sandy Cove when I was a teenager.'

'Oh, there are lots of new things. Sandy Cove has become quite with-it in the last thirty years, you know,' Sharon said. 'The grocery shop is now a mini-supermarket. And there is a fabulous coffee shop at the beach called The Two Marys', run by Mary B and Mary O, who are cousins. Great place for lunch or coffee and cake. And the doctor has built himself a million-dollar home, and those run-down Starlight Cottages are now all done up and have become an artist colony. You'll see, it's quite the boutique little village now.'

'Oh.' Maggie stared at Sharon. 'I'm not sure if that's good or bad.'

'You have to come back here and tell me in a while.' Sharon pointed at the grilled sandwich on the plate. 'But eat up, that's getting cold. And I have to get back to work. Nice to meet you, eh—?'

'I'm Maggie.'

'Hi, Maggie. Have a great stay in Sandy Cove. Say hi to Susie, willya?'

'I will,' Maggie promised and smiled at the waitress as she walked away. She started on the sandwich, musing over what Sharon had said. 'Boutique village' sounded as if Sandy Cove had turned into something from a magazine. Was it no longer the cosy, slightly run-down place she remembered, where everyone was relaxed and easy-going and you could do your own thing and wear whatever you liked in a barefoot beach-comber kind of way? Had that all changed and become fashion-able and upmarket? Would the village be full of tourists and people who wouldn't know her? Her old friends might have moved away and she could find herself in a place full of strangers. In that case, she might be heading into a very lonely few months.

Maggie frowned as she finished her lunch, wondering if booking that cottage for a whole summer had been a huge mistake.

5

It had started to rain when Maggie drove through the village after an hour on long winding roads full of potholes. At least the state of the roads hadn't changed, she thought, as the car bumped along on the uneven surface. But as she reached the main street of Sandy Cove, she realised that what Sharon at the café in Killarney had said was true. The village looked picture-perfect. Gone were the run-down cottages with thatched roofs, the unkempt front gardens and the untidy shopfronts. The thatched roofs of the cottages had been replaced by slate; the front gardens were truly beautiful with well-tended flowerbeds and large tubs of geraniums. The pavements had been resurfaced and baskets of flowers hung from the old-fashioned streetlights. It looked nearly like a village in a storybook and as she wound down her window, Maggie could hear a dog bark and guitar music from an open window. The shop fronts were tidy with quirky signs over the doors and some had benches in front of them painted in various colours. One shop sign in particular made Maggie slow her car, which earned her a tooting from a vehicle behind her. She raised her hand in an apologetic gesture and the car passed her, tooting again, but this time the driver waved and smiled.

'Sorry,' Maggie shouted, sticking her head out the window.

'Okay,' the man at the wheel shouted back. 'No harm done.' Then he drove off up the street and rounded the corner at breakneck speed.

Maggie smiled and shrugged and pulled in at the kerb near the shop, which bore a sign that said SORCHA'S SUPER-MARKET in green Celtic lettering. Maggie stared at the sign. Sorcha? Could this be the same Sorcha she had been friends with all those years ago? Fun, freckly, red-haired Sorcha, her best friend, who had been a real tomboy? She had then turned into a very pretty teenager the boys were mad about. Had she taken over the shop from her parents? There was only one way to find out.

Maggie got out of the car and stretched, stiff after more than four hours at the wheel. It would be good to walk around the village to get her bearings before she headed to Starlight Cottages and her summer rental. And she needed to buy food, of course, so this little supermarket was ideal. Tiny bells tinkled as Maggie pushed the door open and stepped inside the cutest little supermarket she had ever been in.

With its light green wainscoting, the little lamps hanging from the ceiling, the wooden kegs with apples and bananas, and shelves lined with jars and bottles of all kinds, the shop had an old-world charm mixed with modern features like the gleaming deli counter, the freezers along the wall and the shelf with fresh herbs in terracotta pots above the marble counter. There was also a coffee corner with a little wood-burning stove, which Maggie imagined would be lovely in the chill of a winter's day. But now it was summer and the shop seemed cool and fresh and smelled of herbs and apples. This lovely little supermarket was a far cry from the very basic and slightly run-down shop it had been when Maggie was last here.

As there was nobody around, she took a basket and browsed the shelves, picking out milk, bread, butter, marmalade, eggs and other everyday essentials, hoping a shop assistant would appear soon so she could pay and leave. Maggie gave a start as a door opened behind the deli counter and a woman appeared. A woman with short red hair and hazel eyes who Maggie instantly recognised.

'Sorcha?' Maggie said.

'Eh, yes?' Sorcha said, looking at Maggie with surprise. 'That's me.'

'Of course it is,' Maggie said, smiling. 'Do you know who I am?'

Sorcha peered at Maggie. 'I'm not sure...' She stopped. 'You look awfully familiar. But I can't remember where we've met.'

Maggie beamed. 'The last time we saw one another was right here in this shop. Thirty years ago,' she added. 'We were saying goodbye and crying.' Maggie smiled again as she remembered that day. She was joking about it now, but then it had seemed like a tragedy. The family had just closed the door to the cottage and were now going around the village to say goodbye to their friends.

Sorcha had been her best friend since that very first summer when they were both eight years old. During the winter season when they were apart, they had written long letters to each other and then the following summers connected again, so happy to see each other, inseparable all through the holiday. Maggie had appreciated Sorcha's friendship even more during their teenage years, when they had supported each other through thick and thin and shared all those teenage concerns about boys and their looks and school and what they would do when they grew up. And then they had to say goodbye, knowing that even if they stayed in touch nothing would ever be the same. And, of course, they hadn't. Life got in the way and

Sandy Cove and their summer holidays receded into the distance like a beautiful dream that slowly faded.

'We pinkie swore we would stay in touch,' she said as Sorcha stood there staring at her.

'Oh,' Sorcha said, looking as if she was racking her brain. She stared at Maggie and then it seemed to dawn on her. 'Oh, Holy Mother, Maggie?' she exclaimed. 'Maggie Ryan, right?'

'Bingo!' Maggie said, laughing. 'I was wondering how long it would take for the penny to drop.'

'I'm so stupid. How could I not recognise you?' Sorcha grabbed Maggie's hand in a warm handshake. 'How are you? And what are you doing here after all these years?'

'I've come to spend the summer.' Maggie beamed at Sorcha as the years disappeared and she saw her as the young girl she had known. 'It's been so long, hasn't it?'

'It has indeed.' Sorcha smiled and shook her head. 'Silly of me not to recognise you. But you do look quite different with long hair and, well, we've both matured, haven't we?'

'A little worn and dented by life, I suppose,' Maggie said. 'I'm really sorry about not staying in touch like I promised.'

'Me too,' Sorcha said with a regretful smile. 'But you know how it goes. Life and stuff happen and we just slide into a different mode or something.'

'I suppose,' Maggie said. 'But I would have known you anywhere. You haven't changed much, except for cutting your hair. I remember it being so long you could nearly sit on it.' Maggie sighed wistfully. 'I was jealous of that red mane, you know.'

Sorcha laughed. 'And it was the bane of my life. All that washing and brushing and conditioning. I finally got sick of it and had it cut off when I had a baby. I couldn't cope with it then.'

Maggie nodded. 'I can imagine. Babies have a habit of

turning everything upside down, don't they? So you have children?'

'That's very true. And yes, I do.' Sorcha looked around the shop. 'There's nobody here, so how about a cup of coffee in my café corner so we can catch up?'

'Great,' Maggie said and put the basket on the counter. 'I'll finish my shopping afterwards.'

They settled down on the green-and-yellow painted chairs in the café corner after Sorcha had made them both a cup of frothy cappuccino from the machine. Maggie breathed in the smell of coffee and took a long sip. 'Thank you so much, Sorcha. It was a long trip.'

'I know. It's a bit of a hack from Dublin all right.' Sorcha drank from her cup and put it on the table. 'So... where do we begin? Last time was in this shop, you said. I think I remember you and your mother coming to say goodbye to my parents and that you were very sad.'

'And that was around thirty years ago and I had just had the best summer of my life,' Maggie said with a wistful smile.

'It was a great summer, as far as I remember. We were all so young with our lives ahead of us.' Sorcha sighed. 'And then we went out there and faced the world with all those hopes and dreams.'

'I know.' Maggie took another swig of coffee. 'I have been wondering what happened to all of that, and all the friends I made here. So you go first. What have you been up to since then?'

'Oh my God, that'll take a while to tell you,' Sorcha said with a laugh. She paused for a moment. 'I went to business school in Cork and got myself a diploma and all. Then I met this young man and married him only three months after we met,' she continued wistfully. 'Then I got pregnant and then... Lots of hard things happened all at once, actually...'

Maggie watched her friend and nodded. They'd missed so

much of each other's lives – so much happiness but so much sadness too.

'My father died and I had to come back here to help my mother run the shop.'

'I'm so sorry you lost your father,' Maggie said. 'I remember him so well. Such a kind man, who always slipped extra sweets into our bag at the till.'

'He was a darling,' Sorcha agreed with a sad little smile.

'And your mum. She was so nice too.'

'They were both wonderful. And now they're together in the next life,' Sorcha added. 'I miss them but I know they'd be happy that I keep the family business going.'

'I'm sure they would be,' Maggie agreed, feeling a pang of sadness at Sorcha's loss.

'What about your parents?' Sorcha asked.

'They're still alive,' Maggie replied. 'And playing golf in the Algarve. They bought a little house there when they sold the cottage. Now that they're both retired, they spend most of the year there.'

'Must be nice for them,' Sorcha remarked.

'Oh yes, they're happy. I've been to see them there a few times. But as I'm not into golf, it's a little boring. But hey,' Maggie continued. 'Back to you. So you decided to stay and run the shop?'

'Well, it was supposed to be a temporary arrangement until Mum was on her feet again,' Sorcha said. 'But I stayed a lot longer than planned and had my baby in Killarney. And then Mum died and... well, I felt this was where I wanted our son to grow up. Richard, my husband, wanted to leave, to go to Dublin and get started on his career as an economist and consultant in business development. He even got himself a job in a consultancy firm. So he went and I was supposed to follow when my mother was better. But then I just couldn't bear to leave after she died. We split up when our little boy was only five.'

'Oh, I'm sorry,' Maggie said. 'I know how hard that must have been.'

'At the time, yes,' Sorcha said. 'But later on I came to realise how unsuited we were to each other. And he was still a good father to Fintan, who's in college in Dublin now. Studying environmental science,' she added.

'You must be so proud of him,' Maggie said, touched by the pride in Sorcha's eyes.

'I am. But I miss him at the same time,' Sorcha admitted. 'What about you? Have you any children?'

'Yes,' Maggie replied. 'A boy and a girl. Jim, my son, is twenty and Orla is twenty-two.'

'Nearly the same age as my Fintan,' Sorcha said. 'What are they doing?'

'Jim is doing an extension of his gap year in Australia,' Maggie replied. 'I have a feeling he's very happy there, so he might stay and study there. And Orla is doing a very long internship at the European Commission headquarters in Brussels. Both of them are doing well and all grown up. Their father and I broke up last year,' she said quickly, not wanting to get into the details of that painful event. 'I'm still trying to recover,' she added just to explain how she felt.

'It takes time,' Sorcha agreed. 'Been there myself, so I know. But hey, you're still young and good-looking, so life isn't over, is it?'

'Absolutely not,' Maggie said, as the defiant glint in Sorcha's eyes made her feel suddenly better. 'But go on. I want to know what has happened in the village.'

'This and that,' Sorcha said. 'The village has become a popular place to live. People who left have come back and have restored a lot of the old houses. This shop is now making us twice the money it did before. I extended it into the house next door that was being sold and made the flat upstairs a lot bigger.' She paused. 'Do you remember my cousin Brian?'

Maggie nodded. 'Oh, yes. He used to hang around with my brothers. What's he doing now?'

'He realised his dream and became a vet. His surgery is just up the street. You should pop in and say hi when you have the time.'

'I will,' Maggie promised, remembering Brian with the lovely brown eyes and cute boyish face. 'I liked him a lot. I remember how he used to have such a soft spot for stray dogs and cats.'

'He still does. He's a nice guy,' Sorcha agreed. 'Then we have the girls in Willow House. Maeve and Roisin. Remember them?'

'Yes, of course. Lovely old house. And their aunt and uncle were a fun couple.'

'Both passed away, sadly. But Maeve is now living in the house with her family. Three children and a lovely husband. Roisin and her husband had a campervan business but they sold up and are now travelling around Europe in their very own campervan.'

'Amazing,' Maggie said. 'And here I am renting one of the Starlight Cottages for the summer. We're all back where we used to be. I saw the ad by chance on Facebook, but I have noticed that they are no longer the slightly run-down cottages they once were.'

Sorcha laughed. 'Not at all. You wouldn't know the place now. All smartened up and restored. Mostly inhabited by artists, except Jason's place that he rents out in the summer. The very same house your family used to own, actually.'

'I know. That's where I'll be staying,' Maggie cut in.

'Oh, of course! You'll find it very different. All done up and with all mod cons. Jason, who owns it, is a furniture designer. Lydia, his wife, is actually old Nellie's grand-niece. She inherited the cottage when Nellie died.'

'Nellie? That nice woman who lived next door to us?' Maggie asked. 'That's sad. I was hoping to meet her again.'

'Well, she'd be over a hundred if she were still around,' Sorcha remarked.

'I suppose,' Maggie said with a laugh. 'How silly of me. I forgot that so many years had passed. She was around seventy that last summer. I used to call in to her for a cup of tea and a chat. I found her such great company.'

'Oh, yes she was,' Sorcha agreed. 'So inspirational too. I loved talking to her. She was like an agony aunt to us girls around here.'

'I remember that,' Maggie said. 'She was a great help when Paul left and I was so sad.'

'Oh, yes, I remember him,' Sorcha said. 'Gorgeous guy. You two were so in love.'

'I suppose we were.' Maggie sighed. 'I thought my life was over when he left. I never forgot him. One of those regrets about what could have been.'

'Ah, yes. I know,' Sorcha said sympathetically. 'We all have them. But you have never forgotten him, have you?'

'No. A bittersweet memory that hits me from time to time.'

'Maybe it wasn't meant to be?' Sorcha suggested. 'And if you met him again, you'd probably think it was a lucky escape. He might have turned into a hard-drinking pot-bellied man with a bad temper or something. Isn't it better that he stays in your memory as this gorgeous guy who loved you, even if it was only for one summer?'

'That's what Nellie Butler said to me when I was crying into my mug of tea that day.'

'She was right, I'd say.' Sorcha sighed. 'What a great old bird she was. Such a rock of sense to us girls. Always there with good advice.'

'She was,' Maggie agreed. 'But she wasn't very positive about you and I getting married and having children. She thought that would impinge on our independence. No idea why she was so against it.'

'Ah, well, women had it tough in her youth, I suppose,' Sorcha remarked. She finished her coffee and got up. 'But now I have to get going. The evening rush will start in a minute and then I have to add up today's takings and put it all in the safe. Pauline, my assistant, will come in to help out in a minute. But it was lovely to see you and catch up, Maggie. Give me your number so we can keep in touch. But I'm sure I'll see you around a lot.'

'I hope so.' Maggie read out her number while Sorcha typed it into her phone.

'Great,' Sorcha said and put her phone into the pocket of her jeans. 'It'll be great to catch up some more.'

'I'm looking forward to a quiet, restful summer and to meet up with the people I used to know.'

'It might not be as restful as you think,' Sorcha said with a grin. 'This village is not the sleepy backwater you might remember. There is a lot going on under the cheerful surface.'

'Like what?' Maggie asked, intrigued.

Sorcha waggled her eyebrows. 'Planning and plotting and scheming,' she said. 'A revolution is brewing around here.'

Maggie laughed. 'Oh yeah? In what way?'

'In every way. Especially in one quarter.' Sorcha turned to look at the door that was just opening. 'I'll tell you about it later,' she whispered. 'You might be able to infiltrate them and flush out the guilty party.' Then she turned and smiled at the customer who had just entered. 'Hello there, Maureen. Grand evening, isn't it?'

Maggie went to gather up her shopping and paid at the little checkout desk where a young dark-haired girl had just sat down.

'I'm Pauline,' she said as Maggie put her credit card into the machine. 'Welcome to Sandy Cove.'

Maggie smiled at the girl. 'Thank you. I'm Maggie, by the

way. I've been here before many years ago. So I have a lot of catching up to do.'

'That should be fun,' Pauline said as she helped Maggie put her shopping into a paper bag with the shop's name. 'See you soon, I'm sure.'

Maggie said goodbye to Pauline and smiled and waved to Sorcha as she left the shop, her heart beating faster after the reunion. How wonderful to meet again and feel the years roll back. They had both aged but after a few minutes they had seen each other as the young women they had been all those years ago. They had lived a whole life since then, becoming mothers, bringing up children, suffering break-ups and worked hard to make a living. Marked by life but still the same, somehow. The old friendship was now starting up again, Maggie felt with a warm glow as she put her shopping into the boot of her car.

She glanced up the street and saw the sign that said VETERINARY PRACTICE above a blue door. On a whim, she walked up to it and pushed the door open to a waiting room full of people with various pets. It seemed so busy Maggie decided to leave but before she had opened the door again a man in dark green scrubs appeared at the reception desk. Maggie instantly recognised Brian, even though he was much older. But there was no mistaking those kind eyes, the boyish face and the dark hair flopping into his eyes.

'Can I help you?' he said, looking curiously at Maggie.

'I just looked in to say hello,' Maggie said. 'But it can wait as I see how busy you are.'

'Hello?' he said, looking confused. 'Do we know each other?'

'We did once upon a time,' Maggie said, suddenly aware that everyone in the room was staring at her. 'You used to play with my brothers.'

Brian looked at Maggie for a moment and then he laughed. 'If it isn't Maggie Ryan!' he exclaimed, coming forward and grabbing her hand in a tight grip. 'It's been like a hundred years, hasn't it?' He looked at the people in the waiting room, smiling broadly. 'Folks, this is Maggie, who I used to know when we were kids. What are you doing here, though?'

'I'm going to spend the summer here,' Maggie replied.

'Excellent,' Brian said.

'I hope to see you soon,' Maggie said. 'But I think I'll leave you to your patients. We can catch up some other time.'

'We certainly will,' Brian said. 'Where are you staying?'

'In the cottage we used to own,' Maggie said. 'Isn't that strange?'

'How amazing.'

'But I'll let you get on with your work,' Maggie said. 'See you soon, Brian.'

'See ya, Maggie,' Brian said. He turned and smiled at a young girl with a black Labrador. 'So, Clodagh, what's wrong with Holly today? Come into the surgery and we'll take a look at her.'

Maggie left the surgery and got into her car, the reunions with Sorcha and Brian making her smile. How wonderful to find her old friends so quickly and feel that true friendship never dies. It made her feel alive again and the beginning of a new, happier life seemed suddenly real.

A few minutes later, Maggie pulled up outside Starlight Cottages and sat there, looking at the row of houses. They were so different, yet the same. Gone was the flaking paint, the cracked window frames and the warped front doors, some of which didn't even close properly. Instead, here was a row of lovely cottages with climbing roses over the newly painted front doors, sash windows that had been repaired and now added to the charm of these old houses, the roofs having been repaired and the chimneys replaced. It was heartening to see that the period feel had been carefully preserved and Maggie imagined that the houses now looked very much like they would have when they were built over a hundred and fifty years ago.

As she sat there, she remembered the very first time she had seen the cottages when she was a little girl. The trip from Dublin had taken most of the day on bad roads, crammed in a car with her sister and brothers. It seemed suddenly such a short time ago instead of more than forty years. What a different world this had been then. But Maggie saw it all clearly in her mind's eye.

—————

6

'Here we are,' Maggie's father, Paddy, had said as they drew up outside the cottages. 'Starlight Cottages. Our very own summer paradise.'

Bleary-eyed after having slept with her head on Claire's shoulder in the back seat, Maggie stared at the house. 'This is it?' she asked. 'The house you bought? But it isn't a paradise, it's just a house.'

'You'll see,' her father said as he opened the door. 'It might not look like a palace, but I can assure you that this place will be the best summer holiday house we have ever been in.' He got out, taking a big key from his pocket. 'Come on, kids, let's explore our new abode,' he shouted over his shoulder.

Still hot and sleepy, moaning and groaning, the children clambered out of the car, their mother opening the boot to take out the bags. They followed their father inside, looking into the big old-fashioned kitchen with its huge solid fuel stove and Belfast sink, down the short corridor to the living room where there was a sofa bed against the far wall, fireside chairs beside the fireplace, a desk and an empty bookcase. There was a wheel with a handle attached beside the fireplace – a kind of bellows, their father explained, to fan the flames if the fire died down.

He walked to the glass-panelled door at the end of the room and opened it to a sunroom with views of the ocean that made them all stop and stare.

'There's a storm,' Maggie said, pointing at the waves crashing onto the rocks far below them, sending foam high in the air.

'Just the tide coming in,' her father explained, taking her hand. 'Let's go outside and take a closer look at the view.'

They all went out through the door to the little garden, which was overgrown with ferns and wild flowers. 'Something for Mammy to do up,' Maggie's father said. 'And I'll paint all the walls inside and put up shelves.'

'Where will we sleep?' Maggie asked.

'There are two bedrooms upstairs,' Breda Ryan said as she came inside carrying a box with books and board games. 'You and Claire can have the back bedroom and Daddy and I will sleep in the double bed in the other one. Sean will take the sofa bed and we have an extra fold-out bed for Danny.'

'Everyone will have a bed,' Paddy said.

'But where are the boys?' Breda asked, looking around. 'They were here only a minute ago. Paddy, go and look for them. They might have already gone down to the beach, but that path is quite steep.'

'Don't worry,' Paddy reassured her. 'They're strong boys. Let's go and have a look. Maggie, do you want to come with me?' He held out his hand and Maggie grabbed it, excited to see that path to the beach.

'Come on, Claire,' she shouted as they went out the gate.

'I'll stay here with Mammy,' Claire shouted back. 'You go on with Daddy and the boys.'

And off they went, down the steep path, Maggie holding on

to her father's hand for dear life, while they made their way to the little beach below the cliffs, where Sean and Danny were already shouting and whooping, running in and out of the waves even though they were still in shorts and T-shirts. Maggie laughed as she watched them, still holding on to her father's hand, not being as brave as her big brothers. She would become more daring later, and by the time she was ten, she was swimming with them and even having surfing lessons at the surf school on the main beach of the village.

Oh, those summers, Maggie thought as she sat in the car looking at the house. How magical they were, running wild on the beaches with all the other kids, swimming, surfing, fishing, playing rounders. Then tea and sausages in the evening and playing board games in front of the fire, toasting marshmallows and then being carried by Mammy or Daddy up the stairs and into the bedroom where she and Claire were lulled to sleep by the sound of the waves. Such simple pleasures that had seemed so amazing. Did anyone play board games anymore? Maggie wondered. Or toast marshmallows over the glowing embers of the fire? Children of today wouldn't understand how you could have fun without tablets or phones or even a TV. How lucky they had been not to be dependent on all of that and having to make their own fun by using their imagination.

Maggie was slowly pulled away from her memories as the door opened and a pretty blonde woman smiled at her. Maggie got out of the car and walked to the front door, shaking hands with the woman, stepping from the past into the present.

'Hello. I'm Lydia,' the woman said. 'Welcome to Starlight Cottages.'

'Thank you,' Maggie replied. She shook her head and laughed. 'I was sitting here remembering the old days when I was eight and my parents had just bought this cottage.'

'Jason said your family owned it before. It must have been

quite different then,' Lydia remarked. 'My great-aunt lived next door to this one, and now I own it.'

'I knew your great-aunt,' Maggie said. 'We called her Nellie. Such a nice woman. We all loved her.'

'That's amazing,' Lydia exclaimed. 'I barely knew her but I've found out a lot since I moved here. You must tell me what you remember of her.'

'I will,' Maggie promised as she stepped into the small hall, where the wainscoting was painted white and the floor had been laid with terracotta tiles. 'Gosh, this is really gorgeous,' she exclaimed.

'Wait till you see the rest,' Lydia said. 'But I'll leave you to settle in. Give us a shout if you need anything. We're right next door. And you have a nice neighbour on your other side. Saskia is Dutch and she designs jewellery. Next door to her is Ella, who is an artist. Her husband, Rory, is a solicitor.'

'Lots of artists,' Maggie said. 'Except me.'

'And me and Rory,' Lydia said with a laugh. 'I'm a fundraiser by profession. What about you?'

'I'm a PE teacher without a creative bone in my body,' Maggie replied. 'Except I love dance. But I won't be doing much dancing here, of course. I'll be trying out my surfing skills instead.'

'That'll be fun.' Lydia handed Maggie a bunch of keys. 'Here you go. Two keys to the front door. The smaller one is to the back door and that little black one is for the gate. But we never lock our doors here, you know. Foolish, perhaps, but there hasn't been any break-ins or serious crimes here since anyone can remember.'

'Just like when we spent our summers here,' Maggie said. 'The big bad world seemed so far away.'

'It still does,' Lydia declared. 'I love that, even though it's such a close community. Everyone knows everyone's business even before you have said anything. But there are a few bad eggs, of course.'

'How do you mean?' Maggie said, lingering in the hall, even though she was dying to see the rest of the house.

'Oh, you know, people who think they know best and want to be important.' Lydia smiled and shrugged. 'About silly little things like power struggles in the parents' association and other little groups. Best not to get involved, though, even if you want to tell some people off. Right now there is a downright war going on in one of them. But I'll say no more. I don't want to ruin your holiday.'

'Nothing could,' Maggie said. 'It's so great to be back.'

'I'm sure it is,' Lydia said warmly. 'You'll be remembering all the happy summers you had here, I'm sure.' She seemed about to leave but stopped in the door. 'Talking about remembering... We found a tin in the attic when we were doing up the house to let it. Could it be something to do with your family, I wonder? It's a biscuit tin and there seemed to be something in it. Not biscuits but maybe someone's hidden treasure. We didn't open it but kept it in case someone would want it. I put it on the table in the sunroom. If it's not yours, just give it to me and I'll put it away.'

'I'll take a look,' Maggie promised. 'I don't remember a box like that, but it was a long time ago, so maybe it's something we forgot when we moved out.'

Lydia nodded. 'Could be. Let me know in any case. Bye for now.'

Maggie said goodbye and when Lydia had left opened the door to the corridor and went past the stairs, glancing into the kitchen that had been painted primrose yellow. She was delighted to see that the original stove was still there and had been repainted a deep green. Beside it was an induction hob with a fan oven underneath. The cupboards were the same as before, but now painted white. A small round table and four chairs stood by the window from where one could enjoy the view of the mountains behind the house.

Maggie walked on, into the large living room that had once been so cluttered. There had been a sofa bed, a folding bed, fireside chairs, a bookcase and a large cupboard where they had stored books, board games, sketchpads, colouring books, crayons and pencils and all kinds of other paraphernalia during the summer months. She remembered a large pine table and chairs that had been nearly too big for the room. But all that was gone and the room had been transformed into something completely different.

Maggie stopped dead and stared around her in awe. The worn lino had been replaced by polished oak planks; the walls had been painted white with a hint of blue and hung with prints and watercolours depicting various parts of Kerry. A large blue curved sofa stood in front of the fireplace, the mantelpiece replaced by a length of timber that looked like driftwood. A flat-screen TV had been mounted on the wall over a table with a lamp. There was a square dining table at the far end with six chairs and a sideboard, all painted a distressed white. The whole room was light and airy and seemed to flow seamlessly into the sunroom and its stunning views of the ocean. Maggie could see a pair of wicker chairs and a small table where she spotted the biscuit tin Lydia had mentioned.

Her heart beating, she went into the sunroom and looked at the tin. JACOB'S ASSORTED, it said on the top and pictured an array of different biscuits and cookies. She stared at it for a moment. Then she remembered. It was her secret tin, the one where she put her cards and letters and her little diary and then hid it under her bed so the boys wouldn't find it and tease her. She had a faint memory of putting it in the attic that last summer, when Paul had left and she had been so devastated, thinking she would never see him again. Well, she had been right about that.

That tin... What it contained would jolt her back to those days. Should she open it or just throw it away and not indulge in nostalgia that could make her sad about what could have been? She stood there, unable to decide, but then felt she should at least take a look. What harm could it do?

7

Her knees suddenly weak, Maggie sat down on one of the wicker chairs and picked up the tin. The lid was stuck and it took her a while to wrench it open. A waft of mould hit her nose but she hardly noticed as she stared at the contents. There was a pile of letters and cards, a dried, pressed rose, a watch with a blue strap and at the bottom a small leather diary.

Ignoring the cards and letters from friends, Maggie picked up the diary and opened it. It was from 1990. She flicked through the early months and could see events like 'Mammy's birthday' and 'France-Ireland rugby with Claire' mentioned. Then the summer and the ballet classes in Dublin and then... That train journey where she had met Paul. 'Met amazing guy on Dublin-Killarney train, how strange is that?' she had scribbled on 26 June. Then pages through the following weeks with 'no sign of him' and 'no Paul yet', until two weeks later where she had written 'FINALLY! PAUL IS HERE!' surrounded by hearts. Maggie's smile widened as she remembered that day when Paul arrived in Sandy Cove.

As it was a sunny morning, Maggie was in the back garden having breakfast at the rickety table just outside the sunroom.

Everyone had already left for the beach, or to play golf in Waterville after the usual mayhem of getting ready, packing swimsuits and towels and golf clubs. Their mother served them tea, toast and sausages while complaining that they had never got around to building the terrace that the back of the house was 'crying out for'. But now it was too late as the house was going to be sold. 'It'll be much better organised in Portugal,' her father had promised, to which they had all laughed. Then everyone had gone off to their various activities while Maggie lingered over her tea and toast, deciding to have a lazy day reading in the sunshine.

It would be good to have a bit of peace, she thought, while the rest of the rowdy family went off to have their fun. Even if a big family was great most of the time, you never had any space to yourself. Well, this morning she would, she decided. It had been hard these past weeks to smile and pretend she was enjoying herself when she was constantly thinking about Paul. She had been hoping he'd come to Sandy Cove, but it didn't look as if he would. Well, maybe his long-lost relatives in Beara were more fun, she assumed. It was a pity they didn't have a phone in the cottage, so she could have given him a number to ring. But maybe he wouldn't have bothered even then. She needed to be alone to lick her wounds and try to think of other things. She had a Jackie Collins novel she hadn't read yet, and a bar of chocolate hidden away so she wouldn't have to share with her siblings. The weather forecast had promised continued warm sunshine, so when she had done her chores, she would settle into a deckchair with her book and her bar of chocolate and a tall glass of cold homemade lemonade. Perfect.

Maggie was deep into the story and the hero had just carried the heroine into the bedroom, when she heard the noise. Slowly pulling out of her fantasy world, she put her glass on the table beside her and listened. What was that? The doorbell? Oh, yes, there it was again.

'I'm really not at home, so this had better be important,' she said as she swung the door open.

'That depends,' came the reply from the person on the doorstep.

Maggie gasped and stared at him. 'Paul!' she exclaimed, shocked to see him there smiling at her, just like that. She had been ready to wrap her arms around him, but stopped herself in time. They had only met once, even though they had been talking for hours during that train journey. But as she met those sloping green eyes, she wondered if he was as attracted to her as she was to him and holding back as well. 'Hi,' she said instead, and stepped aside. 'Welcome to our house. Do you want to come in?'

'Just for a moment,' he said. 'I'm on my way to a relative who has offered me a bed. But then I thought...'

'Come in,' she urged and walked ahead. 'I'm in the back garden reading. Everyone else is out, so I was enjoying being alone for a change.'

'But then I'm disturbing you,' he said behind her.

'Not at all,' Maggie protested. 'I'm very happy to see you. I was wondering what you were up to. How was Beara?'

'Great,' Paul said as they reached the back garden. 'Beautiful and wild.' He stopped and stared at the view, putting on a pair of aviator sunglasses. 'But, wow, this is awesome. Just as beautiful and wild, but not as bare, if you know what I mean. Those mountains, the ocean and those islands out there. They look incredible.'

'That's the Skelligs,' Maggie said. 'Very famous. There is an old monastery on the biggest one. Skellig Michael. You can take a boat tour out there if you're interested. It's a fishing boat, old and rickety, so the trip is a little scary if you're not used to rough seas. But it's a fabulous trip, so you definitely should.'

'I will, that's for sure,' Paul said.

'Great.' Maggie stood there looking at him, both excited and awkward. 'Sit down,' she finally said, gesturing at the other deckchair. 'Would you like a cup of tea?' she asked in her best hostess voice. 'Or coffee? Or a Coke and a packet of crisps?'

'I'm good,' he said. 'Sit down, will ya? I'm getting tired standing here. I've been taught not to sit down while a lady is still standing.'

'Oh,' she said and started to laugh. 'I'm impressed. You're so well brought up.' She sank down on the deckchair. 'There. I'm sitting.'

'Okay.' He sat down and looked at her. 'Great to see you again, Maggie. Sorry about not being in touch but once I got pulled into the rounds of visiting all the relations, I had very little time. It was tea, tea, tea all the time, with pints with the lads mixed in. Those old women sure can put away a lot of tea and soda bread, not to mention the egg sandwiches and sausages. And the guys – wow. Talk about a capacity for pints.'

'I know what you mean,' Maggie said as she drank in his gorgeous face, wide shoulders and long legs encased in faded jeans. She glanced at his rucksack. 'So who is this relative you're staying with, then?'

'Not really a relative of mine,' he said. 'More like the cousin of a cousin. You know how it is down here. Everyone knows everyone else for miles around and most of them are related in some way. I'm staying with someone called O'Connor on a farm just outside the village.'

'I know them. That's my friend Sorcha's aunt and uncle,' Maggie said. 'Their son, Brian, is a friend of my brothers. Nice family. And Brian is great. Pity you couldn't stay with us, but the house is full at the moment. And we're packing up before selling it in September,' she added with a sad little grimace.

'I suppose that'll be a bit of a wrench,' he remarked. 'But you'll be doing other things and going to other places from now on, leaving your childhood behind.'

Maggie nodded, impressed by his empathy. 'Oh, yes. I'm

going off on a bit of a European tour with my girlfriends next year. We'll be interrailing all over Europe.'

'Sounds great. I'll be either at university or officers' training school. Not sure yet, but I'm beginning to lean more towards university.'

'Will your father be disappointed?'

He shrugged. 'Maybe. But Mom is great. She thinks we should all follow our own star. The trick is to find it.'

'I know what you mean,' Maggie replied. 'I hope you find yours.'

'I'm sure I will,' he said, fixing her with his gaze. 'So, Maggie Ryan, where do we go from here?'

'Eh, uh, you go and find the O'Connors and settle in there?' Maggie said. 'And then we could all go and do something tonight. I think there's a disco in the community hall. It's a bit amateurish but great fun. Brian's the DJ, actually. I think he's very good at it, even though he's only fourteen.'

Paul nodded. 'But how about going to the pub first? Just you and me?'

Maggie nodded. 'Yeah, that'd be great. The Harbour Pub is nice.'

'Let's go there then. If you're free, I mean,' he added.

'Of course I am. I can be there around seven, if you like, and then we'll go on to the disco.'

'Great.' He rose from the deckchair. 'I'll go and find this cousin of a cousin and let them know I'm here.'

She shot up. 'I'll see you out.'

They walked through the house, coming to a stop at the front door. Paul looked at Maggie, his hand on the door. 'I'm so glad to see you again, Maggie.'

'Me too,' she said, suddenly aware of his eyes on her.

He leaned forward and kissed her cheek. 'I think you're gorgeous,' he murmured into her ear before he opened the door and left.

Weak at the knees, Maggie leaned against the door, touching the cheek he had just kissed, still feeling the light touch of his lips. 'You're gorgeous, too, Paul O'Sullivan,' she whispered to herself.

Maggie smiled at the memory, touching her cheek, nearly feeling that light kiss there. She had fallen in love so quickly, the way one does at that age. And then, all through those summer weeks, she had been walking on clouds, spending every waking moment with Paul. And now, she was suddenly glad she had experienced it, that she had met him and got to know a person who could have been her soulmate for life. Even though it had never been, it was as if that experience had become part of who she was. She had carried the memory of being loved that way in her heart all through her adult life.

Maggie leafed through the rest of the diary, but the pages were blank. She hadn't bothered to write down anything after Paul had arrived and probably forgotten about the diary and just left it with the rest of the things in the box that consisted of a few postcards, letters from friends and one from her grandmother in Dublin and two tickets to a rock concert in Cork she vaguely remembered going to with her brothers. So much for a treasure trove of memories.

Maggie's phone pinged from inside the house and she went to find it in her handbag. A text message from Sorcha that said:

If you're not too tired after your trip, how about beer and pizza at the Harbour Pub with me and my friend Susie? I close the shop at seven and then I'm ready for a bit of craic. How about you? Sorcha x

Maggie laughed as she read the message. Sorcha hadn't changed a bit. Always ready to have fun. And how great to get an invitation from a friend on the very first night. What a good idea it had been to come here to this friendly place rather than spending another lonely summer in Dublin. She suddenly felt like living again as she typed her response:

See you then!

Deciding to throw away all the things in the box except the diary, Maggie went upstairs to look at the bedrooms before she unloaded the car. She knew she would pick the bedroom she had shared with her sister all those years ago, the one at the back overlooking the ocean. It was a lovely room, where you could watch the sun setting into the sea and then look at the stars glinting in the slowly darkening sky. Going to sleep listening to the waves would be so soothing after hectic days in the summer sun. She braced herself for a wave of nostalgia as she opened the door, but stopped dead as she saw the room. It had been completely transformed, with oak floorboards instead of the old lino, a double bed with a white headboard and a large framed print depicting a summer meadow above it. Curtains with blue-and-white stripes framed the window where the sun streamed in, and the ugly brown wardrobe had been replaced by a white one with louvred doors. The whole room was bright and inviting and Maggie resisted the urge to sink into the bed among the many pillows piled there. But not yet. She had to unpack and settle in and then get ready for that drink with Sorcha and her friend, whoever she was.

After a further look around upstairs, Maggie discovered that the tiny shower room had been incorporated into the little boxroom to create a big, luxurious bathroom with both a bathtub and a shower, which was a delightful surprise. The other bedroom to the front was equally comfortable and beautifully decorated. She thought that this meant that the ghosts from the past had been completely obliterated and there would be no lingering memories. But as she opened the window in what was to be her bedroom and leaned out, she still felt a pang of nostalgia as the breeze from the sea and the smell of seaweed mixed with woodsmoke brought her momentarily back.

Maggie pulled her head inside and decided to stop moping and get started on making the house her very own. She ran downstairs and started to carry her things inside, hanging her rain jacket and anorak on the pegs in the hall, placing her wellies and walking boots underneath. Then she lugged her suitcase upstairs but decided to make up the bed before she started to unpack. She found sheets and towels stacked in the hot press on the landing, and tuned the little radio on the bedside table to Radio Kerry to have some music while she worked.

Soon the cheery voice of the presenter filled the room and Maggie smiled at his accent. He was talking to a reporter who was interviewing visitors to Killarney, asking them about their impressions of Ireland in general and Kerry in particular. First, a woman from Texas declared that Killarney was 'the cutest town I've ever been in', then a couple from France said that Ireland was 'unique and wonderful and the people – oh la la, so friendly'. Maggie laughed as the reporter moved on and started to ask the next person – a man from New York – some questions.

'What brings you to Ireland?' the reporter asked. 'I mean, apart from looking for your roots and the pubs and the music and all that. Is there any other reason?'

'I'm here on business,' the man said. 'But also to look for my youth. No, I mean, for someone I met in my youth,' he corrected himself. 'Someone who meant a lot to me then.'

'I'm guessing it's a woman,' the reporter said with a flirtatious laugh. 'A lovely Irish colleen you fell in love with when you were here – how many years ago?'

'Around thirty,' the man said. 'Yeah, you're right. It was a pretty Irish girl. We met by accident. One of those things, like ships passing in the night or something.'

Maggie sighed, the sheet she was holding fluttering to the floor. How romantic. Two people meeting like that when they were young and then perhaps meeting again years later... Just like her and Paul. Only they would never meet again, she was sure of that. She turned up the sound on the radio and listened intently to the rest of the interview.

'Then what happened?' the reporter said.

'Then we went our separate ways as she was going to her family's summer house and I was going to catch up with my relations,' the man said. Maggie felt her heart contract as she remembered her own story so similar to the one she was listening to. But the same thing probably happened a lot everywhere. A summer romance long forgotten.

'And you never saw her again after that first meeting?' the reporter asked.

'I did,' the man replied. 'I went to find her and...'

'And—?'

Maggie gripped the sheet. *And—?* she thought, waiting with bated breath for what he would say.

'We spent some time together. Some lovely few weeks in a beautiful village in this area. But we both had commitments after the summer and had to say goodbye, thinking we'd meet soon again.'

'But you didn't?' the reporter cut in. 'Whyever not?'

'I don't know. Life took over, I guess. I went back home and she started college, you know how it goes.'

'And you have a wife and children now?' the reporter asked.

'I'll pass on that question,' the man said with a laugh.

'Sorry,' the reporter said. 'Didn't mean to get so personal.'

'That's okay,' the man said. 'But I think that's enough for me. I'm happy to be here whatever happens. Ireland is a wonderful country.'

'That's lovely to hear,' the reporter said. 'Thanks for talking to me. Good luck with finding your lovely colleen. What's her name?'

'Can't tell you that,' the man said. 'I don't want to compromise her – or me. I'm not sure why I'm standing here on the street being on some radio programme anyway. Why did you pick me?'

'Oh, we just wanted to interview people who looked like tourists,' the reporter said. 'You do look very Irish, but there is something very American about you all the same.'

He seemed to smile. 'You're a very good detective. And why are you asking people all these questions?'

'To find out what they think of Kerry and what they're planning to do and so on,' the reporter said. 'I thought you looked like you had an interesting story.'

'Well, thank you,' the man said, sounding as if he was smiling. 'That's nice to know. But I'll say goodbye now. Nice to meet you.'

'Yes, but—' the reporter started, obviously trying to get the man to keep talking. 'He walked away,' she said into her microphone, as Maggie's heart sank. 'Pity. That would have made a great story. But you can't force people to tell you stuff if they don't want to. If the lovely colleen is listening, get in touch so we can get your side of the story.'

'Don't think that's going to happen,' the presenter in the studio said.

'I know,' the reporter replied. 'Anyway, he was a very attractive man, so I'm sure the lovely colleen will be very happy if ever they do meet again.'

'We wish them the very best luck with that,' the presenter said. 'And now we'll play you some nice trad music to finish this "Out and About" hour.'

Maggie sat on the bed with the sheets, staring into space as the music filled the room. That interview had given her more than a jolt and reminded her of her own summer romance. How would she feel if that man were Paul? If he were really here, looking for her? How would she react if they met again? All kinds of questions went through her mind. What did he look like now? Fat and bald? Grey-haired and stooped? And what would he think of her as an older woman? she wondered, deciding that meeting him again would not be as wonderful as she might imagine. Better to keep the lovely memories where they belonged – in the past.

Maggie got up and resumed making the bed, deciding to stop second-guessing and get on with her own holiday. Life was weird and who knew what might happen.

8

'Pizza and beer,' Sorcha said as they sat down at a table in the Harbour Pub, which was situated at the pier where the fishing boats lay at anchor. 'How does that sound?'

'Like the old days,' Maggie replied, looking around the cosy pub where a group of customers were gathered at the bar. A golden light from the setting sun spilled in through the windows, shining on the old wood panelling and the flagstones, and there was a smell of herbs and spices from the pizza oven. 'I don't think we used to come here much in the old days, did we?'

'No. Not that often. We couldn't afford it. We used to party on the beach,' Sorcha said. 'And get frozen pizzas that we cooked at home and brought with us. Or grill sausages over a fire. Pretty primitive, wasn't it?'

'But fun,' Maggie said as a tall man with broad shoulders appeared at their table. 'Hey,' she said, studying his face. 'You're Sean Óg.'

'I sure am,' he said, looking at Maggie for a moment. 'And you're... you're... Sorry, can't quite place you.'

'Maggie Ryan,' she said and held out her hand. 'But it's

been thirty years, so I don't blame you for not knowing who I am.'

'Maggie Ryan,' he said slowly, taking her hand. 'Of the Ryans at Starlight Cottages?'

'Bingo!' Sorcha exclaimed, laughing. 'God, that took you long enough. I got it straight away when she walked into my shop.'

Sean Óg grinned and squeezed Maggie's hand. 'Welcome back, Maggie. How's life been treating you since you left? Quite well, I see,' he continued, answering his own question. 'It's great to see you. Hey, let's get Nuala to guess who you are. Nuala!' he yelled over his shoulder. 'Come over here for a sec, will ya.'

A tall woman with dark hair appeared from behind the bar and walked over, coming to a halt at the table. She looked at Maggie and beamed her a broad smile. 'Hi there, Maggie Ryan. I heard you've come to spend the summer. Lovely to see you again after all these years.'

Sean Óg stared at Nuala. 'How did you know?'

'I listen to what people say,' Nuala replied, putting her arm around Sean Óg. 'My husband is only interested if it's about the GAA tournaments or rugby. Anything else goes in one ear and out the other.'

'Husband?' Maggie said. 'So you two got married? I remember you dating lots of girls, Sean Óg, but I always knew you and Nuala were meant to be together.'

'Yeah, sure he went through the female population like a dose of salts,' Nuala said. 'But I bided my time and waited for him to grow up. Didn't take him long, I have to say. And here we are, thirty years and three kids later and soon to be grandparents. Isn't that something else?'

'And they run the best pub in Ireland,' Sorcha filled in.

Sean Óg winked at Sorcha. 'Are you looking for a free drink?'

'Could be,' Sorcha said casually.

'First drink on the house for you both,' Nuala cut in. 'As a welcome back gesture to Maggie. You haven't changed a bit, I have to say.'

'Oh, God, I'm sure I have,' Maggie protested, feeling herself blush.

'Not at all,' Nuala said. 'Same baby blue eyes and cute little button nose. Not to mention that slim body that I always hated you for. But I forgive you for being so cute,' she added.

'Everyone's cute at that age,' Maggie remarked.

'Not me,' Nuala said.

'Yes, you were,' Sean Óg countered. 'But hey, my sweet, we have a pub to run and thirsty customers so we have to leave you ladies. We'll send some beers over and then you can let us know what you want on your pizzas.'

'See you later, lads,' Nuala said and followed her husband to the bar where there was already a crowd.

'So fantastic to meet them,' Maggie said with a happy sigh. 'What a great couple they are.'

'Fab,' Sorcha agreed. 'Nuala is a lucky woman.'

'Hi,' a breathless voice said beside them. 'Sorry I'm late, but the last client took a long time to dry.'

Maggie looked up and discovered a petite woman with short pale blonde hair standing by their table. 'You must be Susie,' she said.

'I am indeed,' Susie said and shook Maggie's hand. 'The late-as-usual Susie. Hi, Maggie, lovely to meet you. Sorry I'm late.'

'No problem,' Sorcha said as Susie pulled out a chair and sat down. 'You nearly missed the free beers, though. But here they come,' she added as a waiter arrived with three bottles of lager on a tray.

'What kind of pizza do you want?' he asked as he placed the bottles on the table.

'We'll have a margherita, a Neapolitan and—?' Sorcha looked at Maggie. 'I forgot what your favourite was.'

'No idea what I used to like then,' Maggie said. 'But I'll have a marinara if you do those.'

'Of course,' the waiter said. 'With shrimps and mussels.'

'Perfect,' Maggie said, smiling at him. 'It's so nice to be back,' she added with a happy sigh.

Susie smiled and nodded. 'Must be amazing. Sorcha told me you used to spend the summer here a long time ago.'

'I did,' Maggie said and reached for her bottle. 'And now I'm ready to take a trip down memory lane.'

'Ah, but the road ahead is much more exciting,' Susie said, taking a sip from her bottle. 'I find memory lane a bit repetitive. You know what happened so there are no surprises.'

'Except the happy memories are nice to linger over,' Sorcha cut in. 'But you are just a baby of thirty-two, compared to us, so your memory lane is still being built.' Sorcha turned to Maggie. 'Susie was born here but then her family moved to Dublin when she was around ten and then when she was all grown up and a trained hairdresser she came back and now she's making us all beautiful and cheering us up along with Gerry, her partner at the salon.'

'Business partner,' Susie cut in. 'Gerry has a boyfriend. His name is Philip and he runs an interior design shop in Killarney. They're such a great couple. I love them.'

'Me too,' Sorcha said. 'And Gerry is the best therapist ever. I always come out with great hair and my problems solved. That salon is unique.'

'Maybe we should call it "Susie's and Gerry's Hair and Therapy"?' Susie suggested.

'That sounds incredible,' Maggie said, touching her hair that she had put up in the usual ponytail. 'I should really do something with mine.'

'Problems or hair?' Sorcha asked with a smile.

'Well, I'd tackle the hair first.' Maggie sighed and sipped her beer. 'I'm trying to leave those problems behind and just have a great holiday. I know coming here might revive some painful memories, but it'll also take me back to a time when I was very happy.'

'I know what you mean,' Susie said. 'When I came back, I felt as if I was landing in a soft feather bed. Starting the business was hard work, but it all worked out well because people are so incredibly helpful around here. Everyone came to have their hair done. Even Dr Pat, who has very little hair left. "Trim what's there and polish the rest," he said and then he came in once a week just to get a shampoo so he could help me get started. Now I have more work than I can cope with, especially in the summer with all the weddings.'

'Business is great and now we're working on finding her a husband,' Sorcha interrupted.

'Ah, stop it, Sorcha,' Susie protested. 'The right man will come around when the time is right. I'm prepared to wait and see for now.'

'What's wrong with having a little look around?' Sorcha asked. 'You can't just sit there and wait for Mr Right to fall into your lap. Before you know it, you'll be a bitter auld woman with no man.'

Susie laughed. 'Oh yeah? Like you?'

Sorcha winked. 'That's what you think. I might be having a secret pash with someone, for all you know.'

'You do?' Susie asked, staring at Sorcha. 'How come nobody knows? I mean, any kind of romance is out there before you've even had your first kiss. You know what this village is like. Everyone knows everything before you even know it yourself.'

'Not if you're clever,' Sorcha said. 'I will say no more for the moment.' They were interrupted by the waiter arriving with three huge pizzas that he placed before each of them.

'Fantastic,' Maggie said, breathing in the smell of garlic and herbs.

'The best.' Susie fell on her pizza and devoured two slices before she turned to Maggie. 'You know what? I just remembered something now when you were talking about walking down memory lane.'

'What?' Maggie asked, sensing it was something important. She stopped eating for a moment while she waited for Susie to speak.

'There was someone from America in the village a couple of days ago,' Susie started. 'He was just passing through, he said, when he came into Sorcha's shop to buy a bottle of water and some buns. Sorcha was out just then. But he asked about Starlight Cottages and who lived there now. Said he'd been here before way back when he was a student. So I told him that the cottages had all been sold and now had new owners. Then he shrugged and said something about being silly to expect anyone to still be around after all these years, or something. Didn't think much about it until now.'

'Could it be...?' Sorcha said, staring at Maggie. 'I mean, that guy you were dating the last summer you were here.'

Maggie stared at Sorcha and swallowed a bite of pizza that nearly got stuck in her throat. 'Oh, God,' she whispered when she could speak. 'It could be. And you know what? I heard this guy on the radio today being interviewed about being here when he was young. His story was nearly exactly like mine. He said he met this girl thirty years ago in Killarney...'

'Oh, yes!' Sorcha exclaimed. 'I heard it too while I was closing up the shop. Sounded like such a romantic story. You mean, that might have been *him*?'

'Maybe,' Maggie said. She leaned forward staring at Susie. 'What did he look like? The man who came into Sorcha's shop?'

'Tall,' Susie said, putting down her knife and fork. 'Nice

eyes. Green, I think. Short grey hair and a neat beard. Lovely smile.'

Maggie nearly choked again. 'Green eyes?' she spluttered. 'Paul had green eyes.'

Susie slapped Maggie on the back. 'Who was Paul? Don't tell me yet. Take a deep breath and try to calm down.'

'I'm okay,' Maggie said, taking a slug of beer as she regained her composure. 'It's just such a shock to hear this. Paul was an American boy I met thirty years ago. We were together for a few weeks during my last summer holiday here in Sandy Cove.'

'Like that story on the radio?' Susie said, looking excited.

'Something like it,' Maggie replied. She stared wildly at Sorcha. 'I mean, Paul, here, looking for me? Could it be true?'

'It certainly could,' Sorcha said.

'Oh,' Susie exclaimed, clasping her hands to her chest. 'Isn't this romantic? It's making me all teary-eyed. Lovers meeting after many, many years apart and falling in love again. It's like a movie.'

'Stop it,' Maggie said, halfway between laughter and tears. 'We weren't lovers back then.'

Susie lifted an eyebrow. 'You weren't? Why not?'

'Because of the nuns,' Sorcha said between bites of pizza. 'It was still holy Catholic Ireland then. We both went to strict convent schools, you know. The nuns put the frighteners on us about doing anything remotely... eh, intimate before marriage. We would roast in hell forever, if we did.'

'Oh,' Susie said. 'That must have been a bit sad.'

'Not really,' Maggie remarked, cutting into her pizza. 'In a way it made things easier. There was a rule book we all knew about. Nothing you'd discuss, but there was less pressure, if you know what I mean. And Paul was a real gentleman. So considerate.'

'And boring?' Susie suggested.

'Anything but.' Maggie felt hot all over as she suddenly remembered how he had kissed her. 'But let's not go into that.'

'Okay,' Susie said, holding up her hands. 'Let's not get too personal.'

'I wonder if he's married,' Maggie said, looking at Susie. 'Was he with anyone?'

Susie thought for a moment. 'I didn't see anyone. His car was parked outside but I got the feeling he was alone. So maybe he's still single. Except...'

'He's probably been holding a candle to you all these years,' Sorcha suggested.

'Except what?' Maggie said, staring at Susie. 'What were you going to say?'

'He was wearing a ring. But on his right hand. A gold signet ring of some kind.'

'But that doesn't mean he's married,' Maggie remarked.

'Maybe he's an aristocrat?' Susie said, pushing her plate away. 'He could be a sir or a lord or something.'

'He couldn't be,' Sorcha argued. 'He's American of Irish descent.'

'I suppose you're right.' Susie looked disappointed. 'You'll have to ask about that ring when you meet.'

'I don't think we will. I'll never find him,' Maggie said with a long sigh. 'And he's already been by the cottage and found out I'm no longer there. So I might as well just forget him. Can we have more beer?'

'Coming up.' Sorcha snapped her fingers and a waiter appeared as if by magic. She ordered more beer and they finished their pizzas, eating more slowly, chatting about other things while Maggie's mind was full of what Susie had said.

Paul had been in the shop, asking about her... It made her both happy and sad. Happy because he obviously still cared about her and the relationship they had had. And sad because she was sure she'd never find him. He must have moved on, maybe down to Beara and his relations there, or even back to New York, having given up on the idea of finding her. *Ah well,* she thought. *That's life. Full of things that could have been but never were, hopes and dreams and promises not fulfilled.* As she looked across the pub at people chatting and laughing and Sorcha and Susie deep in conversation, her thoughts went back to that day, their last day together and the promise they had made to each other.

9

'I can't believe it's the end of August already,' Maggie had said to Paul when they sat on the little beach below Starlight Cottages. They had had a long swim and then shared sandwiches that Maggie had brought. Now it was late afternoon and Paul had to go back to Brian's house to pack his bags before he left for Shannon Airport the following morning to catch the flight back to New York. The summer had come to an end. It was already cooler and the days shorter with the leaves turning golden on some of the trees.

'I know,' Paul said. 'This summer has gone so quickly.' He brushed crumbs from his mouth and drank from his bottle of water. Then he looked at Maggie sitting there in her blue swimsuit and a white sweatshirt over her shoulders and touched her hair. 'I love you like this, your hair messy and your face tanned and those blue eyes...' He leaned forward and kissed her. 'I'll never forget this summer. Or you.'

Maggie kissed him back, her lips cold after her recent swim. 'I'll never forget you either. But there is no danger of that, is there? I mean, we'll see each other again next year, won't we?'

'Of course we will,' he promised. 'I'll let you know what I

decide to do and then we'll take it from there. If I go for the army, I might not have a lot of leave, but whatever happens I'll be back.'

'Or I'll come to you,' Maggie suggested, knowing he didn't really want to go to West Point, but would just to please his father. 'I'll see if there are any cheap flights to New York during the winter and pop over to see you.'

'That would be terrific,' he said, smiling tenderly at her. 'I'll be counting the days.'

'And we'll write to each other all the time and maybe talk on the phone,' Maggie said, taking his hand. 'I might even see if I can get a student visa to work in New York during the summer.'

'I thought you were going camping in France,' he reminded her with a teasing smile.

'Was I?' Maggie asked. 'Well, that was before I met you. I have different plans now.'

'I hope you do.' Then he looked at her with a serious expression. 'Maggie,' he started, putting his hands on her shoulders. 'You are so dear to me. These past weeks have been the most important time in my life. I think... I think I love you.'

Maggie looked into his earnest green eyes and felt a deep emotion that made tears well up. 'Oh, Paul,' she whispered. 'Me too. I love you, I know I do. I've never felt like this before. It's like an ache in my heart. I think of you when we're apart and dream about you at night. You're like a drug to me.'

He laughed and pulled her close. 'That sounds serious. But I know what you mean. Every time we say good night, I can't wait to see you again. And now I'm leaving and we'll be apart.' He sighed and shook his head. 'What are we going to do?'

'I don't know,' she replied, taking his hand and putting it to her cheek. 'I can't bear the thought that you're leaving. I'm scared that I'll never see you again.'

'Sweetie,' he said. 'Please don't worry. We will be together again. And one day we will be together for good.'

She looked at him, as hot tears ran down her cheeks. 'You promise?'

'I swear.' He pulled her to her feet. 'Let's make a pact and promise each other that we'll meet again as soon as we can.'

Maggie nodded, feeling cold despite the warmth of the sun on her back. She took both his hands in hers and looked into his eyes. 'I, Maggie Ryan, swear that I will keep in touch with you, Paul O'Sullivan, and make sure we can be together for good one day.'

He gripped her hands so hard it hurt and took a deep breath. 'And I, Paul O'Sullivan, promise that I will never forget you, Maggie Ryan. We will be together for good one day and nothing will separate us.'

Maggie sighed as she remembered those words that had been etched into her heart and mind. She had believed him with every fibre of her body and soul. What he had said helped her through their separation the next day and the following weeks and months. He went back home and started officer training at West Point and Maggie embarked on her first year at Dublin University. They wrote to each other nearly every day until Christmas. But then, after the New Year, there were no more letters from him. They just stopped coming for no apparent reason. Maggie used to check the post in the hall every day when she came home from college, but there was no airmail envelope with American stamps. She became increasingly worried, wondering what had happened, writing several letters and even a telegram. But there was no reply. It had eaten into her heart and she found it hard to eat or sleep. But after a month or two, she became angry both with Paul and herself and slowly managed to put it behind her and move on, even though the lingering sadness and worry took a long time to heal.

'What really happened?' Susie's question pulled Maggie back to the present.

'How come we never saw each other again, you mean?' Maggie asked.

'Yes. Why didn't you write to each other or something?'

'We did,' Maggie replied, sitting back on her chair. 'We wrote often, at first. I think I wrote to him every day for a while. I got a letter from him once a week or so. We even talked on the phone just before Christmas. I remember how lovely it was to hear his voice. He had just started the officers' training course at West Point. Then we kept writing until the Christmas holidays. I was planning to go over to New York in January when he had some leave, but there was a snowstorm over there and all the flights were cancelled. So we kept writing and planning to meet when the weather improved. And then at the end of January, there were no more letters from him. I tried to call the number he had given me but I couldn't get through. I think I even sent a telegram, but got no reply.' Maggie felt a wave of sadness as she remembered how desperate she had been to find out what had happened to him. 'I thought he had been killed in the Gulf War in Iraq that had just started.'

'Oh, no,' Sorcha exclaimed. 'How terrible.'

'I used to watch the news about it on TV,' Maggie said. 'Wondering if his body was in one of those coffins wrapped in the American flag. I mean he was in the army, so...'

'But just a trainee, then,' Susie suggested. 'They would hardly have sent a cadet to war after just one term, would they?'

'I suppose not,' Maggie agreed. 'But I thought that might have been the reason he stopped writing.'

'But it seems like he's very much alive and looking for you,' Susie insisted. 'So we have to find him.'

'It's very kind of you to take an interest like this,' Maggie said, warming to the young woman she had just met. There was a kind, caring aura about her that made Maggie like her even more. Susie seemed so eager to help and to listen.

Susie sighed and looked at Maggie. 'I get the feeling that

this is very important to you. And it's exciting at the same time. I'm a true romantic, you see. I believe in karma and serendipity. Maybe you were meant to part and then meet again? It could be something that was written in the stars.'

Sorcha shook her head. 'How many beers have you had, Susie?'

'Only three,' Susie replied, unperturbed by Sorcha's comment. 'But that's not why I feel like this. I just had an idea. A bit like putting a message in a bottle and throwing it into the sea...'

'How do you mean?' Maggie asked, feeling a buzz that Susie's suggestion had ignited.

Susie leaned forward, looking excited. 'I thought you could contact the radio station and ask if they had any information about him, and perhaps tell them you might be that woman the man was looking for.'

'But it might not be him,' Maggie argued.

'I feel in my bones it is,' Susie said with great conviction. 'It all fits, doesn't it?' She counted on her fingers. 'Thirty years ago, he said. A girl he met somewhere in Killarney—'

'We met on a train,' Maggie cut in.

'Yeah, but the train stopped in Killarney and he might not have wanted to give all the details on the radio,' Susie argued. 'He spent some weeks with her in a lovely village nearby, he said, right? Couldn't be anywhere else but Sandy Cove. Could it?'

Sorcha looked doubtful. 'Any village in Kerry would be lovely to an American. They have such romantic notions about Ireland.'

'I'll do it,' Maggie suddenly heard herself say.

'What?' Sorcha asked.

'I'll call them,' Maggie declared, feeling a buzz of excitement. 'I don't know why I'm saying this, but I feel that I should try to find him. I want to meet him again and ask him what the hell happened,' she said hotly. 'Why did he suddenly stop writing to me? I want to know. Then I can get the closure I feel I need and stop thinking about it.'

'Good for you,' Susie said, nodding. 'I would do the same. I mean, how dare he just stop writing like that and renege on his promise and make you think he was dead? That seems so unfair to me.'

'There might be a good explanation,' Sorcha cut in.

'In that case, I want to hear it,' Maggie declared. 'I need this, I really do. And it's not three beers that makes me say it. What Susie said made me think. I want to *do* something instead of just staying the way I am with all these unanswered questions.'

'Sleep on it, in any case,' Sorcha suggested. 'You might feel differently in the morning.'

'I don't think I will,' Maggie replied. She suddenly felt a wave of fatigue. 'Talking about sleeping, I think I'll go home. It's been a long day with all the driving and settling in.'

Susie nodded. 'It is a long drive from Dublin. I'm not surprised you're tired.'

'I'll go with you,' Sorcha said. 'Neither of us are twenty-one anymore. I need my beauty sleep. And...' She hesitated, looking around the pub. Then she leaned forward. 'I have a date tomorrow. We're going for a drive down to Cork for lunch.'

'With your mystery man?' Susie asked. 'Okay, I won't ask, even though I'm dying to know who he is.'

'I'll tell you when the time is right,' Sorcha said, getting up. 'If you're ready, I'll go with you a bit of the way, Maggie. What about you, Susie?'

'I see some people I know at the bar,' Susie said. 'I think I'll go over and join them for a bit.'

'Okay,' Sorcha said. 'And we'll pay at the till on the way out.' She looked at Maggie. 'We always go Dutch. Is that okay?'

'Of course,' Maggie said, happy to pay her own way. 'That's a great idea.'

'Yeah, because otherwise there'd be a lot of confusion about whose turn it is,' Susie said, getting up. 'And we go out quite often. Lovely to meet you, Maggie. Let us know what happens with your long-lost boyfriend.'

'I'll keep you posted,' Maggie promised. 'Nice to meet you too, Susie.'

'Bye, Sorcha. See you around, lads,' Susie said and waved as she left them and went to join a group of people gathered at the bar.

'Nice girl,' Maggie said as she and Sorcha went to the till.

'She's lovely,' Sorcha said, handing money to the waiter. 'Keep the change,' she told him.

Maggie did the same and then they walked out of the pub and into the mild starlit night.

'Hey there,' a voice said in the darkness. 'Maggie and Sorcha out on the tear just like in the old days.'

'And Brian at our heels as usual,' Sorcha said as the man came into view, his face illuminated by a light on the corner of the pub.

'Hi, Brian,' Maggie said, stepping forward. 'How nice it was to see you after all these years.'

'Hi, there, Maggie.' Brian smiled and held out his arms. 'I was so happy to see you back. How about a hug?'

Maggie laughed and fell into his arms, hugging him tight, looking up at the sweet face and the brown eyes she remembered so well. 'You haven't changed a bit. You look just like the boy who used to hang around with my brothers.'

'I was fourteen,' Brian protested. 'I hope I've matured at least a little bit since then.'

'Yes, but that cute face is still the same.' She pulled away. 'And you became a vet just like you wanted. That's so great.'

'You missed our pizza party,' Sorcha said. 'What are you doing here at this time of day?'

'I've just been out on a call,' Brian said. 'A sick calf at the farm up the road. It took me a while to get it sorted and now I'm dying for a pint and a bit of craic.'

'Plenty of that inside,' Sorcha said. 'But we're off home, being a little too long in the tooth to stay up late.'

'Ah you're not that old,' Brian said. 'Maggie, you wouldn't fancy going back in and having a drink with me?'

'Thanks, Brian,' Maggie said. 'But I'll have to take a rain check on that. I have to admit I'm tired after the drive here and I need to settle in properly. But another time I'd be happy to have drink with you.'

'I'll hold you to that,' Brian said. 'Just to say thank you. After all, you're the one responsible for me becoming a vet.'

'Really?' Maggie asked, surprised. 'In what way?'

'Didn't you know I had a crush on you back in the day?' Brian asked. 'You said to me I'd make a great vet when I helped rescue a dog who had cut his leg up in the mountains. I took that to heart and decided to do just that so you'd be impressed. If you had said I'd make a great astronaut, I'd have given that a shot as well.'

'Thank God she didn't,' Sorcha cut in as they all laughed.

'But you left before I could tell you I did it,' Brian said, looking at Maggie with mock sadness. 'And it's taken you thirty years to come back.'

'But now I'm very impressed,' Maggie said.

'About time,' Brian remarked. 'Well, I'll go in now and have that drink. See you soon again, Maggie,' he added and opened the door to the pub.

'See you, Brian,' Maggie replied as the door closed behind him. Then she stood there for a while listening to the whisper of the wind and the waves lapping against the pier, the clucking of the water against the hulls of the fishing boats at anchor. The smell of garlic and herbs from the pizza oven mingled with the tang of salt and seaweed. 'It's so lovely to be back and meet old friends again,' she said. 'I don't know why I stayed away so long.'

'Neither do I,' Sorcha said and stuck her hand under Maggie's arm. 'I was so happy to see you when you walked into my shop. It didn't take long before the years rolled back and there you were again, my dear summer friend.'

'That's how I felt too,' Maggie said as, arm in arm, they wandered slowly up the lane from the harbour and onto the main street. 'Brian made me laugh with that joke about having had a crush on me.'

'I don't think he was joking,' Sorcha argued. 'He did have a crush on you that last summer. But all you saw was that American guy. You have no idea how Brian moped after you had left.'

'Oh, God. Poor Brian,' Maggie said, taken aback. 'Now I feel guilty. But he seems to have recovered very well.'

'He's quite content, I'd say, living in his old family home with the dogs and cats, even though he hasn't found anyone to share his life with yet. I think he's too busy and maybe too fussy. And he loves his job,' Sorcha said. 'It's his passion.'

They stopped outside Sorcha's shop. 'Well, this is where I live,' she said. 'In the flat above the shop. Do you want to come in for a cup of tea?'

'Thanks,' Maggie said. 'But as I said to Brian, I'm really tired and I want to settle into the house properly.'

'Of course,' Sorcha said. 'You must be exhausted. But...' She paused for a moment. 'I want to tell you something before we say good night. About my date tomorrow. I haven't told anyone, not even Susie. I know she's very sweet and all that but I don't want it to get out yet. And she is inclined to let things slip out as she chats to customers. So it's better not to tell her things you don't want to share. But I need a friend to talk to all the same. I need to tell someone before I explode. And here you are, as if it was meant to be.'

Maggie squeezed Sorcha's arm. 'You don't have to tell me if you don't want to. But if you need a shoulder, I'm here.'

'Not a shoulder, really. It's happy news.' Sorcha sat down

on the little bench outside the shop. 'Sit down just for a minute. There's no one around and it's a warm evening.'

'Okay.' Maggie sat down beside Sorcha. 'What is it you want to tell me?'

'It's about Tom,' Sorcha said. 'Tom O'Dea, the village pharmacist. His shop is just up the street. You wouldn't remember him, they moved here after you left. Anyway, he and I started seeing each other about six months ago. And now we're madly in love. He's a lovely guy. Charming, fun, kind, great company.'

'Sounds like the ideal man for you,' Maggie remarked.

'I think he is. Except for one thing. His mother. She hates me.'

'Why?' Maggie asked, wondering how anyone could possibly hate Sorcha.

'We have clashed in the Tidy Town Association. We're both on the committee, you see. And there are opposing sides to some of the improvements that need to be done around here. You have no idea how aggressive some people can be about silly things.'

'Like what?' Maggie asked.

'Like hanging baskets and the colour of Mad Brendan's memorial bench and painting some of the buildings and the county council getting involved. It's all a mess, really, right now. Mrs O'Dea is the most militant of the lot. I can't understand how my lovely Tom can have such an unpleasant mother. In any case, we were keeping our relationship secret for now, because she could have made things difficult for me.'

'In what way could she do that?' Maggie asked, mystified by all the drama.

'Lots of ways,' Sorcha said with a sigh. She pointed at the shop. 'She used to own a lot of property in the village. Like this house. I'm glad I managed to get permission to extend my shop and renovate my flat before she bought it. That was before I started dating her son, too. You can imagine what it could do to me if she had decided to end my lease. She's that vindictive. She is also one of those possessive Irish mammies who thinks no woman is good enough for her son. She has ruined so many relationships for him. This is why Tom is still single at the age of forty-seven. But he was determined that this time, nothing will ruin what we feel for each other. So we've been meeting in secret and it's been great fun,' Sorcha said, her eyes glittering in the dark.

Maggie laughed. 'I can imagine. But maybe not in the long run?'

'No, of course not,' Sorcha said, smiling. 'But now we don't have to anymore. Because his mother has sold some of the houses she owns to a big firm in Killarney and they have taken over my lease. So now I don't have to worry about her making trouble. And...' Sorcha beamed. 'We're going to announce our engagement soon.'

'Oh, that's wonderful,' Maggie exclaimed, hugging Sorcha. 'Congratulations.'

'Thank you,' Sorcha said. 'But please don't tell anyone yet. We want it to be a big surprise.'

'I won't tell anyone,' Maggie said. 'But what about your son? Does he know about this?'

'Fintan? Yes, he does,' Sorcha replied. 'He likes Tom a lot. So that's great. They get on really well. Fintan understands why we're keeping it secret for now but he wants us to go public soon. He wants to see me settled and happy with someone so he won't have to worry about me.' She yawned and got up. 'But now I think we both need to go to bed. Thanks for listening.'

'Any time,' Maggie said as she rose from the bench. 'Especially with good news like this.'

'It's so brilliant,' Sorcha said. 'We'll defeat the mammy.'

Maggie had to laugh. 'It's such an Irish thing, isn't it?'

'Ridiculously so,' Sorcha agreed.

'A happy ending for you.'

'I think so,' Sorcha agreed with a smile. 'But enough about me. Listen, Maggie, you really should contact the radio station and see if you can find that man. I'm sure it's your Paul. Wouldn't it be wonderful if you met again?'

'Yes, and very strange. Can't even imagine what it would feel like. I'm not sure I'm ready for that.'

'Sleep on it anyway.'

'Good idea,' Maggie replied.

They said good night and Maggie continued down the street towards the cliffs and the coastguard station, thinking about the evening, remembering what both Sorcha and Susie had suggested. Should she really contact the radio station and tell them she might be the 'lovely colleen' that man was looking for? It could start a series of events that she couldn't handle. But if that man really was Paul, it might help her find him. Was it worth the risk of having their story exposed on the radio?

When Maggie reached the house, she hadn't come to any decision. She would follow Sorcha's advice and sleep on it, she thought, yawning as she put the key in the door.

10

Maggie woke bright and early the next day. The sun shone from a cloudless sky, streaming in through the kitchen window as she made breakfast and put it on a tray to carry out to the deck. How her mother would have loved to have had that deck instead of the rough little garden she had constantly tried to improve. She had only managed to plant a few shrubs and mowed the sparse lawn while looking after the family of four children and a husband who wasn't interested in either gardening or DIY. So the house had remained in its slightly dilapidated state, which was fine for a summer holiday but would never be comfortable if they'd wanted to come for winter breaks. Maggie decided against taking photos and sending them to her mother. It would only make her sad to see what the house could have looked like given some work and dedication. In any case, she and her mother weren't close, and ever since her break-up, Maggie had avoided talking to her parents, as she wanted to heal on her own before she faced them again.

She sat down at the round table just outside the sunroom and put on her sunglasses, gazing out at the ocean, where seagulls glided around, and enjoyed the distant sound of waves breaking against the cliffs below. She turned to look at the path that led to the steps to the little beach, now all securely fenced with a gate at the top. Great idea, of course, but it took away from the wild charm of earlier times.

She remembered carefully picking her way down to the beach where Paul would wait for her. They would go for a swim and then sit on a beach blanket and talk for hours... How magical it had been.

Maggie finished her toast and drank her tea, trying to figure out what she would do. Being here had brought all the memories back more vividly than she had expected and now all she wanted to do was find Paul and ask him all the questions that had been going through her mind ever since he stopped writing to her. Having made that decision, Maggie went to find her phone and looked up the Radio Kerry website, tapping in the contact phone number before she had a chance to change her mind.

A cheery woman's voice answered. 'Hi there. Radio Kerry, Kiara Kelly here. How can I help you?'

'Oh...' Maggie started. 'Good morning. I don't know how to say this, but...' She tried to think of a short explanation of what she wanted to say.

'Yes?'

'Well,' Maggie said, charging ahead. 'I was listening to your "Out and About" slot yesterday afternoon and I heard that interview with the man who was looking for someone he used to know thirty years ago.'

'Okay,' Kiara Kelly said. 'That was me doing that interview in Killarney. We multitask here in this little radio station. I got the assignment for that slot. I just walked up to people who looked like visitors and stuck the microphone in their faces and asked a few questions. Fun job, I have to say. I remember that man. He looked a little sad. Good-looking kind of silver fox-type. Gorgeous green eyes. And a thousand-watt smile.'

'Oh. Yeah, that sounds familiar.' Maggie smiled wistfully as she remembered.

'Does it?' Kiara asked, sounding puzzled.

'Yes. I think he's someone I used to know. Someone I've been looking for.'

'You've been looking for him?' Kiara asked. 'And he was also looking for someone. Are you... could you be the "lovely colleen" we were talking about?' she said, her voice vibrating with excitement.

'I might be,' Maggie admitted.

'Oh my God! Really?' Kiara squealed. 'This is so exciting! Hold on a minute. Ronan,' she shouted. 'Wait till you hear this!' Then she had a muffled conversation before she came back to Maggie. 'Hey, would you be willing to do an interview? On the radio?'

'Oh...' Maggie started. 'When?'

'Right now. We'll just ask you a few questions and then broadcast it in our next slot later today. I mean, it could help you find this man, if that's what you want to do.'

'I doubt he'd listen,' Maggie said. 'I have a feeling he's gone back home. I know he was here in this village, asking about the cottage my family used to own.'

'Which village is that?'

'Sandy Cove. We used to spend all our summers here when I was young.'

'Here?' Kiara asked. 'You mean you're there now? In Sandy Cove?'

'Yes. I'm actually renting the same cottage for the summer.'

'Wow.' Kiara paused for a moment. 'This could make a hell of a story. And if we find this man and you're reunited, we could be there when it happens. It could be filmed and broadcast on TV – wouldn't that be amazing?'

'No,' Maggie said, alarmed. She began to regret having made this phone call. 'It wouldn't be amazing at all.' It could be hugely embarrassing. Paul might not want to be exposed in the media in this way. 'I'd rather it was kept more private,' she replied.

'Oh, okay,' Kiara said, sounding calmer. 'I was galloping ahead here. Got a bit carried away. Sorry about that.'

'That's okay.'

'Let's calm down then,' Kiara said, sounding as if she was trying to rein herself in. 'One step at a time. We'll just do something low-key and see if we can help you find him. What's the name of your lost love?'

'Paul O'Sullivan,' Maggie said with a shiver at saying his name out loud. 'His family came from Beara, so he's more Cork than Kerry, actually.'

'That makes it even more interesting. You know what?' Kiara said. 'How about we just mention this in our "Out and About" slot and then see what happens? Either he will hear it himself or someone who knows him will come forward. Just to start. Keeping it low-key this way. Nothing might come of it, anyway. What do you say?'

'Yes,' Maggie said after a moment's reflection. 'That sounds like a good idea.'

'Do you mind telling me your name?' Kiara asked.

'It's Maggie Ryan. And I'm staying in...'

'The very same cottage your parents owned way back then,' Kiara cut in. 'That's what you said. In Sandy Cove, right?'

'Yes,' Maggie replied, her voice hoarse. Her stomach was in a knot as she considered how this story might look if anyone she knew heard it. Sad older woman looking for the lost love of her youth? Would it make her look like a real loser on the rebound after her separation? What would her children think? And Dermot? Would he laugh at her and tell the new woman in his life how utterly pathetic Maggie was and how he had been right to leave her? All kinds of scary images flashed through her mind as Kiara kept talking.

'Lovely village,' Kiara said. 'Would make a wonderful backdrop for a documentary or a movie based on this story.' She stopped and laughed. 'There I go again, getting carried away. But I'm a hopeless romantic and I get such a buzz from stories like this. Don't worry, Maggie, we'll keep it low-key for now.'

'Great,' Maggie said, smiling at Kiara's upbeat tone. 'That's what I'd prefer.'

'A bit like fishing, isn't it?' Kiara joked. 'Throwing out a bit of bait and then waiting to see if you get a bite.'

'I suppose it is,' Maggie replied.

'So do we have all the details? You met Paul O'Sullivan on a train and then he looked you up in Sandy Cove a few weeks later. And you were in love and then...?'

'We lost touch,' Maggie said, cringing slightly at the mention of them falling in love. It felt a little too personal for comfort.

'Right. And now he's here and you're there and you both would like to meet again.'

'I would, in any case,' Maggie declared.

'So would he, judging by what he said,' Kiara stated. 'Even if he was a bit shy about giving out his name and other personal details. All we're doing is giving him a little push, right?'

'That sounds fine. But I don't want it to be blown up into something that it isn't,' Maggie said, hoping this conveyed her feelings. 'It might not even be him.'

'Of course not,' Kiara assured her. 'Don't worry, Maggie. We'll mention it this evening instead of an interview in next week's programme, and then we'll see what happens. The number you're calling from is your mobile, I take it?'

'That's right.'

'Okay. Then we have all we need. Thanks for calling. I hope the two of you find each other. Keep us posted, okay?'

'I will,' Maggie promised, crossing her fingers just in case.

She wasn't at all sure she'd want to call this woman again and get her all excited.

'Bye for now,' Kiara said. 'And good luck.'

Maggie said goodbye and hung up, the butterflies in her stomach flapping around. She suddenly felt sick with nerves. What had she done? What if Paul heard it and got angry? Or if he was with his wife or partner and it caused a lot of trouble between them? But then she reminded herself that he had been looking for *her*. That was a good sign, Maggie told herself and got up from the table, trying to look ahead and think of what she was going to do today. Just laze around, she thought with a happy sigh. Go for a swim at the main beach and see who she'd meet there. She had been told there was a nice café just off the beach called The Two Marys', run by the two cousins she remembered from her childhood. They had been known as Mary O and Mary B – Mary O being quite a bit older than Mary B, who had been around Maggie's age. They would be able to fill her in on all the gossip and tell her what had happened in the village during all the years she had been away.

Maybe they would even give an insight into Sorcha's secret boyfriend and his controlling mother. Maggie had seen the pain in Sorcha's eyes as she told Maggie about their plight. It sounded terrible that a grown man like this Tom would be so intimidated by his mother. But maybe he was only trying to protect Sorcha? After all, his mother had once owned the house Sorcha's shop was in. That could have caused a lot of trouble should Mrs O'Dea suspect anything was going on between her son and Sorcha. The mother still seemed to be on the warpath. It all sounded so petty and trite, a tiny storm in a teacup, but it could cause Sorcha a lot of pain and misery. She deserved to have a happy ending with the man she seemed so in love with. Maggie promised herself she'd do anything she could to help, even if it meant confronting this unpleasant woman. She didn't like rows, but she also hated to see Sorcha so miserable, so she was prepared to do what she could without too much unpleasantness. And maybe, in some way, she could, as an outsider, be the catalyst that changed things around?

She suddenly felt as if coming here was meant to be. Karma or serendipity or whatever Susie believed in seemed at once quite real. There was now a sense of purpose to the summer that lay ahead. She was here to help Sorcha. And to find Paul.

Later that morning, when Maggie was walking into the village to buy the Sunday papers at Sorcha's shop, she bumped into Brian doing the same.

'Hi,' he said, handing Pauline a few euros to pay for the *Sunday Independent*. 'Nice to see you again. How about a coffee? We can get it to go and sit at the harbour.'

'Why not?' Maggie said as she picked up a copy of *The Sunday Times*. 'It would be nice to catch up over coffee.'

'I'll get them,' Brian offered. 'What do you want?'

'I'll have a tall latte, please.'

'Coming up,' Brian said and went to the machine. 'I'll have the same and a Danish. You want one too?'

'Yes, please,' Maggie replied.

Brian got the coffees and Maggie took the papers and the bag with the pastries and they walked together down the street and out to the harbour, where they sat on a bench outside the pub. The late-morning sun was warm on their backs and the water in the bay was calm with just the odd ripple from the light breeze.

'Gorgeous day,' Maggie said, putting the newspapers on the bench beside her.

'Really nice.' Brian handed Maggie her coffee and took a Danish from the bag she had set on top of the papers. 'How does it feel to be back?'

'Strange but very nice.' Maggie sipped her latte and looked

out over the water. 'I'm trying to get used to how everything has changed. It's a bit like waking up from a long sleep to find you have slept for years rather than just one night.' She smiled and fished her Danish from the bag, looking at him as she took a bite. 'Oh, God, this is delicious,' she said as the taste of freshly baked pastry filled her mouth.

'They're from the bakery up the street. At least they haven't changed,' Brian said. 'They still make the best soda bread in Ireland.'

'That's nice.' Maggie was quiet for a moment, looking at Brian, realising how he had grown from a young boy she remembered into a handsome man in his early forties. But he was still so youthful, with a glint in his brown eyes, the unruly brown hair and that sweet smile she found so beguiling.

He met her gaze. 'What are you looking at? Do I have a smudge on my face or something?'

'No, I was just thinking that you don't look very different from the last time I saw you.'

'I was fourteen and I thought you were a goddess. But you didn't notice me, you cruel woman. I was devastated.'

'Oh yeah, I'm sure you were. I just remember you as a cute boy who used to run around with my brothers and tease us girls like mad.'

'Sean and Danny,' Brian said. 'They were great fun. What are they up to now?'

'Sean is a doctor and is living in Donegal and Danny is a teacher like me. He teaches maths and science at a school in Dublin. Sean is married and has two children, and Danny has just bought a flat and is moving into that with his girlfriend. What about you?' Maggie asked. 'Any partner or girlfriend living with you at the farm?'

'No, not at the moment. I still live in the house, but the farmland was sold when my father died five years ago. My mother lives in Dingle now with her sister.'

'I see,' Maggie said, deciding not to ask any further questions about Brian's love life. It felt strange somehow. 'I remember the house. It was such a nice old place with lots of dogs and cats and even hens.'

'I still have animals,' Brian said. 'Two dogs. A springer spaniel called Jessie and a Jack Russell called Bella. Jessie is going to have puppies soon. You wouldn't fancy one, by the way?'

Maggie sipped her latte. 'Now you're tempting me. Our lovely dog Sally died last year and I miss her terribly. We were going to get a new dog, but then...' She stopped. 'Well, my partner and I broke up so that made it impossible to take on a new dog with that upheaval and stress.'

'And sadness,' Brian said and touched Maggie's shoulder. 'I'm sorry, Maggie. I'm sure that was hard.'

'Still is,' Maggie said. 'But being here helps a lot. It's such a great break from everything, from all the pain and the memories of the family I had. My kids have left home and have their own lives now, so...'

'So you're all alone.'

'Yes.'

'I've been on my own for a long time, but that's from choice, in a way, and something I'm used to,' Brian continued. 'But around here you never feel lonely, you know.'

'I think that's very true. I've only just arrived but here I am, having found Sorcha, who used to be my best friend, and now I'm sitting here talking to another old friend.' Maggie finished her coffee and smiled at Brian, leaning her back against the bench with a dart of wellbeing she hadn't felt for a long time. 'I'm so happy I came here.'

'So am I,' Brian said. 'I hope you'll have a wonderful summer.'

'I already am,' Maggie said, glancing at Brian, realising that here was a man happy in his skin without any hang-ups or attitudes. Someone honest and true. 'I might take one of your puppies,' she suddenly said. 'When are they due?'

'In three weeks,' Brian replied. 'But I have to warn you that they're not purebred. Jessie had a little fling with the sheepdog next door, so it'll be a mongrel.'

'They are the best dogs,' Maggie declared. 'My Sally was a Labrador-Collie mix. A wonderful, kind and loyal dog. My best friend, if that doesn't sound too daft.'

'Not at all.' Brian nodded. 'I know what you mean. Dogs have a habit of stealing your heart so I do understand how sad you must have been when you lost your Sally.'

'Of course you do,' Maggie said, touched by his sympathy. 'You love animals and you understand them. I remember that. I thought it was so sweet the way you talked to dogs and cats when we were kids.'

'Everyone else laughed at me and thought I was a bit strange.'

'I don't think Sorcha did,' Maggie said.

'No, she and I were always very close. Nearly like brother and sister. We still are. And right now, she's trying to sort out a problem with a man she's in love with.' Brian stopped, looking contrite. 'But I shouldn't say any more.'

'You can because she told me all about it last night,' Maggie said.

'Oh,' Brian said, looking relieved. 'I'm glad she did. She needs someone to confide in. Another woman, I mean. A friend like you.'

'I don't think I can do anything to help her. But I'm happy to listen, of course. I haven't met him yet, but I have a feeling it's up to him to put his foot down.'

'Tom is very fond of his mother,' Brian said. 'Even if she's a bit of a battle-axe. I think she's very insecure deep down. People like that often are. They try to control people by being bossy and a little threatening. I'd say she'd come around eventually if someone was to talk to her.'

'That someone being me?' Maggie asked with a laugh. 'Please, Brian, don't try to get me involved. I'm not very good at sorting out conflicts. That's part of my problem, really. I always ran away from arguments and let... some people have their way.' Dermot suddenly popped into Maggie's head, the memory of him always winning a discussion and never listening to her point of view. She had never stood her ground to him, preferring to keep the peace by going along with what he wanted to do, even if it was the complete opposite to her own wishes.

'I have a feeling you're too nice,' Brian said, as if reading her mind. He sipped his coffee and turned his head to look at the view without further comment. Maggie had a sense he was giving her some space.

'Yes,' she said after a while. 'You're right. I have always tried to please people and never make waves. I thought it would be better for the children if there was peace at home.' *And then he left me*, she thought bitterly. *Was that because I was too nice?*

'I see what you mean,' Brian said. 'I'm the same. I hate arguments and fighting. Can't even watch thrillers or read detective stories.' He turned to her and smiled. 'Promise not to tell anyone, but I like watching romantic comedies. I even cry at the sad bits sometimes.'

Maggie laughed. 'I won't tell, I swear. I'm the same. Can't stand hate and shouting and fighting. And yes, me too. Love a good rom-com.'

'*Sleepless in Seattle* made me cry when Tom Hanks talked about his dead wife,' Brian confessed.

'That bit was very sad,' Maggie agreed. 'I'm not sure I cried, but my heart went out to him.'

Brian laughed. 'Aren't we the soppy pair?' He gathered up his newspaper and took Maggie's empty paper cup. 'I have to go. I need to check on a mare that's about to foal at a farm an hour away from here. I'll get rid of the cups.'

'Thanks, Brian,' Maggie said. 'I'll stay here for a bit and read the paper. The view is so lovely and I like the peace.'

'Good idea. Have a nice Sunday, Maggie. I'm so glad you came back to Sandy Cove.'

'Me too. Thank you, Brian. Lovely to chat to you.'

'I enjoyed it.'

Maggie watched him walk away, smiling at their conversation and how they had found a common trait in each other – that of hating conflict and rows. She wondered idly if this was a good thing or if it would be better to be more assertive and less afraid to stand up for oneself. Dermot had been the bossy one in their relationship and the parent who did most of the disciplining of their children, while Maggie was the caring, nurturing mother they ran to when they were hurt or sad or frightened, even as teenagers. They had always been able to talk about anything, even the most intimate subjects that Dermot shied away from. In the end, that had been beneficial for her, as she had such great relationships with both of her children. In a way, she had won without doing anything, and Dermot had lost some of the love of his children by leaving her. *But there is no winning or losing in breaking up a family,* she thought. *Just sadness and misery.*

At least talking to Brian had cheered her up in a strange way, giving her hope and a resolve to look forward to enjoying life again among old friends and new. *And maybe,* she thought, *I will meet Paul again and rekindle some of what we lost. If only I could find him.*

11

Brian and Sorcha were still in Maggie's thoughts as she went home with the Sunday papers. Especially Brian. Back in her teenage years here in Sandy Cove, she had been oblivious of Brian's crush on her. But if she had known, what would she had done about it? She would probably have laughed and thought it slightly ridiculous. He was so young then, and she would have looked at him from the distance of being five years older. She decided it was a good thing she hadn't known. It had been a happy surprise to catch up with him and discover what a wonderful man he had turned into. And a true friend, just like Sorcha.

During the following days, Maggie found herself busier than she had expected. As the weather was still lovely, she went to the beach every morning where she enjoyed long swims in the crystal-clear water that was already warm even though it was still early June. She remembered that this was always the case in Kerry, as the Gulf Stream is so close to the south-west coast. Those long swims were the high point of her day, as she had always loved swimming.

That very first Sunday, after her chat with Brian, she had

gone to the beach where she had met a group of young girls who were training for the Sandy Cove Biathlon later in the summer. Their holidays had just begun and they were keen to train hard and do well as a team. Maggie immediately offered to help out with their training, as they had told her they were looking for a coach. As a result she met them every morning and put them through a series of aerobic and strength exercises which would help them improve their stamina all through the race. She often joined them as they swam across the bay, but turned around when she felt she had had enough, leaving the girls to complete the long distances that would help them in their training.

After lunch at home she would sit on the terrace and read one of the many books she had brought. She hadn't had either the peace of mind or the time to read after the break-up, but now she suddenly wanted to get stuck into the mix of thrillers, romantic fiction and biographies she used to love. Sorcha sometimes dropped in after she had closed the shop and they would go for a walk or a drink at the pub and meet up with whoever happened to be there. It was an easy, relaxing routine Maggie felt was helping her to heal. Even though she was just as alone as in Dublin, here in Sandy Cove, she didn't feel lonely at all.

One afternoon, a little over a week after her arrival, Maggie walked up the long slope to the thatched cottage that housed The Two Marys' café. She had meant to call in but hadn't had the time until now. The view from here was even more beautiful than from the beach below as the Skellig islands were more visible and the expanse of the deep blue ocean seemed even more infinite. She would have loved to sit outside, but being Sunday, the tables on the deck were nearly all taken by a number of family groups. Maggie stepped inside the café and found that it was quieter and a lot less busy. She went to the counter and looked at the menu written on a blackboard on the wall.

'Hi,' a pleasant woman's voice said. 'What do you fancy?'

Maggie turned and discovered a tiny woman with grey hair smiling at her from behind the counter. 'Hello,' she said. 'Are you one of the Marys?'

'Yes. I'm Mary O,' the woman said.

'I thought you looked familiar,' Maggie said and held out her hand. 'I'm Maggie Ryan. We used to come to Sandy Cove on our summer holidays when I was a child.'

'Oh.' The woman laughed and grabbed Maggie's hand. 'One of the rowdy Ryans, were you?'

'I was indeed,' Maggie said with a laugh. 'But the rowdy ones were my brothers. I think us girls were quite well behaved.'

'Possibly,' Mary O said. 'I wasn't here much in those days. Busy gallivanting around the country working in all kinds of jobs and looking for my destiny. And then, after a while, I realised it was here all the time. This,' she said, making a wide gesture, 'is the cottage where my mother grew up. We lived in a house nearby and my granny spent her last days here. And then around ten years ago, we made it into what you see now.'

Maggie looked around at the rough whitewashed walls, the original fireplace with the old bellows still intact, at the flag-stoned floor and the window frames painted red. The tables were a mixture of different shapes and timbers and the whole place had a cosy, welcoming atmosphere with the old cottage look still intact. 'You've done a fantastic job. It's so authentic.'

'Authentic? My granny would turn in her grave if she saw it,' Mary O said, laughing. 'It didn't quite look like this in the old days. The floor would have been concrete with a lino over it. And there were several small rooms but we knocked all the interior walls down. It's a bit twee really, but most people love it.'

'I'm sure they do.' Maggie inhaled the scent of sausages and chips and felt her stomach rumbling. 'And the smell is making me hungry.'

'Would you like a plate of sausage and chips with our very own tomato relish?' Mary O asked.

'I'd love that.'

'You go and sit over there by the window and I'll get Mary B to bring it over when it's ready. I'm sure she'll be happy to see you. She was called Young Mary in her youth, when you would have been here on your holidays.'

'Oh, yes,' Maggie said. 'I do remember a Mary we used to play rounders with on the beach. She had fair hair and ran like the wind.'

'That was her,' Mary O said, smiling at Maggie. 'She was on the women's hockey team when she was in her twenties. Then she did a business course in Cork and now we run this place together.' Mary O glanced at the door to the kitchen. 'I'll get her to start your order.'

'Thanks. See you later,' Maggie said. She wandered slowly across the room, looking at the framed black-and-white photos of bygone days on the walls, recognising some of the people in them. There was Sorcha at her first communion, and Brian, her cousin, as a small boy, posing with Mad Brendan and two donkeys. Two young girls outside the library in matching dresses, one blonde, the other with darker hair, were those sisters in Willow House, Maeve and Roisin.

Maggie smiled as the memories of those wonderful holidays came flooding back. What a wonderful place it had been then. Old-fashioned, offering simple pleasures like swimming, fishing, playing rounders and those fun improvised disco parties in the old shed that was now something called the Wellness Centre. And when it rained, they had played Monopoly with games that lasted several days. They had had enormous fun without any modern distractions. What a different world it had been.

Maggie had just sat down when a woman with reddish blonde hair arrived at her table.

'Maggie Ryan,' she said as she placed a plate with sausages and chips in front of her. 'How great to see you again. I wouldn't really have been able to place you if Mary hadn't told me.'

'But I would have known you, Mary B.' Maggie got up and shook Mary's hand. 'You haven't changed much. Do you still run like the wind?'

Mary B laughed. 'Not as much as I'd like to. I have a husband and two kids and this place to look after. But yeah, we do run a bit, hubby and I. We're both running in the Dublin City Marathon later this year. But what about you? How has life treated you all these years?'

'Not too badly,' Maggie said. 'I have a job I love and two lovely kids, both grown up now. Their dad and I broke up a little over a year ago, so that's something I'm trying to recover from.'

'I'm so sorry,' Mary B said softly. 'That must have been hard.'

'It was. Still is,' Maggie replied. 'That's why I'm here, really. I thought this would be a good place to heal.'

'It's the best,' Mary B said. 'But have your lunch and then I'll bring you a coffee on the house and we can have a bit of a chat when the lunch rush calms down.'

'Sounds great,' Maggie said, the delicious smell of the sausages making her mouth water. She dug into her lunch with gusto when Mary B had left, enjoying the rich taste of the sausages, the crispy chips that she dipped into the tomato relish, the best she had ever tasted. Sausages and chips were usually a bland affair, but this was real treat. Locally produced food like this was as good as she remembered.

'Enjoy your meal?' Mary B asked as she arrived back to the table with two cups of coffee just as Maggie had finished.

'It was wonderful.' Maggie pushed away her plate and wiped her mouth on the paper napkin. 'I haven't tasted sausages like this since I was a child.'

'Made by our excellent butcher, Mattie, if you remember his shop?' Mary B sat down on the chair opposite Maggie.

'Of course,' Maggie said. 'Best pork chops in Ireland, my father used to say.'

'They still are,' Mary declared as she sipped her coffee. 'So have you enjoyed meeting the old gang?'

'I've only really caught up with Sorcha so far and just seen some of the others briefly. But I only arrived recently, of course. Plenty of time to see everyone else.'

'The word is out,' Mary said. 'I'm sure they'll be all over you soon.'

'It's been so nice to see some of them,' Maggie said and picked up her cup. 'Can't wait to get together with everyone properly. Funny how you connect even after all these years. It's like we met yesterday after the initial shock of looking at a much older person.'

'It doesn't take long before all the years disappear and you see old friends just like they used to be,' Mary agreed. 'But not everyone from back then is still around, of course. There are lots of newcomers here. And the village is different. Less cosy than it used to be.'

'I heard there are ructions in the Tidy Town Association,' Maggie said. 'All kinds of rows and arguments.'

Mary sighed. 'Oh, yes, don't remind me. Everyone has different opinions and are not afraid to shout them out. I don't know what's going to happen next.'

'I heard there is a certain lady who's very militant,' Maggie said. 'A Mrs O'Dea?'

'Dreadful Darina, you mean,' Mary replied, her mouth twisting into an ironic smile. 'Yes, she likes to throw her weight around, of which there is a lot, if you know what I mean. Thinks she owns the place, which, come to think of it, was quite true until recently. She used to own a lot of property in the area, actually, before she sold most of it.'

'So I gather,' Maggie said as she sipped her coffee. 'Sorcha told me all about it.'

Mary glanced around as the door opened. 'Speak of the devil,' she whispered to Maggie. 'Here she is in person. She likes to get her after-lunch coffee and cake here.'

'Oh.' Maggie looked at the heavyset woman who had just entered the café. She had dark curly hair shot through with grey and was dressed in a cerise linen shirt, wide blue trousers and white lace-up golf shoes. She looked around as she reached the counter, her eyes homing in on Mary B.

'There you are,' the woman said imperiously. 'I was wondering if any of the staff were around.'

Mary got up and took Maggie's plate and cup. 'Hello there, Darina. I was just chatting to Maggie Ryan here, who arrived last week to spend the summer in Sandy Cove.'

The woman peered at Maggie. 'Hello. A summer guest, are you?'

'Well, yes, but...'

'Maggie has been here before,' Mary cut in. 'Her family used to own one of the Starlight Cottages. The one Jason owns now.'

'Really?' Darina O'Dea's eyebrows shot up. 'And now you're renting it for a week or two?'

'For the whole summer,' Maggie said, feeling awkward talking loudly to this woman across the café.

'I see.' Darina O'Dea turned to Mary. 'Could you get me a large Americano and a slice of carrot cake, Mary? And bring it over to Maggie's table.' She looked at Maggie. 'It would be nice to get to know each other, don't you think? As you're going to spend all summer here, I mean.'

'Eh, yes,' Maggie said, not really sure she wanted this kind of company. But it would give her an opportunity to find out what Darina O'Dea was like. 'You're very welcome to join me, Mrs O'Dea.'

'I'll get you a slice of cake too,' Mary offered, rolling her eyes behind Darina's back.

'Excellent,' Darina said. 'And you may call me Darina,' she added as if she had just bestowed Maggie a huge honour.

'Thank you,' Maggie said, avoiding Mary's amused glance, fearing she would start laughing.

Darina marched across the floor to Maggie's table where she pulled out a chair and plonked herself down. 'So,' she said, studying Maggie. 'Where are you from?'

'I'm from Dublin,' Maggie said.

'What part?' Darina asked.

'Glenageary,' Maggie replied. 'It's a suburb in south County Dublin.'

'I know where Glenageary is,' Darina said. 'I know Dublin very well. That's a nice part of town,' she added approvingly, looking at Maggie with more interest. 'So you're here with your family, then? Your husband and children?'

'No. On my own,' Maggie said. 'I'm not married. I'm a teacher,' she continued, to deflect the spotlight from her family circumstances. 'So I have quite a long summer holiday, you see.'

'That's nice,' Darina said. Her chair creaked as she shifted on her seat. 'But you were here some years ago, then? When you were younger, I mean.'

'Oh, yes, I was,' Maggie replied and told her all about her family owning the cottage. 'It was very different then.'

'Of course it was,' Darina agreed. 'We came here twenty years ago. My husband had family connections here and he inherited some property about that time. Our son Tom was looking around for a pharmacy so it suited him to take over the one we owned. He still runs it.'

'So I heard,' Maggie said.

'You did?' Darina stared at Maggie. 'From whom?'

'Oh, I don't remember exactly,' Maggie said airily. 'I've been catching up with old friends since I arrived. Mary here is one of them. We used to play on the beach when we were kids.'

'Did you now?' Darina turned to look at Mary coming across the floor with a tray. 'And here she is with our cakes.'

Mary smiled and placed Darina's coffee and the plates with cake on the table. 'There you go. Would you like another coffee, Maggie?'

'Yes, please,' Maggie said, handing Mary the empty cup.

'Put it all on my bill, Mary,' Darina said. 'I'd like to give Maggie a treat as a welcome gift.'

'That's very kind,' Maggie said, smiling at Darina. 'Thank you.'

'You're welcome,' Darina said, picking up her spoon and attacking the slice of carrot cake with gusto. 'So,' she said, having swallowed her first bite, 'who else have you met since you came?'

'I met Sorcha,' Maggie said, studying Darina for a reaction. 'We were best friends when we were children.'

'Were you really?' Darina's spoon with the next bite stopped on the way to her mouth. 'I'm sure she was a bit of a tearabout back then.'

'Weren't we all?' Maggie said with a laugh. 'We were known as the rowdy Ryans then. Even my father was a bit rowdy, actually.'

'Was he?' Darina looked taken aback. 'Did he have a drinking problem?'

'No, not at all,' Maggie protested. 'He just liked to have fun and discuss politics and so on. It could result in arguments in the pub that were quite heated. And he loved pulling people's legs. Still does,' she said, smiling at the thought of her fun-loving father.

'I see.' Darina sipped her coffee while she studied Maggie over the rim of her cup. 'So you were friends with Sorcha?'

'Oh, yes. Very close friends,' Maggie declared. 'I was so happy to meet her again.'

'I'm sure she has changed a lot,' Darina suggested. 'She's a bit contrary, I find.'

'Maybe she's just very independent?' Maggie said, patting her mouth with the paper napkin. 'She probably had to be very assertive as a single parent. Bringing up a child on your own isn't easy.'

'I suppose. But that's all very well in those circumstances. Arguing with people and being stubborn isn't very pleasant generally. She can be very stroppy, you know.' Darina's mouth set in a thin line for a moment. 'But let's not dwell on these things right now. You're probably looking forward to a lovely summer here, meeting old friends and new. And maybe... you might like to join my association?'

'Which association would that be?' Maggie inquired, even though she knew the answer.

'The Tidy Town Association. We're hoping to win the top prize this year, so we're working hard on getting the village spick and span and we need every hand on deck, so to speak. Could be a good way to get to know people around here.' Darina drew breath and looked expectantly at Maggie.

Maggie picked up her spoon and cut off a piece of cake while she pondered the question. Then she looked at Darina and smiled. 'Yes, I think that's a great idea. I love this village and I'd like to help make it look its best for the competition. I'm actually quite busy helping with the girls' biathlon team, but I'm sure I can squeeze in something. I like gardening and painting, so I could definitely do something. Not that I think that the village needs that much improvement. It looks very nice already.'

'There is a lot more to do before it's up to standard,' Darina said, looking shocked. 'We have a meeting on Thursday evening in the community hall. At half past seven. Tea and biscuits afterwards. Would you be free to attend?'

'I have been so busy since I arrived,' Maggie said. 'But I think I'm free then. I'd love to come. Thank you for inviting me.'

'You're very welcome,' Darina said, looking pleased. 'I'm sure you'll enjoy it.'

'I'm looking forward to it,' Maggie said and took a bite of the cake. She looked at Darina, who had taken her phone out of her large handbag and was reading a text message. She was perhaps a little pompous and full of herself but apart from that she had been kind and welcoming, aside from her slightly unkind comments about Sorcha. She hoped she could perhaps help the two of them get along.

Darina turned off her phone and put it back in her handbag. 'Sorry, but I had to take a peep at that message. It was about an urgent matter. You were saying?'

'I said I was looking forward to the meeting on Thursday.'

Darina nodded. 'Excellent.' She fished a card from her handbag and handed it to Maggie. 'My contact details should you need them.' She closed her handbag with a loud snap, drained her cup and rose. 'But now I have to leave you. Wonderful to meet you, Maggie. See you Thursday. I'll reserve a seat for you.'

'Thank you,' Maggie said. 'See you then, Darina.'

Darina nodded and sailed out of the café while Maggie looked at the card that said, *Darina O'Dea, president of the Sandy Cove Tidy Town Association. Chairwoman of the Parish Council.*

'Impressive, don't you think?' Mary B said in her ear.

'Amazing,' Maggie said. 'President *and* chairwoman.'

'Sandy Cove royalty,' Mary B said, her voice full of laughter. 'She rules this village with an iron fist.'

'I'm so honoured to have been asked to the meeting,' Maggie said with a laugh.

'You should be. She gave you the five-star treatment.' Mary held the coffee pot over Maggie's cup. 'More coffee?'

'God, no,' Maggie protested. 'I've had enough excitement. More caffeine would give me the shakes. But you know what? I thought she was quite sweet really. Okay, so a bit... full on... but still so friendly and welcoming.'

'She's looking for allies.'

'Sorcha isn't too fond of her.'

'It's mutual,' Mary B said, putting the coffee pot down. 'Sorcha is the only one who dares contradict her. But I'm staying out of all that. You should go to that meeting, though. We need new blood and a new perspective on things. Darina might listen to you, as you're from Dublin and all.'

'I don't like taking sides or getting into arguments,' Maggie protested.

'You can sit on the fence while keeping your ear to the ground, if you know what I mean,' Mary remarked, winking.

'Sounds a bit like acrobatics,' Maggie said with a laugh.

'Well, you're a keep-fit person, so I'm sure you can manage that kind of exercise,' Mary joked.

'I'll do my best.' Maggie's gaze drifted to the window. 'But I think it might rain, so I'll head off. I've had a gorgeous morning, swimming and then having a lovely lunch here and catching up with you. Now I need to go back to the cottage and do a bit of tidying up.'

Mary nodded and picked up the coffee pot. 'The kids at the surf school will be coming here for their snacks and stuff soon, so it'll be busy. Lovely to see you, Maggie. Drop in soon again.'

'I will,' Maggie promised.

'Say hi to Lydia. She'll be asking you over for a cup of tea later.'

Maggie stopped on the way to the door. 'How do you know?'

'I'm psychic,' Mary said with a wink. 'See ya around.'

Maggie laughed, waved and left the café, running down to the beach to get her towel and swimsuit that she had left there, while the first raindrops pitted the sand. She put the towel over her head and ran all the way back to the cottage, arriving breathless inside the door as the heavy shower smattered against the windows.

Catching her breath, Maggie took off the towel and picked up a piece of paper on the doormat and looked at a message scribbled on it.

How about a cup of tea with me, Jason and the neighbours this afternoon? We'll be looking forward to seeing you at four if that suits you. Hope you can come. Cheers, Lydia.

'Mary truly is psychic,' Maggie said to herself as she went upstairs to have a shower and tidy herself up. She was delighted by the invitation. It would be nice to meet the neighbours who she had glimpsed now and then but never managed to introduce herself to. Having checked her watch, she saw that it was coming up to three o'clock, so she'd have plenty of time to shower and change out of her shorts and T-shirt and even wash her hair. No need to look a mess the first time she met her neighbours.

After her shower, Maggie went into her bedroom and turned on Radio Kerry for some nice music while she changed and did her hair. A catchy Irish tune made her smile and hum along with the song before they switched to the commercials and then a familiar voice came on the air.

'Hi there,' the female presenter said. 'This is Kiara with

some exciting news about that "Out and About" feature we did last week. Some of you might remember the nice American I interviewed recently who was looking for a "lovely colleen" he met on a train some thirty years ago. Well, folks, you won't believe this, but we have found her! She called last Sunday telling us she had met this young American on the train from Dublin to Killarney thirty years ago. She heard the interview and it rang a bell so loudly she nearly jumped out of her skin. And she is right here in Kerry for the first time since she said goodbye to her American boyfriend, and staying in the very same cottage her parents used to own. The young couple spent some weeks together in Kerry before they had to say goodbye and start college in their respective home countries. They promised to stay in touch, but for some reason lost contact and now, thirty years later, they want to meet again. Isn't that romantic?'

'Oh, God,' Maggie mumbled and stopped brushing her hair. She put the hairbrush on the dressing table while she listened, her heart sinking, waiting for what would come next, praying that this Kiara woman wouldn't reveal anything personal about either her or Paul. She hadn't heard anything since she called last week and had begun to think it was all forgotten. Wat was this reporter going to say? Then she breathed a sigh of relief at what Kiara said next.

'I'm not going to read out her name on air, but I would like that nice man to call me back, if he's listening, or... Here's a clue to his identity. Maybe someone on the Beara peninsula who recently had a visit from an American relative could contact us? I don't want to read out his name either, even though I know it, just to keep it private. We will try to put all the pieces of the story together and if they should meet, then we'll be there in the right circumstances. Stay tuned for the next instalment of this truly romantic story.'

Unable to move, Maggie sat there and listened to the first

bars of 'Fields of Gold', which ended the feature. That song had always made her think of Paul and all the memories she treasured. She caught sight of herself in the mirror, her hair still wet, her face pale. If they ever met, would Paul even recognise this woman with the sad eyes and tired expression? Her eyes had been happy then, her face smooth and unlined, her body young and fit. She was still fit, but her body bore the marks of two children and the pain and sorrow from the recent separation must be showing in her face. Not to mention the fine lines around her eyes and a few grey hairs. Maybe it would be better if they never met again and he remembered her the way she was at eighteen: young, pretty, full of energy and so ready to tackle the years at university and the hard work to get her degree, and anything else life would throw at her.

But no, she thought. *I need to meet him, if only to find out why he stopped writing all those years ago.*

12

Maggie rang Lydia's doorbell a little after four o'clock. She could have walked along the path and gone in through the back garden but it didn't seem polite to do so as they didn't know each other that well yet. But she had liked Lydia instantly and hoped they would become friends.

The door was opened by a tall man with greying dark hair and brown eyes. He smiled at Maggie. 'Hi, Maggie. Welcome to our house. I'm Jason. We spoke on the phone when you called about the house.'

'Of course.' Maggie returned Jason's smile as she recognised his deep voice with the American accent, and shook his hand. 'Hi, Jason. Nice to meet you in person.'

'Nice to meet you too, Maggie.' He stepped aside. 'But come in. The neighbours are already here, along with a friend or two who'd love to meet you.'

Maggie entered the cottage, which was similar in layout to hers but quite different in interior decoration. The hall still had the original wainscoting and tiled floor and the corridor was painted a warm yellow, which gave the impression that the sun was shining in despite the dark clouds outside. She followed Jason down the corridor to the living room, which was furnished with two red velvet sofas flanking the fireplace and a Persian rug on the parquet floor. The walls were covered in a mixture of paintings, prints, photographs and posters, which gave the room a rich, cosy feel. It was a room to linger in, to sink into the sofas in front of a roaring fire on cold winter evenings and read a book or simply relax.

'This is gorgeous,' Maggie said as she looked around, not yet wanting to approach the group of people standing by the oval table at the far end where tea and cakes were laid out.

'Thank you,' Jason said. 'All Lydia's work. Sweetheart,' he called across the room. 'Maggie's here.'

Lydia immediately detached herself from the group and rushed to Maggie's side. 'Hi and welcome,' she said. 'Everyone's here, as you can see. Must be some kind of record. They usually arrive so late to a party you'd think nobody is going to come.' She grabbed Maggie's arm. 'Come on, don't be shy. Nobody bites here, except perhaps Rory but he only bites Ella and she bites right back.'

'Oh?' Maggie said as she approached the group with Lydia.

'She's pulling your leg,' a pretty, dark-haired woman said, holding out her hand. 'I'm Ella.' She gestured at the tall broad-shouldered man standing beside her. 'And this is my husband, Rory. He doesn't bite at all.'

'Hi,' Rory said with a broad smile, squeezing Maggie's hand in a tight grip. 'Welcome again, we should say, as you used to live here. Must be strange to be back after so many years.'

'A bit of a Rip van Winkle experience,' Maggie said with a laugh. 'Things have changed a lot, but it's still the same, if you know what I mean.'

He nodded. 'Oh yeah. This village has kept all the best qualities of what it used to be like years ago.' He gestured at a tall, thin woman with long black hair standing nearby. 'But I must introduce you to your next-door neighbour. Saskia, this is Maggie, who has come to spend the summer in Jason's house. As I said, Saskia lives next door to you and then there's Ella and me. So now you've met everyone in Starlight Cottages.'

Saskia shook Maggie's hand. 'Hello. Nice to meet you. I hear you used to spend your summers here when you were younger.'

'That's right,' Maggie replied. 'It's lovely to be back.'

'Saskia makes gorgeous jewellery out of sea glass,' Ella cut in. She gestured at her earrings made of green stones set in gold. 'She made these and Rory bought them for my birthday.'

'Fabulous,' Maggie said as she inspected the jewellery. 'I love the way the glass shimmers when you move.'

'I found those pieces on the beach below us,' Saskia said. 'It always makes me happy when I find something unusual. I like to think it brings me luck in some way or another.'

'It certainly brought me a lot of luck,' Rory remarked as he looked at Ella.

She shoved him in the side with her elbow. 'Luck had nothing to do with it, my sweet.'

They were interrupted by the door to the living room suddenly opening with a bang, admitting an older woman with white hair, dressed in jeans, a Liberty print shirt and silver trainers. 'Sorry I'm late,' she said, sounding breathless. 'But I bumped into DD and she gave me a whole spiel about this new person she has managed to enrol into the Tidy Town Association and how she would now have a majority when we vote on the Mad Brendan memorial bench and a whole list of other items we were fighting about – I mean, discussing – at the last meeting.'

'Oh, God,' Ella said. 'I hope whoever it is won't be joining forces with DD. That's Dreadful Darina,' she said to Maggie. 'A woman who is very difficult to deal with. If she has managed to get a new ally and gets her will, it'll be a disaster for the village. Who is silly enough to be taken in by Darina, anyway?'

'Oh,' Maggie said, feeling her face flush. 'I'm afraid that would be me.'

'What?' Ella exclaimed as the room fell silent. 'You've met her already? And she twisted your arm and enrolled you?'

'Well, eh, not quite,' Maggie tried to explain. 'We just had this conversation at The Two Marys' and she bought me coffee and cake and was quite nice, actually. I just said I'd come to the meeting, that's all.'

'Hmm,' Ella muttered. 'So that's how she bought you. With coffee and cake, eh?' She winked at Maggie. 'But we can buy you right back, can't we? How about pizza and wine? What's your favourite?'

Maggie laughed. 'Oh, I'm much more expensive. Lobster and champagne might tempt me to change over to the other side. Throw me a diamond and I'm yours forever.'

'I don't think we can afford you after all,' Ella said.

'So Dreadful Darina only had to give you coffee and cake?' Rory asked. 'But now the price is higher?'

'I didn't know there was so much at stake,' Maggie retorted. 'And I have had time to think. Had I known there was a war on, I'd have been better prepared. Darina wouldn't have got me that cheaply,' she added, returning Ella's mischievous smile.

Everyone laughed except the older woman, who frowned. 'It's funny now but I can't laugh at what that woman and her supporters are planning to do with this village.' She stepped closer to Maggie and held out her hand. 'I think they forgot to introduce me. I'm Lucille. Rory's mother and Ella's mother-in-law.'

'The best mother-in-law in the world,' Ella said and put her arm around Lucille. 'We're blessed to have her.'

'And the whole village,' Jason cut in. 'I don't know how we managed without her before.'

Lucille laughed. 'Neither do I, Jason.' She turned to Maggie. 'I'm delighted to meet you, Maggie. I heard you used to spend your summer holidays here a long time ago, in Jason's cottage. I'm sure you remember Mad Brendan?'

'Oh, yes, very well,' Maggie replied. 'I was very sad to hear he had passed away. He was such a character. We used to sit on that bench beside him when we were kids and listen to his stories. It was great craic to see him pose for the tourists and tell them stuff that wasn't quite true but probably what they wanted to hear. He looked like a big leprechaun with his beard and that green hat and the tweed trousers he used to wear. And he'd say things like, "Isn't it a grand day, to be sure, to be sure." And, "All the saints of Ireland be with you on your travels." The tourists lapped it all up and gave him great tips. I was really sad to see that bench empty and neglected.'

'But that's one of things we want to change,' Lucille said. 'I never met Mad Brendan – being a recent blow-in – but I think someone like that deserves a memorial. We wanted to paint the bench a light blue and put a little plaque on the back. Ella would paint seagulls and shells around that.'

'That sounds lovely,' Maggie replied. 'It would match the views and also Brendan's love of the sea that he would look at from the bench. He had a little boat in the harbour and used to love going out to fish mackerel in the bay. It would be the perfect tribute.'

'Exactly,' Lydia cut in. 'But Darina and her crowd don't agree. They want to paint the bench green and not put up a plaque at all. It will match the post box, they think. And then they want to dig up the flowerbed outside the library because they think it's messy. There are all kinds of other things they have suggested, which we don't want, but Darina has contacts in the county council, so if they can get a majority vote, it'll all be done. She thinks this will earn the village first prize in the Tidy Town competition as well, of course.'

'That's why she and her crowd blocked the planning application for the new playground,' Ella cut in. 'They thought that would ruin the look of the main street. Never mind that it would be a safe, fun place for kids to play.'

'We have to put our foot – I mean, feet – down,' Lucille said. 'And I think you could be a huge help to us.'

'Oh,' Maggie said, taken aback. 'I had no idea all this was going on. But I don't see how I can help. I mean, I've only just arrived and I thought I'd go to the meeting to find out what's going on in the village and meet people. That was what Darina said, anyway. Tea and buns and a bit of a chat afterwards.'

'Ah yes, she would say that,' Lucille remarked. 'All innocent and friendly, I suppose, just to lure you to her side.'

'Well, I'm not easy to lure,' Maggie said, beginning to feel a little awkward. 'And I don't take sides. I'm not sure I want to go to this meeting at all if it means that there will be arguments.'

'Could we stop this now?' Lydia said. 'I invited you all here to welcome Maggie, not get her involved in our problems. And I was looking forward to her telling us about the good old days when my great-aunt Nellie lived in this cottage. You were next-door neighbours, so you must have known her well.'

'Yes, I did,' Maggie said, smiling at Lydia. 'She was great gas, actually. She'd travelled all over Europe in her youth, just before the war. We found it fascinating to listen to her stories. She was a kind of agony aunt to us teenage girls. She had a very practical view on everything. Especially about men.' Maggie let out a laugh as she remembered. 'She warned us against becoming housewives but that fashion was on the way out then, anyway, which she thought was excellent. If we had broken up with a boyfriend she'd say that we should forget about it and move on. "A husband and family aren't what defines you as a woman," she used to say. But then she was a very interesting woman.'

Lydia nodded. 'Yes, she was. I've heard much the same about her from others. Lovely that she was so helpful to the girls around here. I'm sure she was a huge help.'

'Absolutely,' Maggie agreed. 'It was a great to have a wailing wall when the teenage angst hit us.'

'How lovely.' Lydia suddenly laughed. 'Hey, we have forgotten about the tea and cakes that I put out on the table. Please, everybody, help yourselves while I go and make a fresh pot.' Lydia took the big teapot and left the room, while everyone started to talk and pile their plates with muffins and sponge cakes and assorted biscuits.

Lucille moved back to Maggie while she nibbled on a cupcake. 'So are you having fun catching up with old friends?' she asked. 'It must be strange to be back after so many years.'

'Everyone asks me that question,' Maggie replied. 'And yes, it's a little weird, but nice too. The village has changed so much since I left thirty years ago. Some things are very familiar and other things seem quite new. But the friendly atmosphere hasn't changed at all, which is lovely.'

'Well, that's wonderful,' Lucille remarked. 'Some of the changes have to be for the better, I'm sure.'

'Of course,' Maggie agreed. 'And I love the way it looks now. But in the old days, it was cosier, if a little run-down.'

'I'm sure that was nice, too. But I like things to improve,' Lucille declared. 'And what about the people?' she asked. 'Old friends you must have met up with again? Have they changed a lot?'

'Yes, in some ways, of course,' Maggie replied. 'But not as much as I thought, apart from being older. It's funny, but after a while the years seem to roll back and you see the same person you knew. Especially Sorcha, who was my best friend then.'

'That's wonderful,' Lucille said. 'I have found that too with real, true friends I've been away from for a long time. Not that I have many friends left,' she said sadly. 'At my age, you find yourself losing friends all the time.' She sipped at her tea. 'What about old boyfriends? Have you reconnected with any of them since you came back?'

'No,' Maggie said. 'Except...' She paused, wondering if she should tell Lucille about Paul and the man she had heard on the radio. It seemed strange to reveal such things to someone she had just met. But she had immediately liked this witty, feisty old woman who seemed so wise and truly empathetic. 'I had a boyfriend that last summer. He was American and we were... close.'

'Madly in love, you mean,' Lucille filled in. 'The way one can only be at eighteen. So what happened to him?'

'I don't know,' Maggie said. 'We lost touch. But I never forgot him. Coming here has made all those memories so vivid. And then something strange happened,' she added, proceeding to tell Lucille about the man she had heard on the radio.

'How amazing,' Lucille said, her eyes sparkling. 'And are you that girl he was talking about, do you think?'

'I think I am,' Maggie confessed. 'That man sounded so like my American boyfriend, even though he is a lot older, just as I am, of course.'

'And you want to meet him?' Lucille took another bite of cupcake while she waited for an answer.

Maggie fiddled with the slice of lemon cake on her plate. 'Yes and no,' she finally said, trying to convey how conflicted she felt. 'I'd love to see him again in one way, but on the other hand, I'm not sure it would be a good idea.' She'd been thinking a lot about what she wanted from Paul – of course, rekindling their romance would be lovely, but she also knew she needed to be realistic. 'I do want to know why he stopped writing to me all of a sudden. It has been niggling at me all these years.' She looked at Lucille and noticed the compassion in the older woman's eyes, which gave her the courage to explain. 'We made a promise to each other. A promise to keep in touch and then be together forever when the time was right. But I suppose we both broke that promise. He stopped writing, but I had to move on after that. And then I met someone else and had my children. My summer romance faded into the distance somehow. Except I always wanted to know why the letters stopped coming.'

Lucille nodded and moved to the table where Lydia was pouring tea into cups. 'He owes you an explanation, then. But you have to decide if you really want to meet him as an adult or keep him as a beautiful memory. It could change your life forever.'

'Oh,' Maggie said. 'I didn't think of it that way.'

'Maybe you should?' Lucille asked. 'But perhaps that's none of my – or anyone else's – business. Let's have tea and go and sit on one of those heavenly sofas. You look like you need a rest.'

'We'll all go and sit down,' Ella said. 'I could do with a break as well. And we won't mention the war,' she added with a wink. 'I mean, the row with a certain lady.'

Maggie took a cup with tea and milk from the table and joined Lucille on one of the sofas, closely followed by Ella and Saskia, who sat down opposite them while the men stayed where they were, deep in conversation. 'Hurling final,' Lydia said as she sat down beside Maggie. 'Will Kerry beat Kilkenny next week? They'll be discussing that all afternoon.'

'I don't think they will,' Lucille stated. 'But I'd hate to tell them that.'

'Why ruin a good discussion?' Lydia asked, sitting back in the sofa. 'Let them at it, I say.' She smiled at Maggie. 'Tell us more about the early days. What was it like here when you were a child?'

Relieved the subject of Darina and her campaign was off the agenda, Maggie started to talk about her childhood, sharing all the lovely memories and funny stories while they listened with rapt attention. But while she talked, it wasn't her early childhood that went through her mind, but that summer when she was eighteen. What Lucille had said lodged in her thoughts. Did she really want to meet Paul again? It might rip open wounds that had healed and reveal truths she might not want to hear. It might even ruin the memories of her idyllic summers and her happy homecoming to this lovely village.

13

'I did something you might not approve of,' Sorcha said on the phone later that night.

'Uh, I think I did too,' Maggie said as she sat on the terrace looking at the sunset. Her gaze lingered on the beautiful scenery and it suddenly struck her that she hadn't thought about the break-up from Dermot once during the past week. Sandy Cove was giving her the peace of mind and healing she had craved. Then she cast her mind back to her meeting with Darina, wondering if she might have been a little too friendly.

'Like what?' Sorcha asked, her voice pulling Maggie back to the present.

'No, you first.'

'Oh, okay. Please don't get mad,' Sorcha said. 'But I told Brian about your quest to find Paul.'

'Why did you do that?' Maggie asked. She had avoided the subject during her conversation with Brian for some reason. There had been so many other things to talk about. 'I don't mind at all, though.'

'Oh, good,' Sorcha said, sounding relieved. 'It just struck me that he might be able to help find this guy. He has a cousin who has a cousin on the Beara peninsula, remember? Didn't your Paul stay with Brian during that month he was here?'

'Yes, he did,' Maggie said as a lightbulb flashed in her mind. 'Of course! I should have thought of that.'

'It was a long time ago and you're old,' Sorcha teased. 'Anyway, I spoke to Brian and he's going to contact his cousin's cousin or whatever he is and ask if Paul has been around and if they have any contact details. I should have asked you first, of course, but as usual I went ahead without thinking. Sorry.'

'No need to say sorry,' Maggie reassured her. 'It was a great idea. I've decided that I really want to meet Paul again, if only to get the closure I need.'

'And then you'll fall in love again,' Sorcha said dreamily. 'Just like in the movies.'

'Nah, this isn't the movies,' Maggie said, laughing, even though that thought had been flickering through her mind. *Wouldn't it be lovely if...* she had thought and then dismissed it. 'Things like that don't happen in real life,' she declared.

'You never know,' Sorcha said. 'Sometimes you have to give fate a helping hand. Now it's your turn. So what did you do that I won't like?'

'Don't get mad now, but I kind of made friends with Darina. Well, not friends exactly, but she treated me to coffee and cake at The Two Marys'. And then, before I knew it, I agreed to come to the meeting on Thursday. So now she thinks I'm going to be on her side.' Maggie drew breath. 'I don't know how it happened, to be honest.'

'I do. Darina can be sweet and charming to beat the band if she wants you to do something for her. And then she'll make you feel guilty if you don't deliver.'

'I know the type,' Maggie said. 'But what makes it worse is that I met some people at Lydia's this afternoon who seem to dislike her. Ella and Lucille, for example. Rory wasn't too fond of her either. So now I don't know what to do. I don't feel like going to that meeting. I thought it would be a great way to catch up with people I used to know and meet some new ones. But...'

'Oh, do come,' Sorcha urged. 'It'll be fairly civilised even if Darina and her gang get bolshy. And then there's tea and buns afterwards, which is usually fun. I need your support, in any case.'

'But Darina seems to think I will support *her*.'

'You can pretend. The voting is closed so nobody will know what you voted for anyway. And...' Sorcha paused. 'You could be a huge help to me and Tom this way.'

'How?'

'Well, you could humour her and be her friend and then maybe see if you can brainwash her into liking me and thinking I'll be perfect for Tom.'

'Yeah, that'll be easy-peasy!'

'I mean it. You can be very persuasive. I remember how you could get permission from your parents to do practically anything. Like us cycling to Killarney to go to McDonald's.'

'We were ten,' Maggie remarked.

'I know, but you probably still have it in you.'

'I doubt it. In any case if I do look like her friend, everyone else will hate me.'

'You could be her secret friend. She'd love that.'

Maggie laughed. 'Have you been drinking?' she asked.

Sorcha chuckled down the phone. 'Maybe I'm just drunk on the memory of my perfect day with Tom.' She sighed wistfully. 'We had a magical day walking around the lakes in Killarney. And then we had lunch in a very romantic spot. And we talked and talked. I wish we could be together all the time. And we will. We're going to choose the ring next week and then we'll announce our engagement. Tom is very excited about, but he's a little worried about what Darina will say. He loves his mother and doesn't want to upset her. He's an only child, you see. So Tom is all she has.'

'I think I'm beginning to understand what's going on,' Maggie said.

'Yeah.' Sorcha was quiet for a while. 'It's my bad luck to fall for a mammy's boy.'

'Maybe he's just being considerate.' Maggie suddenly felt truly sorry for Sorcha. She had been through a lot of sadness having gone through a divorce and now finding herself all alone after her son had left home. And then she'd fallen in love with a nice man whose mother wouldn't let him go. 'I'll help you,' Maggie suddenly said. 'I'll try my best to get into Darina's good books and then I'll tell her how wonderful you are. She'll think you're Mother Teresa by the time I'm finished.'

'Ah well, I wouldn't go that far. But thanks, Maggie. You're a true brick.'

'You're welcome. Happy to help.'

'But let's not forget that other matter,' Sorcha continued. 'Brian will be in touch very soon and maybe he'll have a lead on yer man in Beara.'

'That would be terrific.' Maggie suppressed a yawn. 'Sorry. Must be all this sea air and the swimming. I should go to bed.'

'Me too,' Sorcha said. 'Good night, Maggie. Sleep tight.'

When she had hung up, Maggie slowly walked upstairs thinking about what Sorcha had said, and also about Brian. That old crush seemed so sweet now that she remembered his big, sad eyes on her at times when they met up with the gang. But she hadn't thought it was anything to do with her. He had been so young, only fourteen and she had been nearly five years older, which was a huge age gap at that age.

She had been so mesmerised by Paul – looking into those green eyes she hadn't been able to pay attention to anyone else. And now Brian was ready to help her find the man that had stolen her away from him in some way. She promised herself to make it up to him in any way she could.

As if reading her thoughts, Brian called early the next day.

'Morning, Maggie,' he said. 'Hope I didn't wake you up.'

'Not really,' Maggie said as, still in bed, she put the phone on speaker mode while she got up and pulled back the curtain. Then she got back in bed and sat back against the pillows she had propped up. 'I was just about to get up.'

'It's only just past seven thirty,' Brian said. 'But I have a few farms to visit before I open the surgery at nine, so I thought I'd give you a quick call before I set off.'

'Mmm?' Maggie mumbled, still sleepy.

'I'll try to see if I can find the contact details of those O'Sullivans that Paul visited back then. They might be able to help you find him.'

'That's very kind of you,' Maggie said, touched by his concern for her. 'Especially considering the way I treated you then.'

'Ah sure, I was only a kid and you were besotted with someone else,' Brian said with a teasing note in his voice. 'Blinded by love.'

'Yes, and I thought it was the love story of the century,' Maggie said with a laugh. 'But then he left and after that it just fizzled out. He just stopped writing. Probably met someone else. It nearly tore me apart at the time but then I moved on, the way you do when you're young. The love I felt for Paul became just a sweet memory.'

'That's frustrating...' Brian replied quietly. He paused and there was a slightly awkward silence. 'Strange that he didn't explain, wasn't it? Seems like he didn't have the guts to—'

'I don't think it was a lack of courage,' Maggie interrupted, annoyed by the insinuation. 'There must have been a reason for what happened. I'm sure he just couldn't...' She stopped.

'Yeah, maybe,' Brian said without conviction. 'I didn't mean to imply...'

'I know. I think I just need closure.' She didn't want to tell Brian that a part of her hoped she'd see Paul again and they'd fall back in love. That would be so lovely, such a perfect conclusion to their romance that had been so vivid in her mind ever since she came back to Sandy Cove. 'And I'm so grateful for any help you can give me.'

'Could be great to get that closure,' Brian said. 'I want to help you. Just for old times' sake. And because it's important to me too.'

'Why?' Maggie asked.

'Hard to explain.'

'Maybe you could try? When we have that drink?'

'Maybe,' Brian said, sounding hesitant. 'But now I have to go. I'll call you when I have any news.'

'Thanks, Brian.'

Maggie hung up, frowning. Brian had sounded a little distant. It made her feel bad that she had been so dismissive of him in her youth. He was kind and generous with his time – she could see what an important part of the community he was and she liked him all the more for it.

Brian had been part of the fabric of friends and family in those days. Now she realised that she didn't have that kind of security net anymore. The family was split up and most of her friends had drifted away during the year after her separation. She had felt bereft and lonely thinking she was doomed to spend the rest of her life on her own. But here, in Sandy Cove, she was beginning to pick up the threads of the old friendships, which was truly comforting. *Funny*, she thought, *how I feel so at home here already after all these years. Things have changed, people have moved on, but there's still that feeling of togetherness.*

Maggie vowed there and then to try to be part of the community, even if it was only for this summer. She suddenly looked forward to the meeting on Thursday. It would take her mind off her search for Paul, which was quickly becoming an obsession.

14

The Tidy Town Association meeting took place in the community hall next to the church. Several rows of chairs had been placed in front of the podium, where Darina, dressed in a yellow shirt dress, was flicking through a stack of printed pages. The members were trickling in as Maggie entered feeling a little self-conscious. She had walked slowly through the village enjoying the little gardens with their flowerbeds, yet again amazed at the transformation of the village.

Once inside the building, she looked around the hall, wondering if the people there would feel she was intruding on a meeting that, strictly speaking, only concerned permanent residents, not someone who was just here for the summer. But Lydia and Ella greeted her enthusiastically, while Sorcha shot her a conspiratorial smile. Saskia was helping out at the tea table at the back of the room, placing plates with buns, cakes and biscuits beside rows of teacups. Maggie went across and asked if she could help, but Saskia told her all was already done.

'Go and sit down,' she suggested. 'I think Darina is about to call everyone to order. We're going to vote on a number of issues, so it might get a little rowdy. I'm playing tea lady so I can stay out of any fracas,' she added with a wink.

'I'm sure it won't get that bad,' Maggie said. 'And as a newcomer, I'll just observe and say nothing.'

'I hope you can,' Saskia replied. 'But I think Darina has already registered you as a new member. Go on.' She waved her hand. 'Get a chair somewhere at the back.'

'That's my plan,' Maggie said. 'See you later.'

Maggie went to the back of the room, where Sorcha had already settled down. 'Is it okay if I sit here?' she asked a smiley lady with grey hair who was chatting to Sorcha.

'Absolutely,' the lady said and patted the chair between her and Sorcha. 'I'm Catriona Mulloy, and you're Maggie Ryan. I remember your family very well.'

'The rowdy Ryans,' Maggie said with a laugh.

'Ah sure, all the kids were a little rowdy. Nothing wrong with that,' Catriona said. 'Welcome back, by the way. I hear you're staying the whole summer.'

'Oh, yes, I'm looking forward to it.' Maggie smiled and sat down, then looked up as Darina clapped her hands, which stopped the general chatting.

'Good evening, everyone,' Darina said. 'I was going to say "ladies and gentlemen", but as there are only ladies here, there's no need. Pity. We do need a few men.'

'They're all hiding in the pub,' Ella volunteered. 'But that way we can sign them up for all the jobs and they won't be here to protest.'

There was communal laughter while Darina appeared to scan the room. Then she smiled as her gaze landed on Maggie. 'First of all, I want to welcome a new member. Maggie Ryan, please stand up so we can see you.'

'Oh, God,' Maggie muttered. But she stood up and waved. 'Hi,' she said in a voice squeaky with embarrassment while

Sorcha giggled beside her. Then she sat down, her face burning while everyone applauded.

'Maggie is a summer guest,' Darina said when the applause had died down. 'But her family are well-known in the area and she plans to stay the whole summer, so I've decided to let her join.'

'As if it's a huge honour,' Sorcha whispered in Maggie's ear.

Darina glared at Sorcha and then launched into a long speech about what needed to be done in the village, most of which her support group in the front rows met with 'hear, hear,' and nods and smiles. Maggie tried to concentrate while Darina droned on about flowerbeds, hanging baskets, mowing lawns, cutting hedges and picking up litter, but sat up when she came to the subject of Mad Brendan's memorial bench.

'We, I mean, the majority here, think that that bench should be painted green,' Darina stated. 'None of this airy-fairy nonsense with seagulls and clouds and whatever else Ella has dreamed up. It doesn't go with the general look of the village, we feel. Green is the traditional colour of Ireland. And that plaque isn't really necessary at all, in fact. We all know that's where he sat and, well, it's not as if he was Oscar Wilde or anything, is it?' She paused, looking at the members, as if waiting for applause or at least approval.

'Brendan wasn't too fond of her,' Sorcha whispered in Maggie's ear. 'He said she was a busybody and a know-it-all. She didn't like him much either. She used to say he was common and he pretended not to hear when she told him to go home and stop blathering to tourists.'

'But he was lovely,' Maggie whispered back. 'Such a character.' She suddenly saw Darina in a different light after the rude comments about Ella's designs and the sneer at Brendan himself, who had been so loved by all in the village.

Darina looked at them, her eyes like hard pebbles. 'What are you whispering about back there?' she asked.

Maggie looked at Sorcha for a moment. Then she stood up, realising that she should take the heat from Sorcha. 'We were saying that we were very fond of Brendan, Darina. I was really sad to hear he had passed away. I remember his stories and his funny turns of phrase. I know he was doing a bit of an act for the tourists, but they loved it. There wasn't a bad bone in his body, you know. He was the epitome of this village, with his kind heart and wonderful wisdom and humour.' She looked around nervously. 'So why not remember him with a plaque on the bench he used to sit on?'

The hall was silent as Maggie sat down, beginning to regret having said anything. She was, after all, supposed to pretend to humour Darina. 'Sorry,' she whispered to Sorcha. 'I was going to placate her so you didn't get told off but I had to stand up for Brendan.'

'Good for you,' Sorcha whispered back. 'Never mind buttering her up.'

Then Darina opened her mouth 'A small plaque could be acceptable,' she said graciously. 'On a bright green bench, of course.' She smiled as her supporters gave her a brief applause.

'Darn,' Maggie muttered. 'I lost that one, didn't I?'

'No,' Sorcha hissed in her ear. 'You managed what nobody else has. We have the plaque. You did well.'

'But she's sticking with the bright green,' Maggie mumbled. 'That's not what I call victory.'

'We'll get there,' the nice lady called Catriona whispered on Maggie's other side. 'The plaque is just a start. It'll be fine.'

'I hope so,' Maggie said, wondering if it was really worth fighting for the colour of a bench. But she felt there was more to this than met the eye. Sandy Cove had always been a very peaceful, friendly place, but now it looked like that peace was about to be shattered by this woman who seemed so set on calling all the shots.

Darina wound up the meeting, saying the subject of the

memorial bench would be discussed in further detail at the next meeting the following week. As the formalities finished, everyone started to talk and move towards the table. But then the door opened with a crash and a man entered.

'Hold everything,' he shouted, waving a stack of papers. 'I have just discovered something we need to address right away.' He elbowed his way through the crowd and jumped up on the podium. 'Listen,' he called. 'Be quiet for a moment.' He handed the stack of papers to a woman at the front. 'Could you distribute these, please?' Then he stood for a moment while the papers were being handed out. 'What you will see is an application for planning permission to build—'

'A hotel?' a woman shouted as she looked at the piece of paper.

'That's right,' the man at the podium said. 'Planning permission is being sought for a fifty-room hotel to be built on the headland between Wild Rose Bay and the main beach, with a path leading down to the little beach at Wild Rose Bay, plus a car park in front. They've already had an access route approved by the county council.'

There was a stunned silence in the hall. 'Is this some kind of joke?' Ella asked, staring at the piece of paper she had been handed.

'No,' the man shouted back. 'It's real. I saw the notice put up on a pole that had been driven into the ground beside the path that runs from The Two Marys'. Seems to have been put there in the past day or so. I took a photo with my phone and printed out these copies you have now.'

'Oh my God,' Sorcha whispered, staring at her copy. 'If this happens, the village will be ruined. And that beautiful beach and the headland and all the flora and fauna and lovely walks...'

'And wild swimming at our beach,' Lydia said. 'The peace and tranquillity... Oh, no. I can't even bear to think about it.'

'Who is doing this?' Catriona asked the man. 'I know the

land was sold recently, but to whom? It says the company is called...'

'Hy Brasil,' Sorcha said, looking at Maggie with huge eyes. 'But that's the company who owns my shop.' Her gaze drifted to Darina. 'That's the outfit you sold the house to, isn't it?'

Darina didn't reply for a moment. 'Yes, but I had no idea,' she finally mumbled. 'I thought... They said they were buying some property as an investment and to make improvements in the area.'

'Some improvement,' Ella said with a snort. 'It's going to wreck the whole area. But who are they? Where are they based?'

'In Killarney,' Darina said. 'They have an office there, anyway. It's not very big, actually. I dealt with a very nice woman who was very stylish and polite.'

'Hmm,' Catriona said. 'That doesn't tell me anything.'

'We have to fight this,' Ella said. 'Never mind Mad Brendan's bench and the flowerbeds and the playground.' She waved the paper in the air. 'This is a disaster,' she exclaimed. 'It's a threat to our village, our way of life and the environment around here. We can't let this happen.'

'You should lodge a protest,' Maggie said. 'If every single resident in Sandy Cove does, that should help dissuade the county council from going ahead.'

'I'd like to organise a protest march,' Lucille piped up. 'And then we should chain ourselves to the railings outside the county council offices and maybe even do a hunger strike.'

'That's going just a tad too far,' a woman argued. 'Let's just lodge the protest and see if we can get the media to report this. The local newspaper, for a start, then the national press and TV. If there is public outrage, I'm sure the politicians will do something to stop this.'

'Our very own Mick O'Dwyer is a member of the Irish

parliament,' Lydia said. 'I'm sure he'll be happy to help. And he's a local who grew up here.'

'He's Dr Pat's son,' Sorcha told Maggie. 'Used to be an actor.'

'Oh, yes,' Maggie said. 'I know who you mean. Quite high profile in politics, isn't he?'

'Very much so,' Sorcha replied.

The man who had broken the news still stood at the podium. 'Okay,' he said, 'could we all agree to lodge a protest? That's a good start, I think. I would also like to know who's behind this company that call themselves Hy Brasil. Ridiculous name, if you ask me. Sounds like something out of a Paddy-whackery Hollywood movie.'

Maggie laughed. He was right. A company that called themselves after a mythical island said to lie somewhere in the sea off the west coast of Ireland seemed quite OTT. 'Maybe they're hoping it'll rise out of the mist every seven years like in those fairy tales,' she said.

'I bet they don't even know what it means,' Sorcha said. 'The old Irish myths have been long forgotten by the younger generation.'

'Let's have tea and talk about it,' Ella said. 'I could do with a cuppa after all this excitement.'

Everyone agreed and gathered around the tea table, helping themselves to tea and cakes, talking in hushed tones about what they had just heard.

Darina joined Maggie as she was talking to an old friend of her mother's. 'I didn't think you'd be so vocal at your very first meeting here,' she said.

'About what?' Maggie asked. 'Mad Brendan's bench? I just felt I should share my feelings on the matter,' she said. 'As someone who knew Mad Brendan so well.'

'I suppose everyone has a right to express their opinion,' Darina said stiffly.

'Yes, I think so,' Maggie agreed. 'But I think that whole matter will be put on hold for now. That proposed construction of the hotel must be dealt with first.'

'Yes, that's true,' Darina said. 'But once that has been sorted out we'll have to come back to it, don't you think?'

'Yes, of course,' Maggie said in a soothing tone.

'You and Sorcha seem to know each other well,' Darina said.

'We do. She was my best friend all those years ago. And now we've picked up the friendship again, which is lovely,' Maggie said warmly.

Darina pulled at Maggie's sleeve. 'Could I have a word in private?'

'Eh, yes?' Maggie said, glancing at the people around them. She stepped aside. 'What was it you wanted to say?'

'It's about Sorcha,' Darina mumbled in Maggie's ear. 'You said you used to be close friends with her. And now you've connected again, is that right?'

'Eh, yes?' Maggie replied. 'Why do you ask?'

'I have a feeling that she and my son are getting... close. Has she said anything about that to you?'

'Not in detail,' Maggie said airily. 'Just in passing really.'

'So you don't know how serious it is?'

'No,' Maggie replied, beginning to feel awkward. 'But are you not happy about them seeing each other?'

'Not really,' Darina said with disapproving eyes. 'I mean she's... a little older than I had hoped. There'll be no children, should they get married. I had hoped to have grandchildren one day, you see.'

'Oh.' Maggie glanced at Sorcha, who was deep in conversation with Ella. 'Well, maybe that's between the two of them. And in any case,' Maggie added in a flash of inspiration. 'If your son gets married and has children, he'd be too busy and won't have much time to look after you, will he? Parents of small children rarely have much energy for anything else but the babies. I know this from experience.'

Darina stared at Maggie thoughtfully. 'Goodness,' she said. 'I never thought of it that way.'

Emboldened by the hesitant look in Darina's eyes, Maggie decided to go a step further. 'And when you get really old and find it hard to manage, they might feel it would be a good idea if you lived with them. If at that stage, you and your daughter-in-law get on really well, I mean. A lot better than a nursing home, don't you think?'

'Oh,' Darina said, her eyes brightening. 'That would be ideal. Not that I think I'll ever be that helpless, but you never know. It would be good to have such a plan just in case.'

Maggie nodded. 'Exactly. Of course, if they had children they might not have much room. But in Sorcha's case, her son would have left home and have a family of his own by then. Which would mean you'd have yet another family to look after you. Sorcha's son doesn't have a grandmother, so you could fill that role for him, too.'

'Yes, indeed,' Darina said. 'That's quite...' She paused. 'You have made me look at it all in a different light.'

'I'd leave them alone if I were you,' Maggie said. 'Interfering might only cause trouble between you and your son.'

'And it could ruin all those things you have just explained,' Darina said, looking alarmed. Then she smiled and patted Maggie's arm. 'Well, my dear, I was quite cross with you earlier but now I feel we could be on friendly terms again. And I will stop interfering and try to deal with it all. Isn't that what you said?'

'Yes, I...' Maggie started when her phone pinged. She took it out of her pocket and glanced at it. A text from Brian. *I have a lead. Call me.* Maggie gasped and suddenly forgot all about Darina, Sorcha, the Tidy Town Association, Mad Brendan's bench and even the hotel. 'Excuse me,' she said and started to move towards the door. 'I have to make an urgent phone call.'

Darina said something Maggie didn't hear as she quickly left the hall, punching Brian's number as she went.

'Hi,' Brian said. 'That was quick. How was the meeting?'

'Strange. I'll tell you later,' Maggie stammered, her heart beating like a hammer in her chest. 'You have a lead? You've found Paul?'

'Yes,' Brian chortled. 'And I have a number and all. I'll text it to you and then you can call him yourself.'

'Me?' Maggie said. 'Oh, God, I'm not sure I want to. What if...'

'What if the sky falls in?' Brian said. 'My cousin's cousin said he's been on a visit to Beara and now he's on his way back up the coast. He's still hoping to find you, my cousin's cousin said.'

'Oh.' Maggie stood there, the phone to her ear while all around her the members of the Tidy Town Association poured out of the community hall, still talking about what they had just found out.

'Call him,' Brian urged.

'I can't,' Maggie said, suddenly thrown back into her own dilemma. 'I'm scared of what might happen.'

'You're worried you'll be disappointed?'

'No, but that he'll be.'

'Why would he?' Brian asked.

'I'm so much older now.'

'So is he. And you look great,' Brian declared.

'No I don't,' Maggie protested. 'I look saggy and baggy and – old. I don't think I want him to see me. Can we forget about it? I'm too nervous to do this.'

'Jaysus,' Brian said, sounding exasperated. 'After all the effort I made to find this guy. I had to make, like, ten phone calls, chat to an auld aunt for an hour about her cat and then promise I'd go all the way to Beara to visit her before she finally put me on to her nephew who knew the whole story. And now you tell me you can't call this guy because you're *nervous?*'

'Well, wouldn't you be?' Maggie countered, weirdly enjoying their exchange despite all her fears.

'I have no idea. I'm not a girl,' Brian said. 'All I know is that you look fantastic and any guy should be so lucky to catch up with you.'

'You're just saying that,' Maggie protested, despite being touched by his comments.

'No, I'm not.'

Confused and frightened by the thought of facing Paul again, Maggie shivered. 'I'm sorry, Brian. I know you've gone to a lot of trouble and I appreciate all your help, I really do. But I'm not sure I can do this.'

'Yeah, right,' Brian muttered. 'You're a big chicken, Maggie Ryan, do you know that?'

'Yes, I suppose I am.' Maggie sighed deeply while Sorcha came through the door, staring at her. 'I need to think about this.'

'I'll text you his number all the same,' Brian said. 'You might change your mind.'

'Maybe,' Maggie said. 'Thanks for your help, Brian. You're a true brick.'

'Hmm,' Brian said. 'Thanks, I suppose. Bye for now, Maggie. Let me know what you want to do.'

Maggie said goodbye to Brian, wondering why he had seemed so grumpy, but most of all, why was he pushing her to meet Paul? There seemed suddenly to be a lot of emotions brewing under the calm, caring exterior. But everyone had some kind of issue, she surmised, and focused on Sorcha, who touched her arm. 'Sorry, what did you say?'

'I just wanted to say thanks for standing up for Mad Brendan in there,' Sorcha replied. 'You were magnificent.'

'Oh, well, I just said what was on my mind.'

'You were great,' Sorcha said. 'Darina seemed impressed, too, even if she didn't approve.' Sorcha paused. 'We're going to the pub for a drink before heading home. We're going to work out some sort of strategy. But I can see that you need to be on your own. Who was on the phone?'

'Oh, I'll tell you later. And yes, I could do with a bit of time to myself,' Maggie said gratefully. 'Thanks for understanding.'

'I'm here if you need someone to talk to.'

'I know,' Maggie said and gave Sorcha a brief hug. 'Thanks for being there for me. And thanks for not asking any questions.'

'You're welcome.' Sorcha smiled and walked off.

Maggie headed back to Starlight Cottages, her head full of what Brian had told her. Paul was still around and she could meet him if she wanted. But did she? Was she strong enough? What if it went wrong? She had dreamed about Paul so many times... what if their reunion didn't live up to her fantasy? Maggie kept wrestling with her feelings as she walked towards the cottage. What on earth was she going to do? Then her phone pinged. It was a text from Brian with Paul's number. *Just in case you change your mind,* he wrote.

Maggie stopped walking and quickly typed a reply. *Very conflicted, but thanks. I'm beginning to lean towards calling him.*

Do it! Brian texted back.

Maggie resumed walking. Brian was beginning to be such a great friend, making such an effort to help her find Paul. His cajoling earlier hadn't upset her; it felt more like the kind of teasing she had done with her brothers when they were teenagers and it made her laugh to think about it.

Maggie's phone rang as she stepped into the house. She replied without checking who it was, assuming as she had been thinking about him, that she knew who it was... 'Brian—' she began but was interrupted.

'Maggie Ryan?' the voice at the other end said. It was a deep voice with an American accent. Maggie blinked and nearly stopped breathing. Knowing instantly who it was, her knees buckled and she had to sit down on the little stool in the hall. 'Yes,' she said in a near whisper. 'This is Maggie Ryan. Who's this?'

'Hi, Maggie,' the man said. 'This is Paul. Paul O'Sullivan.'

15

Sitting on the stool, her stomach in a knot and her hand holding the phone shaking, Maggie was so stunned she couldn't speak. She fought to catch her breath and slow her racing heart. 'Oh, God,' she finally managed to croak. 'It's you.'

'Yeah.' He breathed out heavily.

'How did you get my number?' she asked, still breathless. She couldn't believe this was happening, that she was hearing his voice after all the years that had passed and all the hurt and disappointment, the wondering and frantic searching for him.

'Your friend Brian just called me. He said... well, that you needed to think. But then I guess he felt you needed a push so he gave me your number and urged me not to hang around. I hope you're not mad.'

Maggie sighed. 'At Brian? Who could be? He means well and he probably thought he was being helpful.' She sent a silent 'thank you' to Brian, knowing that if he hadn't done what he did, she wouldn't have had the courage to call Paul herself. Whatever happened next was in the lap of the gods.

'I'm glad he called me,' Paul said. 'And wow, here I am talking to you. Unbelievable.'

'I can't believe I'm talking to you either. It's been a long time,' Maggie replied wistfully, trying to calm herself down.

'Too long,' he said. 'And that's my fault.'

'Yes, I think it is.' Maggie closed her eyes and put her forehead on her knees for a moment, trying to get her racing heart to slow down. Here it was. That moment she had been waiting for. His voice was deeper than she remembered and she found it hard to believe it was really him at the other end.

'I'm sure you have been wondering what happened back then,' he said.

'Yes, I have,' Maggie said, lifting her head. 'For a very long time.'

'I'm sure. I'd like to meet you in person and explain. And maybe...' He stopped and let out a laugh. 'I have no idea what to say.'

'Me neither,' Maggie said.

'Well, that's great, isn't it? We haven't been in touch for thirty years and when we are, we have nothing to say.'

'Oh, I have plenty to say,' Maggie declared with a sudden rush of emotion. 'It's just that I don't know where to start.'

'We have to meet,' Paul insisted.

'I know,' Maggie said, the knot in her stomach tightening again.

'How? Where?'

'Not in public,' Maggie replied. 'And not here in Sandy Cove. I want it to be away from everyone. This village is lovely, but...'

'But everyone knows what you're doing even before you're doing it?' he filled in, his voice full of laughter.

Maggie let out a laugh, warming to his charming voice. 'Yes. This is not exactly New York. Or even Dublin.'

'Where are you right now?'

'In the cottage. I mean, the cottage my parents used to own.

They sold it but now I'm renting it for the summer,' Maggie babbled nervously.

'I know the house.'

'Of course. What about you?' she asked.

'Still with my Beara family. I was planning to go to Killarney tomorrow. Maybe we could meet there? Plenty of nice cafés and restaurants.'

'Yes, I think that might work,' Maggie said, even though she still wasn't sure she wanted to meet him in public. Or at all. 'Look, was it you I heard on the radio?'

'It was,' Paul replied.

'I called the station and said I thought you were talking about me and now they're all excited about you and the "lovely colleen" meeting up after thirty years and... Oh God, I'm sorry, I shouldn't have done that.' Maggie drew breath, waiting for his reaction as he had to be annoyed.

Paul let out that laugh she knew so well. 'I know you contacted the radio station. Brian told me. Don't worry about it. I was kicking myself for even talking to the woman when she was running around with her microphone and then I tried to reveal as little as possible. Let's dodge them and meet somewhere out of the way. Like the gardens at Muckross House. Remember we went there once on our bikes?'

'We cycled around the lake and had tea and buns at the café in the visitors' centre in the old stables,' Maggie said. 'And it rained and we got very wet.'

Paul laughed. 'Yeah, I remember that. Would be nice to go back and relive old memories.'

'It's changed a lot since then. There's a new building with a café and shops near the greenhouses,' Maggie told him. She paused as a thought hit her. 'Are you alone?' she asked. 'I mean, do you have a wife or a partner or anything?'

'No. No wife, no partner. I'm... It's been hard.' He stopped. 'What about you?'

'I'm on my own too,' Maggie said, her voice shaking a little. 'Recently separated and trying to get used to being all alone.'

'Kids?' he asked.

'Two. Grown up and flown the nest.'

'That's tough. I have a daughter and a granddaughter, so I'm an old grandpa,' he added with a laugh.

'Oh.' Maggie was suddenly stuck for words. She couldn't imagine him as a grandfather even though, at around fifty, he was old enough by now. But to her he was still the young man she had been so in love with. 'That must be nice,' she added.

'Sure,' he said. 'So how about us hooking up, then? At Muckross House? Tomorrow afternoon. Three o'clock okay with you?'

'Yes,' Maggie replied. 'That's fine. We could meet by the greenhouses and then walk through the gardens.'

'What if it rains?'

'It won't,' Maggie promised. 'According to the weather forecast, it will stay dry and sunny tomorrow.'

'Great. Okay, Maggie, I'm really looking forward to seeing you again.'

'Me too,' Maggie said. 'Bye for now, Paul.'

'Bye, Maggie.'

He hung up and Maggie sat on the little stool in the dark hall wondering if she was dreaming. It seemed like a miracle that she had just spoken to Paul, the young man she had once thought was the love of her life. No longer young, of course, and probably marked by some tough knocks in his life, just like her. She wondered what he'd been through and why he suddenly wanted to meet her after all these years. She should be angry with Brian for giving Paul her phone number without asking her, but if he hadn't, she'd still be dithering and Paul might have gone back home before she made up her mind.

Maggie slowly got up from the stool, feeling she was at some kind of crossroads in her life. She caught sight of her face in the mirror and stepped closer to look at herself. What would Paul think if he saw her now? Maggie picked up her phone from the small hall table and dialled Sorcha's number.

She answered straight away. 'Hi, Maggie,' she said above the sound of voices and glasses clinking. 'Have you changed your mind about the pub? I was about to head home but I could stay on if you want to come over.'

'No,' Maggie said. 'I don't. It's... Something happened. He rang me.'

'Who? Oh, you mean *him*.'

'Yes. Him. Paul O'Sullivan. Brian gave him my number without asking me, but, well, it was a good thing. I'd still be trying to make up my mind if he hadn't called.'

'So what happens now?' Sorcha wanted to know.

'We're meeting tomorrow. In Killarney.'

'Really?' Sorcha almost shouted. 'That's amazing!'

'Yeah, I suppose,' Maggie said glumly. 'Except...'

'Except what?' Sorcha asked. 'Isn't this terrific? So exciting.'

'I'm not sure,' Maggie said, still looking at her reflection in the mirror. 'I think I need a facelift or something. I look terrible. Old and frumpy.'

'No, you don't,' Sorcha argued. 'I thought you looked great tonight when you stood up and made that statement about Mad Brendan's memorial. All sparkly and fiery.'

'Oh that,' Maggie said, feeling it had happened years ago. 'I got a bit carried away. But that was then, this is different. Where can I get an emergency makeover before three o'clock tomorrow?'

'Oh, I see,' Sorcha said. 'That's not a problem. We'll get Gerry at Susie's salon on the case. He's an amazing stylist. He can make anyone look ten years younger and a hundred times prettier in a few hours. He styled my mother's cousin's daughter for her wedding last April. A plain woman, to say the least, and he made her look so good the groom didn't recognise her and nearly fainted when she walked up the aisle.'

Maggie laughed. 'That sounds amazing. Maybe Gerry can make me look a little less drab then.'

'He'll turn you into Miss Ireland in half an hour,' Sorcha said. 'I'll call him tonight and explain and then I'll text you with the appointment. I'm sure he'll be delighted to style the "lovely colleen".'

Maggie smiled. 'I wouldn't aim that high. I just don't want to look like I've been dragged through a hedge.'

'On it,' Sorcha said. 'Stay tuned for the appointment.' She hung up.

Maggie walked into the kitchen, still smiling. Sorcha was a true star, and so were all the people she had met since she came back, with the exception of Darina. She would be a tough nut to crack, but like everyone else probably had a soft spot. In Maggie's experience, people who acted like Darina had often a reason for their behaviour towards others. Darina seemed like someone who wanted to be in control all the time. Not a control freak as such, but perhaps she had been bullied or badly treated sometime in her youth or childhood. Maybe she would soften if someone managed to crack open that hard shell.

Maggie forgot about Darina when her phone pinged with a text from Sorcha.

Gerry will see you at the salon at 9 tomorrow morning. He jumped at the chance of making you look fabulous when I said it was an emergency. S xx

Maggie sent a quick 'thank you' back before she went out onto the terrace and sat down looking at the stars that were beginning to appear in the darkening sky. As she sat there, she remembered how they had sat in the creaky deckchairs when they were children, wrapped in blankets on chilly August nights, and looked at the stars, pointing out the constellations, gazing at the swathe of the Milky Way across the blackness up there. It had always made her shiver at the infiniteness of the universe and made her feel tinier than a speck of dust. And here she was, meeting Paul again tomorrow. What would he think when he saw this older woman he had known as a young man of twenty-two?

Did it matter at all in the scheme of things? she wondered as a breeze laden with the smell of salt and seaweed cooled her hot cheeks. Maybe not, but now she wanted to meet him. And when she did, she wanted to look her best. Would the chemistry, the *feeling* between them still be there? Or would they be like strangers who had changed beyond recognition?

16

Gerry, a dapper young man with short platinum hair and several earrings in each ear, greeted Maggie enthusiastically the next morning.

'Sit here, lovely lady,' he said, indicating one of the chairs in front of a wall of mirrors in the small salon. 'Let's take a look at you and see what we can do.'

Maggie sat down and smiled back at him, trying to feel positive despite the tired face she saw in the mirror. She had slept fitfully all night, the butterflies in her stomach refusing to settle down. All she could think of was meeting Paul and wondering what he would think of her. Not much, she decided as she looked at her pale face with dark circles under her eyes and her flat hair. 'I need a lot of work,' she said with an apologetic smile. 'I'm sorry to barge in on you like this at the last minute, too. It's so kind of you to fit me in.'

'It's Friday morning and the big rush won't be until tonight,' Gerry said. 'I have plenty of time. And Susie usually sleeps late so we'll be all alone and can discuss what needs to be done in peace and quiet.' He shook out a light blue cape and put it on Maggie with a great flourish. 'There.' He placed his hands on her shoulders and looked at her in the mirror. 'Right,' he muttered. 'Let's see what we can do. What kind of look are you after?'

'I'm not sure,' Maggie said, her voice a little shaky. 'I want to look fresh and young – or at least younger,' she said. 'Natural but still polished. And maybe more alive,' she added. 'But as you can see it's going to take a bit of a miracle.'

Gerry nodded. 'Fear not, my dear. I love a challenge.'

'Then this is your lucky day,' Maggie said with derisory laugh.

Gerry patted her shoulder. 'I'll have you looking fabulous in no time. There's good material here, I can see. It's for an important date, Sorcha told me.'

'Very important,' Maggie replied. 'I'm meeting a man I haven't seen for thirty years.' She paused. 'I don't know if you listen to Radio Kerry, but—'

'But of course!' Gerry exclaimed, looking excited. 'Do I take it that you're meeting that man I heard being interviewed recently and that you are indeed the "lovely colleen"?'

Maggie let out a snort. 'Oh yeah, the "lovely colleen", that's me. As you can see there's nothing lovely about me at all.'

'Don't be hard on yourself,' Gerry said, his hands still on her shoulders and his eyes kind as they met hers in the mirror. 'You have fantastic bones and lovely eyes. I'll have you looking fabulous in no time at all. But I think you should be doing this for *you* and nobody else. You can't truly love someone else until you love yourself, I always feel.'

'I never thought of it that way,' Maggie said. 'But I think that's very true.'

'Of course it is,' Gerry agreed. 'I see a lot of good points here. Lots of great material to work on. You have a good face and gorgeous blue eyes.' He lifted up a strand of her hair. 'Your hair is nice and thick but a little sad. It's too long, I think. And the colour needs to be jazzed up.'

'Jazzed up?' Maggie exclaimed, putting her hands on her head. 'I don't want pink streaks or anything.'

'Fear not, pretty lady. I'm thinking caramel and honey highlights. It'll look fab against that golden skin. And then we'll apply a little make-up to make those blue eyes blaze like sapphires. We use a special brand of natural products that are made in Ireland. You'll look as fresh as a daisy by the time I've finished with you.'

Maggie laughed. His good mood was so contagious she immediately felt both hopeful and happy. 'I'm looking forward to this.'

'So am I,' Gerry said. 'So, darling girl, will we get going, then?'

'Do your worst,' Maggie said. 'And I don't want to look until you've finished.'

'Great idea,' Gerry said and twirled her chair around. 'I'll face you this way, then. We have no clients until eleven, so we can work in peace until Susie comes.'

'Brilliant,' Maggie said.

Gerry worked in silence as he mixed the colour and applied the highlights, wrapping strands of her hair in foil. 'This bit is the trickiest,' he said. 'You want to balance the colours and make sure the product stays in exactly the right amount of time. So please don't say a word until this is finished. Close your eyes and think of happy things and then I'll shampoo and condition when I take the foil out and then we can start cutting.'

'Okay,' Maggie said, pleased to have this moment to relax and think. She closed her eyes and went through the conversation with Paul in her mind. It had been wonderful to hear his voice and he had sounded like someone whose company she would enjoy. Nice, considerate, maybe even interesting. And she was relieved to hear that he was unattached.

But what about her? Would he find her interesting too? She felt she hadn't changed that much since she was young, at least her interests hadn't. She still loved sports and dance, animals and nature and was still passionate about the environment, especially marine life. Her bookshelves were stacked with books about the flora and fauna of Ireland, biographies and a romantic novel or two. She was older and wiser but mentally scarred and wary of men after what Dermot had done to her. She had felt she couldn't open her heart to anyone after that. But since she had arrived in Sandy Cove, she had begun to feel more alive and a lot less lonely. And now she was looking forward to meeting Paul with both trepidation and excitement.

'There,' Gerry said in her ear. 'Wakey, wakey. Time to remove the foil strips and shampoo and condition. Follow me to the basin.'

Maggie walked across the salon to the basins and sat down, tipping her head back, closing her eyes again as the warm water washed over her hair.

'I'll give you a head massage,' Gerry said as he applied shampoo. 'I do this to Kate, our doctor, when she comes in for a trim. I did a fab job on her hair a few years ago,' he added proudly. 'It totally transformed her. But now I'm going to focus on you. You'll love the massage. Very relaxing and good for the circulation of your scalp.' He proceeded to gently rub his finger-tips around and around on Maggie's scalp, while a slow ballad played on the tin whistle wafted from the loudspeakers in the ceiling.

'Oooh,' Maggie sighed, feeling her whole body relax. 'This is wonderful.'

'Good for the soul,' Gerry said, rubbing in the conditioner. 'And now once I have rinsed this out, it's time to cut.' He wrapped Maggie's hair in a towel and she followed him back to her chair by the mirrors.

Gerry combed out her hair and looked into the mirror. 'Sorry, dear, but I think you'll have to look. I was thinking short but not too short. Like a bob with a few layers and a cropped neck. This will flirt with your eyes and soften the jawline. What do you think?'

'Sounds great,' Maggie said. 'Go for it.'

'Will do.' Gerry nodded and took his scissors from a pouch on the shelf.

They were quiet while he cut and chopped and combed and cut again, ruffling her hair and then snipping around the edges. As she watched him work, Maggie realised how skilled he was. Amazing that such a stylist was to be found here in this small village.

'All finished,' Gerry said. He grabbed a hairdryer from the shelf and plugged it in. 'This just needs a little bit of work and you're done.'

The door opened when Maggie's hair was nearly dry and Susie walked into the shop, panting. 'Oh my God, Maggie,' she exclaimed. 'You look fabulous!'

Maggie blinked and stared at her image in the mirror. The new style that Gerry was just finishing was shorter than she had imagined, with a fringe across her forehead and the ends in line with her jaw. But it was the colour that delighted her the most. Her own light brown was enhanced by honey and caramel high-lights that complemented her blue eyes and lightly tanned face. Gone were the drab strands and flat hair to be replaced by shiny curls that shimmered and bounced when she shook her head. Her face looked a lot less tired too, because of the head massage and the feeling of being pampered. 'Oh,' Maggie said in a near whisper. 'It's a miracle. Gerry, you are a true genius.'

'I know,' he said, grinning. He ran his fingers through her hair. 'So easy to style, too. It's a masterpiece, wouldn't you say?'

'Oh, yes!' Susie clapped her hands. 'Bravo,' she shouted. 'Five stars to you, Gerry.'

'But we're not finished,' Gerry said. 'A little dab of mascara, blusher and just a hint of pink on the lips, I think. What do you say, Susie?'

'Perfect,' Susie said. 'Is that okay with you, Maggie? We could use the new products from the Irish brand we've just bought in. Very popular with brides as it stays on all day and is tearproof.'

'I'm not planning to cry,' Maggie remarked with a laugh. 'But yeah, why not?'

'Great,' Susie said. 'Hey, Gerry, make us all a coffee and I'll do Maggie up.'

The make-up Susie applied did wonders as it gave Maggie a glow and polish without making her look too made up. She had even managed to magic away the dark circles under Maggie's eyes.

Maggie smiled as she looked at herself, prettier, a little younger and a lot happier. She shook her head to make her hair dance around her face and suddenly felt that she was beginning to love herself, just as Gerry had suggested. This makeover was for her and nobody else. No matter what happened with Paul, she was ready to face the day.

Maggie arrived at Muckross House and gardens a few minutes before three o'clock. The rain had held off as she had predicted and the sky was nearly all clear except for a few clouds over the mountains. She could see the lake glimmering in the distance as she drove into the car park. She found a place at the far end, which she knew would mean a long walk to the greenhouses, but she had no choice. She would a be a little late, but maybe that was a good thing. This way, she wouldn't look too eager. She laughed at herself and ran a hand over her hair. She still wasn't used to her new look and had been glancing in the mirror all through her drive to admire herself, which was a new feeling that made her smile. How silly to be so happy about a new hairstyle at her age, she thought, as she got out of the car. But as she slammed the door shut, the butterflies started to dance in her

stomach again. Not from fear but from excitement. She felt
somehow that this day would change her life. She only hoped it
would be for the better.

Maggie started walking across the car park towards the café
and greenhouses, scanning the crowd of visitors to see if she
could spot anyone who looked like Paul. But she saw no man on
his own among the couples and families walking around. *He's
probably already there, waiting for me*, she thought, her heart
beating and her hands cold.

Like a robot she walked around the big café and boutique
towards the large Victorian greenhouses on the vast expanse of
lawn. She saw someone sitting on a bench under a tree and
stopped for a moment to catch her breath. But he had seen her
and stood up. Frozen to the spot, Maggie stood stock still,
staring at the man walking towards her. The shape of his head
and the square set of his shoulders were familiar, but his greying
hair and beard made him look like a stranger. He came closer
still and she saw those green eyes fringed with black lashes and
the smile that lit up his face. Then he stopped and they looked
at each other across the expanse of lawn and all the years that
had passed.

'Maggie,' he said and held out both his hands. 'Is it really
you?'

She stepped forward and took his hands. 'Yes. It's me.' She
saw that his face was lined and that he had a scar that ran down
his left cheek. His shaggy hair was nearly all grey and his beard
was closely cropped. It suited him, she thought.

His gaze scanned her face. 'You look wonderful.'

'I'm older, of course,' she said, pulling her hands out of his
grip. She felt suddenly awkward under his intense gaze. This
was too weird, even though it was incredible to meet him again.
But it felt suddenly overwhelming. She didn't want to rush into
his arms and start some kind of love affair again. Not with this
man who had lived a whole lifetime after they had parted all

those years ago. They weren't the same people, she realised, as she looked at him and saw a stranger.

'We're both older,' Paul said.

'And maybe wiser,' she said.

'Hopefully.' He gestured at the bench. 'Do you want to sit here so we can talk? Or do you want to go to the café and have coffee or something?'

'Let's sit here for a moment,' she said. 'I don't want to be among people right now.'

'Me neither,' he said.

She sat down. He joined her and they faced each other. 'It feels so strange,' she said. 'It's you but then not you – the young man I said goodbye to.'

'I know. It was such a long time ago.' He looked out across the garden. Then he turned to her. 'But then, in some way, it's like it happened yesterday.'

'I know. I was so sad when we said goodbye,' Maggie said, that moment suddenly so vivid in her mind that her eyes filled with tears. 'I think I was sad for months.'

'So was I. For a while anyway.' He paused for a moment. 'You see,' he started, 'it felt like I was leaving a part of me behind. And, of course, I was in a way. A little bit of my heart was still with you. Then I came back home and I tried to adjust to that, and to being back in the States and doing what I was expected to do. So I passed all the exams for West Point and left home to start my officers' training course. Thought I'd be honouring my father and the family and so on. I was even convinced I really was officer material.' He sighed and shook his head. 'But it turned out I was wrong.'

'Oh?' Maggie said, sad to hear that Paul had agreed to do something just for his father's approval. 'What happened?'

'I was kicked out. They thought I lacked leadership or something like that. I think it was because I couldn't take the bullying and the brutal way we cadets were treated. So I went home with my tail between my legs. My father was disgusted and didn't talk to me. Refused to pay for the university course I wanted to take instead. So my dream of studying psychology ended there and then.'

'Oh, God,' Maggie said. 'How hard that must have been.'

'Yes. It was. Very hard. I left home and went to work at my uncle's insurance company in Chicago, and then, after a few years I became an insurance broker. I married a girl who worked in my office, but it didn't work out. We divorced a few years later. We had a daughter we named Pauline, who I brought up on my own when my ex-wife left to live in Texas. She married someone in the oil business later on and then she took over the care of our daughter.' He stopped and looked bleakly at Maggie. 'But I've always felt bad about breaking my promise to you. You must have been wondering why I cut you off like that.'

'Yes, why did you?' Maggie asked. 'Was it because you thought I'd think badly of you for not following your dreams?'

'No. I knew you'd understand that bit. You had told me I should do what I wanted. But I had some kind of breakdown when my father became so hostile towards me. I was depressed and wanted to leave everything behind. Even you. I thought I'd contact you later, when I was in a better place. But it took a long time for me to heal after that. And I had moved to Chicago, and well, my life took such a different turn that I felt I had become someone else. I didn't want to burden you with my problems. And at that time I didn't have a cent to my name.'

'I see.' Maggie looked back at him and tried to understand what he was saying. She had thought at the time that he had been at West Point and perhaps gone to war. She had imagined all kinds of reasons for him to cut her off, but not this. 'I suppose,' she said, 'that as time went on and you *meant* to contact me again, I receded further and further in your memory. All the things you were going through probably obscured everything else as you struggled to survive.' She drew breath and looked at him, waiting for a response.

He nodded, his eyes serious. 'Yes. There was so much to deal with and my mental health wasn't the best. I'm glad you understand.'

'I'm trying to,' Maggie said, knowing that she would never have forgotten him whatever she had been through. But he was different and maybe their romance hadn't meant as much to him as it had to her. 'Why did you come back?' she asked. 'Why did you want to find me?'

'Oh,' he said. 'So many reasons. I have always wanted to go back to Ireland and see my family here again. And then there was you. I found your letters in my mother's house when she was clearing it out. She was moving into an apartment after my father died last year.'

Maggie put her hand on his arm. 'You lost your father? I'm so sorry.'

'Thank you.' He put his hand over hers. 'It's okay. I'm dealing with it. We managed to mend a lot of fences before he passed away. We were okay and there was peace between us. That helps a lot.'

'Oh, that's good.'

He removed his hand and sat back. 'Yeah. I'm fine. Sad but calm. Accepting it, you know? That's the most important part.' He cleared his throat. 'But back to why I came here this time and why I wanted to meet you. I read your letters again after all this time and it all came back to me. The way I felt about you then, I mean. And the promise we made.' He laughed softly and shook his head. 'We were so young and romantic. We thought everything was possible. And you loved me so much.' He groped in the pocket of his leather bomber jacket and pulled out a wad of envelopes tied together with a rubber band. 'Here they are, if you want to read them.'

Maggie looked at the letters and shook her head. 'No, I don't think I do. There's no need. I remember most of them.'

He nodded and put the wad back in his pocket. 'Beautiful letters so full of love and hope. And I read them and then... I cut you off and forgot all the things we meant to each other. And our dreams. How sad that must have made you.'

'I thought you were dead,' Maggie whispered. 'I thought you'd gone to war in Iraq and never came back. I tried to contact your family but I had only that phone number and no address. I wrote to West Point but the letters were returned with a "not known here" or something scribbled on it. That was after Christmas. You must have left then.'

'Yes. I was already in Chicago.'

'I see.'

'Yeah.' He sighed and shot her a look she couldn't quite decipher. 'And here we are, thirty years later, different people,' he ended.

'Do you really think so? That we're so different?' Maggie asked. 'The raw material must still be there, though. And then what we have experienced made us a little cynical, or jaded, I mean,' she tried to explain. 'But I'm still me inside, the girl you knew back then. My personality hasn't changed. It's just that what I've been through has made me less...'

'Innocent?' he asked. 'More suspicious? Less optimistic?'

'Something like that.' Maggie laughed. 'I'm not sure how to express it. I think we need to get to know each other as adults. But maybe you don't have the time? How long are you staying in Ireland?'

'I was planning to stay another two weeks,' he said. 'I took a long break and left my assistant to run things while I'm away. And we're in touch all the time so I can keep an eye on things. I took over from my uncle when he retired, you see. He left his entire company to me. And now it's grown and we're into all sorts of other businesses.'

'Oh, that's amazing,' Maggie said. 'So you did succeed after all eventually.'

'Too late to impress my father,' Paul replied with a wry little smile. 'But yeah, I'm doing well. I've branched out in all kinds of areas and we're a big company now.' He focused on her. 'But what about you? I know nothing about your life. What did you end up doing?'

'I'm a PE teacher and I love it,' Maggie replied. 'I always wanted to do that. Sports and everything to do with exercise and dance is still what I love the most. And teaching young kids and teenagers is incredibly rewarding.'

He nodded as he placed his arm along the back of the bench behind her back. 'I remember you saying that. I'm glad you got to realise your dream. And what about your personal life? You have kids, you said?'

'Yes. A son and a daughter I'm very proud of. Jim and Orla. I love them to bits and think of them every day. But I'm separated from their father,' she continued, feeling a dart of pain as she said it. 'He left me last year. I'm still trying to deal with it. It's not easy.'

'Of course not. Is that why you came back to the village?'

'Yes.' Maggie looked away from his gaze. 'It just happened by accident. I saw an ad for a cottage to rent and it happened to be the one my parents used to own. As if it was meant to be. Karma and all that,' she added with a smile, thinking of what Susie had said. 'And now here I am, with you.'

'Amazing.' His gaze didn't leave her face. 'What an idiot,' he muttered.

'Who?'

'That man who left you. I mean, you're so pretty. I don't get how any man wouldn't want to be with you.'

Maggie felt her face flush. 'Thank you,' she said, feeling suddenly awkward. His remark sounded flirtatious in a way she wasn't used to. But he was probably just being kind and hadn't meant it the way it came out.

'So what do we do now?' he asked. 'Do you want to go over to the café and have tea and scones or whatever it is you have at this time of day?'

'Yes,' she said, suddenly overwhelmed by what he had told her, including the remark about her looks. 'That would be great.' She got up, hoping her face had cooled down and tried to regain her composure. She suddenly wanted to be among people. Being all alone and so close to him was too much suddenly. She felt the same chemistry between them as when she was young, but not the same meeting of hearts and souls. It was too early to think that way, she told herself. They needed to get to know each other before she could judge their relationship to each other.

He jumped to his feet and they walked across the lawn to the café, where they joined the queue at the counter. Paul loaded a tray with scones, cream and jam and ordered two pots of tea, paying with his credit card before Maggie had a chance to get out her wallet. 'I'll get this,' he said.

'Thank you.'

'You're welcome. I don't feel comfortable about a woman paying for my food. I'm an old-fashioned kind of guy,' he added. He took the tray and started to walk across to the conservatory where he found a free table. 'Despite the forecast, it looks like it's going to rain, so we'll sit here. Okay with you?'

'Perfect,' Maggie said. 'The weather in Kerry is so unpredictable. Even the experts get it wrong a lot of the time.'

They sat down, and as the rain began to smatter against the glass roof, they continued to talk in a less personal way, simply chatting about this and that, looking at each other and pretending it was completely normal to sit here together after thirty years of separation.

Just as Maggie was beginning to feel exhausted by all the

emotions she had been through in the last hours, her phone rang. She excused herself and replied without thinking, giving a start as she heard the voice at the other end.

'Hi, there. Kiara here from Radio Kerry. Just wondering if you have any news?'

'Uh,' Maggie said, looking at Paul. 'Hi, Kiara. Hold on just a moment.' She covered her phone with her hand. 'It's Kiara. That woman from the radio station. She wants to know if I have any news. I don't know what to say to her.'

'I do.' Paul grinned and snatched the phone from Maggie. 'Hi, Kiara,' he said. 'Paul O'Sullivan here. I'm the guy you interviewed the other week. I'm happy to say that I found the "lovely colleen" and we've just met. So I just wanted to say a huge thank you for interviewing me and helping Maggie to find me.' He listened for a while and then handed the phone back to Maggie. 'She wants to talk to you.'

'I'll put the speaker on,' Maggie said and clicked on the speaker sign. 'Hi, we're both listening now.'

'Oh great,' Kiara said, 'I'll record this if you don't mind?'

'Go ahead,' Paul said before Maggie had a chance to reply. 'It'll be great to share this with everyone who might be listening.'

'Fabulous.' Kiara chortled at the other end. 'I wish we could film you. But as that's not possible I just wanted to ask how you're both feeling right now? It must have been so amazing to meet again after all these years.'

'Incredible,' Maggie said. 'And weird at the same time. But in a happy way,' she added.

'Did you recognise each other straight away?' Kiara wanted to know.

'Not quite,' Maggie said. 'But after a while the years seemed to disappear. Paul was familiar and a stranger at the same time.'

Paul's smile was warm as he looked at Maggie. 'Ah, but

Maggie is just as gorgeous. I couldn't understand why we lost touch like that. How could I let such a beautiful woman go?'

'Yes, why did you?' Kiara asked.

'Ah well, it was just one of those things,' Paul said. 'Life took over and the memories faded.'

'But now you've found each other again,' Kiara said dreamily. 'What happens next, do you think? Another love story but with a happy ending this time?'

'I don't think so,' Paul replied, winking at Maggie. 'Too much water under the bridge and all that. We're just catching up and then I'll go back home in a few days. Back to my wife and kids. And Maggie's in a relationship too. But it was nice to meet up.'

'Of course,' Kiara agreed, sounding disappointed.

'So all's well in the end,' Paul said. 'We've managed to close this chapter and then we'll go back to our lives having had a very pleasant time catching up.'

'Lovely,' Kiara said. 'Thanks for telling me. Have nice stay in Kerry, Paul.'

'I will indeed,' Paul said. He said goodbye and gave the phone back to Maggie.

She hung up, shaking her head, laughing. 'Great stuff, Paul. You managed to kill that story stone dead. Not that I approve of lying, of course.'

'I thought it was the best thing to do. Now we won't have anyone breathing down our necks or staring at us wherever we go. She seemed to have lost interest completely.'

'I hope so.'

Paul nodded and checked his watch. 'I'm having dinner with some friends in a little while. And I'm sure you'll want to get back to Sandy Cove.'

'Yes. It's getting late.' Maggie rose from her chair.

Paul got up and they stood there, looking awkwardly at each

other. 'I'd love to see you again,' he said. 'I mean... of course if you don't want...'

'I do,' she interrupted. 'Of course I do. I feel we need to get to know each other again as adults. Don't you?'

'Yes. There's so much more to talk about. So much to discover.'

'There is,' Maggie agreed, feeling she knew more about him now than ever before.

He leaned forward and kissed her cheek. 'I'll be in touch. See you soon, my sweet Maggie.'

'Bye,' Maggie whispered and walked away, his kiss still burning her cheek, feeling as if she was walking on clouds as she reached her car, wondering if she was dreaming. But it had really happened and he had begun to redeem himself to her. She could see more clearly now – understand what had happened to him, which must have been so hard for a young man. And she forgave him instantly, the old grudge softening and disappearing, making her heart feel light as that burden of resentment and hurt she had been carrying floated away. She felt suddenly free and joyful, looking forward to seeing him again and sharing her own story with him.

As she drove away through the park, she went through their meeting and what they had said to each other. She realised that he had done most of the talking and that – apart from telling him she was separated and had two children – he knew absolutely nothing about her life. His story was naturally the more important, as he had to explain why he had stopped writing to her. When they met again, he would want to hear her story and she would tell him everything. But would they connect again the way they had thirty years ago? Then they had been so blindly in love and thought nothing could stop them having a life together. But this time around, they were older and more careful. At least she was.

Can I fall in love again, just like that? she wondered as she continued down the road to Sandy Cove. What Dermot had done to her had shaken her confidence and now she was afraid of letting go, of feeling that way again for a man. But meeting Paul had made her feel alive again and given her a buzz of excitement. She couldn't wait to see him next, whatever happened in the end. He was going back home in two weeks.

But so what? she thought. *Even if all we have are a few short weeks, isn't that better than nothing?*

Maggie glanced at herself in the rear-view mirror and smiled. The reunion with Paul had driven her to have a makeover that made her look like her old self, that woman she had been before Dermot left her. She wanted to be that woman and not the sad creature who had come to Sandy Cove to lick her wounds. Seeing Paul again gave her hope and a feeling of closing the door on all the sadness. He had looked at her in a way that gave her a buzz of excitement. Maggie turned on the radio and sang along with Bruce Springsteen, as a sudden wave of pure joy surged through her. Life was for living and loving, not moping and crying. The summer seemed full of the promise of something new and exciting. Life wasn't over yet. It was just beginning.

17

The following week started with glorious weather and a phone call from Paul. 'I want to come to Sandy Cove,' he said. 'And stay for a while. I'd love to see that gorgeous village again and meet everyone who's still around. And be with you, of course.'

'That would be great,' Maggie said, as she sat in the kitchen just finishing her breakfast. 'Uh, um, do you want to stay with me? I have a guest room, but...'

'No. Better not,' Paul said after a moment's hesitation.

'I suppose,' Maggie agreed, mentally kicking herself for even suggesting it. The mere thought of him here in the house actually made her feel very odd. She was suddenly unsure about her feelings and started to wonder if she was looking forward to seeing him again or not. On the one hand, she was dreaming of some kind of romance, but on the other she was wary of what would happen when they had to say goodbye again, which was inevitable. Maybe she shouldn't see him at all now that he had given her the closure she had so desperately wanted. But then her heart started to beat faster as she remembered how he had looked at her. He was right, though. If they stayed in the same house, it could throw them together in a way she wasn't ready for and maybe never would be. 'We shouldn't force anything,' she said. 'Or...'

'Or put temptation in our way and make things happen that we might regret later.' He stopped. 'Sorry, I didn't mean I wouldn't want it to. But we've only just met again and we should be careful not to rush anything. I just want to be with you and for you to get to know me better.'

'Of course,' Maggie agreed. She glanced out the window as she spoke, her spirits soaring at the sight of the sun shining on the mountainside covered in wild roses and the blue sky with only a few fluffy clouds. It was one of those stunning days only Sandy Cove could deliver. And now she would spend it with Paul. It seemed like a dream come true.

'I've already booked into a B&B in Ballinskelligs,' he continued. 'I don't think I could ask what's-his-name? The guy whose family I stayed with back then?'

'Brian,' Maggie said. 'No, I don't think that would be possible. He's a vet and has a lot of animals. Three dogs and two cats and there's an old horse out to grass behind his house, too.'

'I'm not that into animals,' Paul said with a laugh.

'You're allergic?'

'Not really, dogs and cats just aren't my thing,' Paul replied. 'Never got why people have to have pets. Do you?'

'Yes, I do,' Maggie said, feeling disappointed at his lack of love for animals. 'I love dogs in particular. Our dog died just before... before the separation. I'm going to get a new one as soon as I get back. I might even find one here. Brian's springer spaniel is going to have puppies soon, he told me. I might take one of them.'

'Oh,' Paul said. 'I had no idea you were one of those dog-ladies. Don't tell me you hug trees as well?'

'Not really,' Maggie replied, joining in his laughter. 'I haven't gone that far yet. But why not? Trees are beautiful.'

'And you don't have to take them for walks or pick up their droppings.'

'That's true. So where are you now?' Maggie asked, wanting to leave the subject of dogs and trees.

'I'm actually already in Ballinskelligs,' he replied. 'Just checked into the B&B. So what are you up to today?'

'I was going to join the Tidy Town Association work force, picking up litter on the beach this afternoon with Sorcha, if you remember her, and some other friends. But I can cancel and say I have a guest to take care of or something.'

'Hell, no,' Paul exclaimed. 'Why don't I join you? That way I can meet some of the old gang. That would be fun. And then we can go for a swim when we've finished the litter-picking. Maybe have dinner somewhere later?'

'That would be great,' Maggie replied, only a little disappointed he hadn't suggested that they'd be on their own. 'Do you want to meet at the beach?'

'I'll pick you up just after lunch,' he said. 'I want to see the cottage first.'

'Okay,' Maggie said, her spirits lifting. 'I'll give you a tour of the house. It's been beautifully restored.'

'See you later, then,' he said and hung up.

Maggie put her phone on the table and finished her breakfast, trying to gauge Paul's mood and the way he was planning their day. He didn't seem to want them to spend the day together on their own, preferring to meet the people he had known when he was last here. Did it mean that he had been disappointed in her when they met? Had she seemed old and frumpy to him despite her new look? Or was it simply a case of him seeking atonement for the way he had cut her off and now that she seemed to understand and forgive, he was off the hook and could enjoy his Irish holiday? The phone ringing interrupted her thoughts. It was Brian, she saw from the caller ID.

'Hi,' he said. 'How did it go last week? Did you meet the man of your dreams and pick up where you left off?'

'After thirty years? Are you joking?' Maggie asked, knowing he was teasing her. It took her by surprise just how much he made her smile sometimes.

'Yes,' Brian said. 'I was. Sorry. That was tactless. I just wanted to know if it was what you hoped. I know how I felt when I saw you again, so I was sure he'd be just as stunned. And maybe you were happy to meet him again. Did it feel like you were meeting the same person?'

'Yes and no,' Maggie said with a sigh, warmed by his comment about how he had felt when he saw her again. 'It was weird. We were strangers in one way but close in other ways. As if there was a huge hole in our relationship. Or a ravine between then and now and we were trying to meet in the middle. He wants to join the litter-picking on the beach this afternoon.'

'Not the most romantic of dates,' Brian remarked. 'I mean, litter-picking? I'd be more for a champagne picnic for two or something if I was him.'

'I didn't know you were the champagne type.'

'I can be any type you like,' he said, his voice flirty.

'I bet,' Maggie replied, blushing. She quickly changed the subject. 'But I think Paul wants to take it nice and slow. Do things together first before the champagne and other stuff. And the beach needs to be cleaned. Are you coming?'

'Just for half an hour,' Brian replied. 'To show my face and support the effort. And now I get to take a peek at yer man too. We didn't know each other that well in them old days when he stayed with us, as he was much older. But he didn't like dogs as far as I remember. We had this big black shaggy thing called Jack. Paul didn't like him at all. Said he was dirty and hairy, which was true, I suppose.'

'I do remember Jack,' Maggie said. 'He was a lovely fellow.'

'He was,' Brian agreed. 'I cried buckets when he died. Not very manly of me, but that's the way I am.'

'Nothing wrong with that,' Maggie declared. 'As I told you, we lost our Sally last year and I'm still sad.'

'You should definitely take one of Jessie's puppies,' Brian suggested. 'That'll help you with the loss of your friend.'

'I'm very tempted,' Maggie said.

'Someone at the door of the surgery,' Brian said. 'I have to go.'

'See you at the beach later, Brian.'

'See ya, Mags,' Brian said and hung up.

Maggie smiled at the old nickname and got up, glancing at her image in the mirror as she went into the hall. Did she look okay, or should she dress up? No need for that, her T-shirt and shorts were fine for litter-picking, if not spectacular. But why should she fuss? They were cleaning up the beach, not dining in a fancy restaurant. And if Paul didn't like her the way she was, he wasn't the same person she had known in her youth, when what any of them wore was of no importance at all.

When the doorbell rang later that afternoon, Maggie opened the door and smiled as Paul came into view. 'Hi, welcome to my rented summer home.'

'Thank you,' he said with that wide grin that had never failed to make her heart beat faster. He was dressed in a faded blue Ralph Lauren polo shirt, shorts and scuffed Docksider loafers. *The picture of casual style*, Maggie thought.

He glanced around the hall. 'This looks a lot more elegant than I remember.'

'You're telling me,' Maggie said with a laugh. 'It's been turned into a boutique cottage by the architect owner who lives next door. American, actually. From Boston.' She opened the door wider. 'But come in. I'm sure you'll want to take a look around before we go to the beach.'

'Thanks,' he said, stepping across the threshold. 'Can't wait to see the improvements.'

'Come this way.' Maggie walked ahead of him into the living room and out onto the terrace where she stopped, waiting for him to catch up with her.

Paul stepped onto the terrace through the door of the sunroom and looked at the view. 'Wow. This is still as awesome as it was. But the house has been done up so much I don't recognise a thing. And this used to be a scruffy little garden with rickety deckchairs and a few shrubs. But now it's like something from an interior design magazine. A great improvement, I have to say.'

'I wasn't so sure at first,' Maggie said. 'It was a bit of a shock to see it all transformed, but now I love it. The comfort of a hot shower, a modern kitchen and smooth tiles under my feet is hard to beat. Especially now that I'm a little older. You can't stay stuck in the past, you know.'

Paul looked at her and smiled. 'That's my motto. I love everything modern and shiny.'

Maggie laughed. 'Then you must have been disappointed when you saw me. I'm not what you'd call new and shiny anymore.'

'I was delighted to see you,' Paul protested. 'I knew you wouldn't be eighteen, so it wasn't a shock at all. And now that I'm used to you as a mature woman, I like what I see.'

His eyes on her made her blush and she suddenly didn't know what to say. 'You're not bad yourself,' she countered, trying to joke away her nerves. 'But maybe we should get going? They'll all be at the beach by now and as I promised...'

'Sure,' he said and started to go back inside. 'Thanks for the tour, Maggie. And the compliment,' he added over his shoulder with a wink.

They left the house and walked up the lane towards the main beach where a number of people were standing around holding large blue plastic bags. As they drew nearer, they saw that Darina, dressed in white Bermudas and a blue-and-white stripy top, was shouting out orders. Maggie suppressed a giggle when she saw that Darina had a whistle on a string around her neck.

'Oh, God,' Maggie whispered, 'she's organising the troops.'

'Who is she?' Paul asked, looking at Darina. 'Some kind of navy person?'

'No, she's Darina O'Dea, self-appointed queen of Sandy Cove,' Maggie muttered back. 'We're all terrified of her.'

'Is that so?' Paul said, looking amused. He walked up to Darina and waited for her to finish.

Darina turned and looked at Paul. 'Hello,' she said. 'I don't think we've met.'

'We haven't,' he said and held out his hand. 'I'm Paul O'Sullivan, a friend of Maggie's from America and I've come to help with the clean-up of the beach.'

Darina brightened and shook his hand. 'Oh, that's wonderful. Welcome to Sandy Cove, Paul. So happy you offered to help us with the clean-up. We need all hands on deck.' She handed him a blue plastic bag. 'Here you go. Maybe you and Maggie can join forces as we're a little short of bags.' She pointed at two large black bins. 'Plastic to the left, paper to the right, when you come back with your load.'

'Excellent,' Paul said. 'I see you have the situation under control.'

Darina beamed. 'I do,' she said proudly. 'And if everyone follows orders, this will be the cleanest beach in Ireland by the time we're finished.'

'Impressive,' Paul said. He looked at the group gathered around them. 'I see some people I used to know a long time ago. Don't remember all the names, but maybe they remember me...'

'Oh, yes,' a man in a fisherman's sweater said beside them. 'Paul O'Sullivan, I do remember you. I'm John O'Mahony. Nice to see you again after all these years. Hey,' he shouted into the crowd. 'How many of you were here in the early Nineties? If you were, come and say hi to an old friend from the States. The O'Sullivan Beare from New York.'

Maggie stood mesmerised while Paul shook hands with everyone in turn, chatting and laughing and answering questions. He looked like a politician in full campaign mode and seemed to forget all about Maggie as they all shared stories of that summer when he had been part of the gang for a short few weeks. She vaguely remembered how he had been so popular with everyone and joined the games on the beach, the sing-songs at the pub and all the other activities, Maggie hanging on his arm sharing some of the limelight with the charming young man.

It had delighted her then that he seemed to be so at home with Irish people and made her feel he might even be open to living in Ireland for good if circumstances allowed. But now, thirty years later, she watched him through different eyes and wondered why he was suddenly so eager to catch up with these people again. Why had he come here at all? She had thought it was because he cared about her and had been reminded of his promise to her when he had found her letters, but as she watched him, she wondered if he had ulterior motives.

'What's up?' Brian, who had just arrived, said in her ear.

Maggie twirled around. 'Hi, Brian,' she said, delighted to see him. Dressed in baggy shorts and a denim shirt that had seen better days, he was the opposite to Paul's polished appearance. But his strong tanned arms and legs and his shaggy brown hair made him look both cute and oddly dependable. *Someone to lean on in a storm*, she thought, feeling lucky to have found such a dear friend in him. 'Nothing much going on,' she added with a laugh. 'Just Paul being Prince Charming to everyone, as you can see.'

Brian smiled as he followed her gaze. 'Yeah, well, that's kind of nice. And look, Darina is joining in too.' He turned to Maggie. 'Amazing to see you two together, I have to say. Does it feel like the old times? The old chemistry kicking in?'

'It was so strange. Still is,' she said, watching Paul talking to a dark-haired woman. 'I can't believe he's here like this, catching up with the old gang. Everyone seems to love him. He even has Darina eating out of his hand.'

'She looks quite smitten from here,' Brian said. He opened the blue plastic bag he was carrying. 'I wasn't one of the gang when he was here in those old days as I was so much younger. So I'm not as besotted as everyone else.' He looked at her, smiling. 'I think the latest arrival is much more interesting.'

'Ah, stop,' Maggie said. 'You're only saying that to make me feel good.'

'I'm saying it because it's true,' Brian stated. He bent to pick up a bottle from the sand. 'Anyway, I'd better get going on the clean-up as I have to go on a call soon.'

'I'll help you,' Maggie said. 'Paul and I were supposed to be a team but he seems to have forgotten,' she said, looking at a small group led by Paul picking up all kinds of litter that had blown into the dunes.

'Great. Come on, then,' Brian said. 'We can do the other side of the beach.'

They walked away from the main group and started picking up bits of paper and plastic bags, remains of picnics and other bits and pieces that had blown in from the sea. 'Terrible how people don't seem to clean up after themselves,' Brian muttered, bending to pick up a plastic tub. 'Local people are generally tidy, but we get a lot of visitors in the high season.'

Maggie put a Styrofoam container into the bag. 'I know. I hate plastic. I know what it does to birds and marine wildlife.'

Brian put down the sack and brushed his hair back, gazing out at sea. 'Me too.' He looked at her. 'But what about this latest scare? The hotel being built on that headland.' He pointed up the slope. 'It's going to kill The Two Marys' as the bulldozers will be going up that hill.' His eyes were full of sadness as he looked at Maggie. 'It's going to wreck the whole village and our way of life. We can't let that happen.'

'How can we stop it?' Maggie asked. 'A few protests aren't going to do it. If the county council gives it the go-ahead, that'll be it.'

'There has to be a huge campaign. We have to alert the media and get the politicians to do something. I'm going to talk to Mick O'Dwyer tonight. I called him and Tara, his wife, asked me to dinner. Do you want to come?'

'Oh, but...' Maggie said, looking down the beach, noticing that Paul had dumped his plastic sack and was walking towards them.

'You have plans with Paul?' Brian asked with a slight edge to his voice.

'Not yet, but I might.'

'I understand,' Brian said. 'You need to be together. I'll keep you posted.'

'I could call Kiara at Radio Kerry,' Maggie offered. 'I could say Paul and I are going to join forces to try to save the village from the developers. Make it into an interesting story connected to us.'

'That would be great,' Brian said. 'It could start the ball rolling.'

'Hi, there,' Paul interrupted, coming closer. 'Brian, isn't it?'

'Yes,' Brian replied. 'Hi, Paul. Nice to see you again after all these years.'

'Terrific,' Paul said as they shook hands. 'You were a skinny kid as far as I remember. But now you're taller than me. Must be all that good Irish food.'

'Must be,' Brian replied.

'But I was interrupting something,' Paul continued. 'The two of you look a little glum.'

'We were talking about the planning permission that's being sought for a hotel up there,' Maggie said, pointing up the slope. 'It's going to be quite big and there'll be a car park and a walkway to the little beach on the other side. Wild Rose Bay. You might remember that.'

Paul squinted against the bright sunlight as he looked up at the headland. 'Beautiful spot,' he said.

'Yes, and we don't want it ruined,' Brian remarked.

'Well, maybe the hotel will be nice all the same,' Paul said. 'I know it might be a shame to ruin the natural look and all that but you can't live in the past, as you said yourself, Maggie. And wouldn't it provide jobs for this area?'

'Maybe,' Brian said. 'But it's not as if people around here are unemployed.' He grabbed his sack. 'Look, I have to go and do my rounds. I think this part of the beach is pretty clean anyway.'

'I think so,' Maggie agreed. 'Bye for now, Brian. Let me know what Mick O'Dwyer says.'

'I will.' Brian lifted his sack, ready to walk away.

'Who's Mick O'Dwyer?' Paul asked.

'He's the TD for this area,' Brian replied.

'TD?' Paul asked.

'Member of the Irish parliament. We're hoping he'll be able to stop the hotel project. We're also going to try to get the media interested,' Maggie continued.

Paul frowned. 'Media? Why?'

'If there's a public outrage, it could help stop this project. We could even get this area declared as a nature reserve,' Brian replied. He stopped and brightened. 'Wow. That just came out. And now I realise we could get the Department of the Environment on the case.'

'Sorcha's son Fintan studies environmental science,' Maggie

cut in. 'Maybe he knows someone in that department? Or he could get his fellow students interested in joining the campaign.'

'Brilliant.' Brian looked at Maggie with admiration. 'I'll call Fintan this evening. And now I'm really off. Talk to you later, Mags.'

Paul's eyes were amused as he looked at Maggie. 'A campaign? The two of you really got carried away there, didn't you?'

'Did we?' Maggie asked. 'Isn't it important to stop this place being ruined by a huge monstrosity of a hotel?' She pointed up the hill. 'It'll be sitting there like a big lump of concrete and then the little beach on the other side will be destroyed by hordes of people picnicking and I don't know what. No to mention the noise and mess during the construction, with bulldozers and JCBs and trucks going up and down. It breaks my heart to think about it.'

'How do you know the hotel will be a monstrosity?' Paul asked. 'Have you seen the plans? What if it's a building that goes well with this landscape and actually enhances it?'

'Enhances it?' Maggie asked with scorn in her voice. 'How on earth could it? And the beautiful beach – that beach where we walked and swam and were completely alone, with the wild roses covering the slopes and the white sand and...' Maggie's eyes suddenly filled with tears. 'It might mean nothing to you, but it means a lot to me.'

Paul's eyes softened and he touched her cheek. 'Don't be sad, Maggie. It might not happen at all. I do remember that beach. It's a beautiful place.'

'We were happy there,' Maggie said.

'I know.' He looked at the bag he had dropped further away. 'I think we've done enough for the environment today. And I have to make a few phone calls and do a little work on my laptop, so I'll be heading back to the B&B for a bit. But I'd like to take you out to dinner this evening. How about we meet later at that little fish restaurant I saw on the main street? The Wild Atlantic-something?'

'The Wild Atlantic Gourmet,' Maggie said. 'I'd love to have dinner there with you.'

'Great. I'll book a table for eight. Is that too late for you? I can't make it earlier as I have a Zoom meeting.'

'No, that's fine,' Maggie said.

'Great.' Paul patted Maggie's shoulder. 'Cheer up, Maggie. It mightn't happen. Let's go and sort all the stuff I picked up.'

They walked back towards a group of people who were sorting the contents of their bags into the recycling bins. Maggie felt a surge of hope as she thought of what she and Brian had discussed. Paul's reaction had shaken her slightly but she supposed, being American, his ideas of progress and job opportunities were different. And he didn't have the same emotional connection with the village and its surroundings as her. She couldn't expect him to feel about it the way she did. She looked at him as he joined the group and realised what a charming, sociable man he was. Everyone seemed to take to him, and he to them.

But what did he feel about her? Did his heart beat faster when he looked at her? *And what about me?* Maggie wondered. *How do I really feel? I got the explanation, the closure I needed, so now what?* She looked forward to the date with him in that little restaurant. A romantic dinner for two was just what they needed.

Maggie felt a tiny buzz as she arrived home at the thought of her first date since the separation.

18

Over plates of scampi and chips in the cosy restaurant, Maggie and Paul finally reconnected and found each other again. Not in as romantic a way as Maggie had hoped, but as two people who had once been close and now rekindled some of their feelings for each other. Maggie told Paul all about her life and how her relationship with Dermot had ended.

'We were together for twenty-two years,' she said. 'We had a family and I thought we were, if not as madly in love as in the beginning, at least content and happy together. I was, anyway.'

'So it came as a complete surprise?' Paul asked, looking at Maggie with great sympathy.

'Like a bolt of lightning from a clear blue sky. I thought he was joking at first. But then I found out he had been cheating on me with this woman for over six months. Of course, she was younger and prettier than me,' Maggie added with a sigh. 'That same old story.'

'I'm so sorry, Maggie,' Paul said. 'That must have been awful.'

'Yes, it was. More than awful. And it took me a long time to understand that it had actually happened.' Maggie looked down at her plate. Then she stabbed a scampi with her fork and took a bite, looking at Paul, determined to stay positive and not look like a victim. 'You know that old saying that the best revenge is to live well? I think it's true. I feel I'm living well by being here and seeing all my old friends again. It has made me very happy. And now, here I am with you. I feel that's a very good revenge.'

'The best,' Paul said, putting his hand on hers for a moment. 'I don't understand how that man – your ex – could do that to you. But let's not dwell on it. Coming here was the right thing for you, I think. Not only because of us meeting up, but because I think this village is special. You were so happy here when you were growing up.'

'That's true. And my new friend Susie thinks it was karma that brought me here and this is where I will find love again, she says.' Maggie laughed and picked up a chip with her fingers. 'Not sure about that, but you never know.'

Paul looked at her for a moment. 'Maybe she's right,' he said. 'But... well, I'm only here for the next two weeks and then I have to go back to Chicago.'

'Oh,' Maggie said, popping the chip into her mouth. 'Two weeks is better than nothing,' she said when she had swallowed. 'And to be honest, Paul, right now I'm not...' She stopped, not sure how she felt or how to continue.

'I know,' he said with a laugh. 'Me too. I'm a little confused and still getting used to being with you again. I'll have to leave, but I could come back in August, if I get myself organised to work long distance.'

'That'd be perfect,' Maggie said. 'I do need a little space after all the emotions. And I'll be busy with the campaign. My daughter Orla is coming here for a break in July, too. I'm really looking forward to that.' They had had a long FaceTime chat the previous evening during which Orla had told Maggie she had a week off in July and wanted to spend it in Sandy Cove. It would be a lovely mother-daughter time during which Maggie would show Orla all the special places from her childhood and introduce her to everyone she knew. She couldn't wait to see her daughter again.

'And then you can enjoy her visit without me breathing down your neck,' Paul said with a smile. 'I have a feeling you and your daughter are very close.'

'Yes, we are,' Maggie replied, smiling as she thought of Orla. 'She's given me huge support all through the past year. So now I want to give her a wonderful holiday and show her all the places where I had so much fun.'

'Sounds good,' Paul said approvingly.

Maggie smiled and nodded and continued to enjoy the scampi and chips, the crisp white wine and fresh bread. They ended the meal with strawberry cheesecake while their conversation drifted to the first time they met and all the memories of those days.

They left the restaurant as it was getting dark, walking slowly up the quiet street, and after a few steps Paul reached out and held Maggie's hand. It was a sweet moment that Maggie felt brought them closer. But when they stopped outside the cottage, Paul let go of her hand and looked at her for a long moment that still felt slightly awkward. 'So here we are,' he said. 'Thank you for a really nice evening.'

'I should be the one to say thank you,' Maggie protested.

'Not really,' Paul said. 'I enjoyed the evening immensely. I like you a lot, Maggie Ryan. And at the same time, I'm in awe of you.'

'Why?' she asked, confused by the appraising look in his eyes. She suddenly felt she was being assessed.

'You're stronger and more independent than before. You don't seem to need to lean on anyone. And I think it would be very hard to fool you.'

'Why would you want to?' she asked, laughing.

'Why indeed?' he said with a grin. 'I wouldn't dare.' He

leaned forward and lightly kissed her cheek. 'Sleep well. I'll be in touch.' And with that, he walked to his car and got in, driving away up the lane and turning towards the road to Ballinskelligs.

Maggie looked at the rear light disappearing around the corner and stood there in the dark for a while wondering what he had meant about not being able to fool her. Would he want to? And about what? Finding out, it seemed, would be the key to their continued relationship. If there was to be one at all.

Brian called just as Maggie had walked into the hall.

'Great news,' he said, his voice excited, barely giving Maggie a chance to answer the phone. 'Mick is on the case and is going to contact the Minister for the Environment and some other colleagues. In fact, he had already started. He saw the planning application on the headland when he was walking his dogs. Tara is going to take photos to be published in *The Irish Times* later this week. She might even get them on the evening news on RTE in a couple of days. She's a fantastic photographer and will take pictures that will show the beauty of the landscape, which will prove what a sacrilege it would be to build anything there. I think this will be a big story.'

'That's brilliant,' Maggie said, her spirits lifting. It was so wonderful to feel Brian's passion for Sandy Cove.

'And Fintan said he had an idea how to at least get the project delayed. But he didn't want to say too much yet. He'll get back to me when he's read up on a few things, he said. But I think it's looking more hopeful, even though it'll be a slow process.'

'As long as we can stop this, it doesn't matter how long it takes,' Maggie replied.

'You're right.' Brian paused. 'How was your romantic dinner at the Wild Atlantic?'

Maggie bristled. 'How did you know we were there? Or that it was romantic?'

'If you sit in the window looking into each other's eyes, it's hard to keep it a secret,' Brian teased.

'We weren't... I mean, we were just talking about the old days.' Maggie stopped, feeling her privacy was somehow being invaded. 'But it was lovely, thank you very much.'

'Good.' Brian cleared his throat. 'Well, anyway, that was all I wanted to tell you. I know you're as upset as we are about this hotel being built. Oh, and I wanted to ask if you and yer man would like to come up to my house on Friday. I'm doing a barbecue and have invited a few odds and sods. Actually, even though it's supposed to be a surprise, I have to tell you. Sorcha and Tom are going to announce their engagement, so that's why I'm throwing a party for them. But don't let on you know, okay? Darina has to be told before it's official, you see, and that could be tricky.'

'Oh. Of course,' Maggie said. 'I won't tell a soul. I'm so happy for Sorcha, though. And I'm dying to meet Tom. I'm sure Paul will want to come, so I'll accept for both of us. Thank you, Brian.'

'You're welcome. Tell Paul not to let on about this to Darina. They seem to be getting very pally.'

'What?' Maggie asked, puzzled. 'Pally? What do you mean?'

'I saw them chatting outside the pub in the main street earlier as I passed on the way to Mick's. Looked like Paul was bending her ear about something fascinating. At least she looked fascinated, but maybe that was just her enjoying a chat with a good-looking man.'

'Are you pulling my leg?'

'No, just telling you what I saw. But maybe they just bumped into each other and she made him stay to chat. She can be very persuasive, as you know.'

'That's for sure,' Maggie said with a laugh. 'She plied me with cake and coffee and nearly made me promise to go against Sorcha and Ella about the memorial bench. But then I saw the light and stood up for old Brendan. Not that it's much of an issue anymore now that we're trying to stop the hotel project.'

'It'll come up again once we have that sorted,' Brian replied. 'But that's not going to be hard to handle compared to this, I think.'

'I'm sure you're right.'

'Got to go. Early start tomorrow as usual. Bye for now, Mags. See you Friday,' Brian said and hung up.

Maggie frowned as she went upstairs, thinking about what Brian had told her. Then she decided to forget about it. Paul was probably just being polite. But he had obviously stopped the car and got out to talk to Darina for some reason. But whatever it was it didn't seem important. Paul was such a charming, kind man and had probably noticed that Darina was a lonely woman who yearned for human contact and a bit of kindness, even from a stranger. *Nice of him*, Maggie thought, the memory of their evening and that kiss on her cheek giving her a warm glow. Even if all they would have were a few weeks of a summer romance, it was worth it for how it made her feel. And when he finally left, they would stay in touch and maybe see each other again.

Maggie nodded, a little smile playing on her lips. This time it would be different.

19

The old farmhouse stood on a hill overlooking the village and the bay beyond. Maggie knew it well, having spent many summer days there with Sorcha all through her childhood summers, playing with the dogs, helping out with the horses and generally enjoying days at the farm when they had nothing else to do. It had been a haven – a warm, welcoming home that always smelled of newly baked bread. Brian's mother had always kept the door open and there had always been time for a chat and tea and buns at the big kitchen table. Now, thirty years later, Maggie was delighted to see that apart from the absence of cows and horses, the house looked exactly the same.

'A bit of a wreck,' Paul remarked as he pulled up on the gravel beside a row of cars in front of the house.

'It's the most welcoming house I've ever been in,' Maggie said. 'Maybe it's not very modern, but what's wrong with that?'

'Nothing seems to have been done to it since I stayed here,' Paul said as he got out of the car and opened the door for Maggie.

'Ah, Brian's too busy with his practice to do repairs and

upgrades.' Maggie looked at the house. 'The roof is okay, though.'

'That's a relief,' Paul said with a touch of irony.

Maggie glanced at him, but said nothing and turned to look at the sweeping views of the hills, the village and the glittering ocean instead. 'The view from here is fantastic,' she said.

Paul went to stand beside her and draped his arm around her shoulders. 'So it is,' he said. 'And the house is very nice too. I didn't mean to sound critical.'

'I know. It's strange to see a place after so many years. I suppose you see all the flaws a lot more clearly as an adult.'

'I guess,' Paul said. 'But we'd better join the party. There seems to be a lot of people here already, judging by the cars.'

'We might be a little late,' Maggie said and started to walk around the house. 'Thanks for picking me up and for offering to drive me home.'

'That way you can have a drink or two,' Paul said as he followed her. 'I don't mind not drinking tonight. I have to do a little work later anyway.'

Maggie stopped and looked at him. 'Work? What exactly is it you do? You said something about insurance but do you do other things as well?'

'Oh, yes,' Paul replied. 'I'm branching out and investing in a few different things. But let's not talk about that right now. We're here to enjoy ourselves, aren't we?'

'Of course,' Maggie said and continued to the back of the house. 'You can tell me about it later.'

'I will,' Paul promised as they rounded the corner. 'If you're really interested.'

'You bet I am,' Maggie said. Knowing about his work would help her discover more about him and his life, who he really was and what he had become since they parted all those years ago. They walked towards the group gathered around the barbecue on the lawn behind the house. 'Hi,' she said to Brian, dressed in a big white apron over his jeans and polo shirt. 'Sorry we're late.'

'No problem,' Brian said. 'There are more people arriving soon.'

Sorcha came towards them, dragging a tall dark-haired man by the hand. 'Hi, Maggie. This is Tom, my brand-new fiancé. We just did the deed,' she continued with a grin and held up her left hand where Maggie saw a solitaire diamond on the third finger.

'Oh wow, congratulations!' Maggie exclaimed and wrapped her arms around Sorcha. 'That's a gorgeous ring. So happy for you.' She smiled at Tom over Sorcha's shoulder. 'Great to meet you at last, Tom. Sorcha has told me so much about you.'

Tom grinned. 'Oh yeah, and I know all about you, Maggie.'

'Only the good things, I hope.' Maggie smiled, then pulled away from Sorcha and shook hands with Tom. 'This is so wonderful.'

'Congratulations to the happy couple,' Paul said behind Maggie and grabbed Tom's hand. Then he placed a light kiss on Sorcha's cheek. 'Tom's a lucky man.'

'Thank you,' Sorcha said. 'And it's lovely to see you two together as well.'

'How did Darina take the news?' Maggie asked.

'Not too badly, thanks to you,' Sorcha said.

'Except you seem to have suggested we all live together,' Tom filled in. 'So now my mam is looking for a bigger house for us all.'

'What?' Maggie exclaimed, looking sheepish. 'I never said she should do that.'

'He's joking,' Sorcha said. 'Darina is actually a bit shocked even though she was expecting it. But she's taking it on the chin. We might even get on together eventually.'

'She'll be fine,' Tom declared. 'I'm only sorry I was such a chicken not to tell her about us until now.' He pulled Sorcha close. 'But then it's got me to where I am today, with this lovely woman by my side.'

'Oooh,' Susie sighed as she joined them. 'Karma wins again.' She smiled at Paul. 'Hi. Talking about karma, how are you and the "lovely colleen" getting on?'

'Just fine,' Paul replied, beaming her a wide smile. 'We're enjoying catching up and getting to know each other again.' He put his arm around Maggie as Brian came closer. 'Hi, Brian. Need any help with the barbecue?'

'I think I can manage,' Brian said. 'I only just lit the charcoal and I'll put the meat on in about twenty minutes. Sorcha made a potato salad and some other stuff. Please help yourself to drinks,' he added, gesturing at the nearby table with its array of bottles and glasses.

'We will,' Paul said. 'What do you want, Maggie?'

'I'd love a beer,' Maggie replied.

'There you go,' Paul said and handed her a bottle.

Maggie sipped the beer, enjoying the cool, smooth taste of lager. She took a few sips and went to talk to the others around the barbecue, while Paul stayed to chat with Susie.

'Hey, Maggie,' Brian interrupted as he checked the fire. 'Go and say hello to Jessie. She's inside with Bella. I'm sure you'd like to meet them.'

'Ooh, yes,' Maggie exclaimed and broke away from the group. 'I want to meet the mother of my new baby.'

'New baby?' Paul called, turning away from Susie.

'Yes,' Maggie replied. 'I told you that Jessie is Brian's springer spaniel and she's pregnant. I'm going to take one of her puppies. Don't you remember? Can't wait for them to be born. Do you want to come with me inside?'

'No, thanks,' Paul said. 'I'll stay here and talk to these old friends. You go ahead.'

More people arrived as Maggie went inside the house. This was going to be a big party. She had felt tension in Paul as he talked to the others just now and she wondered if the charm and easy banter was put on to hide his real feelings. It couldn't be easy to try to fit in with people who had known each other all their lives. Or... was it something else?

Maggie shook off those thoughts as she walked through the back door into the kitchen that was as warm and welcoming as she remembered, even if a little messy. The large table was littered with boxes of medications, a stethoscope and other vet paraphernalia and the antique dresser beside the stove was covered in books and magazines of all kinds. But the late-evening sun shone in through the windows, casting pools of light on the flagstones and the whole room was like a haven away from the hustle and bustle of modern life. A black cat wandered in through the door and jumped up on one of the chairs, looking suspiciously at Maggie. It was as if time stood still here, and Maggie wanted to sink into one of the chairs in front of the stove and relax with a cup of tea and the cat on her lap, and listen to music from the old radio that used to be permanently tuned to an Irish music station. Then she heard a whimper and felt something brush against her leg and discovered a springer spaniel beside her, wagging its tail and looking at her with melting brown eyes.

'Jessie,' she said and bent down to pat the dog. 'How are you, old girl?'

Another little whine and a small black-and-white terrier came in through the door and trotted to Maggie's side. 'And you are Bella, I bet,' Maggie said and picked the little dog up in her arms, which earned her some enthusiastic licking of her face, while Jessie's tail thumped against her leg.

'I see you've made friends with my girls,' Brian said, walking inside.

'They're gorgeous.'

'They are not alone,' Brian said, looking at Maggie with a glint in his brown eyes. 'That blue T-shirt brings out your eyes.'

'Oh, eh—' Maggie said, suddenly tongue-tied. 'Shouldn't you be minding the barbecue?'

'Yer man has taken over,' Brian said with pretend resignation and took off his apron. 'He's the king of barbecues over there in the States, apparently. He stepped in and told me I did everything wrong so I let him at it. Gives me a chance to talk to you, anyway.' They both laughed.

'I'm sorry,' Maggie said. 'Paul can be a bit... overwhelming. Tends to want to be the star of the show, I've noticed. He wasn't like that before.'

'In them old days?' Brian asked, taking Bella from Maggie. 'I think that's enough licking, young lady,' he said and put the dog on the floor. Then he looked at Maggie. 'How's it going with... everything?'

'Great,' Maggie said, suddenly aware of an odd spark between them. 'We're getting to know each other slowly.'

Brian raised an eyebrow. 'Slowly, eh? I wouldn't have thought Paul was the slow type.'

'Well, maybe in this case he's being careful,' Maggie said. She looked around the kitchen. 'I love this room. I can still smell the cakes and buns your mum used to bake.'

Brian laughed. 'I know. It seems to have seeped into the walls. But I think she'd chastise me for the mess if she could see it. I don't have much time for housework, I'm afraid. But she comes here sometimes and does a big clean-up.'

'It's a nice mess,' Maggie said, taking a step back. She was beginning to feel something strange as she talked to Brian. A faint urge to hug him or something, which surprised her. She glanced through the window and saw Paul at the barbecue, surrounded by people to whom he was chatting and smiling while attending to the meat. She turned back to Brian. 'I miss your mum. We used to call her Auntie Mo, I remember. Lovely woman.'

'Oh, yes, she is,' Brian said with a sad little sigh. 'I miss her too. But she's happy living with her sister in Dingle. I feel her presence here anyway. It's very comforting to be surrounded by all her things. We talk often. I'm the baby of the family, and I think she still sees me that way. Weird, isn't it?' he said with a crooked smile.

'Not at all. I think that's wonderful ,' Maggie said, her heart going out to this lovely man she had become so fond of. There was a certain vibe between them she couldn't ignore, but it was something she didn't want to analyse further. She felt a sudden urge to get out, knowing that if she stayed a minute longer something would happen between them that she couldn't handle. She didn't want to ruin the friendship with him. 'I think Paul needs a little help,' she said and walked to the door.

'Yeah, probably,' Brian said and picked Bella up again. 'I'll settle these girls and get some more beer from the fridge.' He shot Maggie a look she couldn't quite decipher but there was suddenly a tension between them that hadn't been there before.

What's going on? she asked herself as she left the kitchen. *Why do I feel like this? Brian is a friend, nothing more, but ever since he said he had a crush on me I've wondered if he still does... Oh, God, this is not supposed to happen while I'm reconnecting with Paul.*

Maggie joined the group around the barbecue, trying her best not to think about Brian and her sudden pull towards him. It was probably just the beer and the nostalgia as she had remembered his mother and had been brought back to the past by the atmosphere in that warm, welcoming kitchen.

Paul smiled and put his arm around her. 'Nearly done. I've cooked steaks in various shades of black and brown according to requests. Some rare, some medium, some well done. What's yours?'

'I like it quite rare,' Maggie said, her mouth watering at the sight of the steaks Paul had lined up on a board.

'That one should be fine, then,' he said and pointed with a long fork at a thick steak. 'I'll have the one beside it. Maybe you could load up two plates and we'll go and sit at the long table.'

Maggie did as she was told, trying not to look at Brian, who had just come out through the back door. He glanced briefly at her but went to talk to Sorcha and Tom at the round table further down the lawn. Then Paul steered Maggie to the long table and they sat down, soon involved in lively conversations and enjoying the steaks and the rest of the food.

Later on, the conversation turned to the proposed hotel and how horrible it would be if it was allowed to be built. Paul's comment that it could create job opportunities for the area was met with scorn, and when he said he had heard it would be a five-star hotel with a pool and spa, the atmosphere turned nearly hostile.

'Why do we need a pool?' Ella said. 'When we have the ocean? And we already have the Wellness Centre, so we don't need any fancy spas here, thank you very much.'

'Yes, but that Wellness Centre is a bit New Age-ish, don't you think?' Paul remarked. 'It's quite quaint and charming and all that, but this hotel spa will be state-of-the-art.'

'State-of-the-rubbish,' Ella said with a snort. 'Our Wellness Centre is so natural and unique. It goes so well with the environment and all the products they use have come from this area. Actually, from the field above where this hotel is supposed to go. It's pure heaven up there. And when I use the products that come from Cormac's lab, I feel I'm in touch with nature in a wonderful way. Have you tried the bath oil?' she asked Maggie. 'It smells of the roses that grow wild around here.'

'I haven't yet,' Maggie said. 'I must go down to their little shop and get some of the stuff they make.'

'I highly recommend all their products,' Ella said. She

glanced at Paul and smiled. 'Sorry about the aggro, but we all feel so strongly about this around here. We don't want the uniqueness to be ruined by modernity.'

'I can see that,' Paul replied. 'No hard feelings here. I was not really serious, just playing the devil's advocate to tease you. It's good to discuss things and find out where people are coming from, though.'

'Very true,' Ella agreed and lifted her bottle of beer in a salute. 'In any case, you're a hell of a cook. Those steaks were perfect.'

'And Sorcha's potato salad was delicious,' Paul said.

They were interrupted by a clinking of a fork against a glass. At the other table, Brian rose and started to speak.

'I want you all to raise your glasses or bottles of beer to Sorcha and Tom, who have just announced their engagement. Sorcha has always been like a sister to me, and I'm so happy to see her engaged and soon to be married to Tom, who we all know very well.' He held up his glass. 'Here's to Sorcha and Tom.'

'Sorcha and Tom,' everyone shouted, clinking glasses and bottles. Then they all applauded and rose to embrace the delighted couple.

Maggie joined the fun and hugged both Sorcha and Tom and then everyone started to hug each other. Paul gave Maggie a tight squeeze and managed to kiss her on the mouth, which gave her a jolt.

She stepped away, her face hot, not knowing what to say and do.

Paul grinned and then turned to hug Sorcha while Maggie's gaze drifted to Brian standing behind Paul. Their eyes met for a moment, before Maggie stumbled away to her table and sat down, trying to pull herself together. It had been a light kiss, but she could still feel his mouth on hers in a kiss she had expected to happen sooner or later, but not like this, in public and as a result of general excitement. It didn't mean anything, she told herself, he didn't even seem to know who he was kissing at that moment. Her own emotions were in turmoil and she couldn't quite understand what was going on between them. She had never felt so confused in her life.

Much later, as Paul drove her home, he was as friendly and breezy as before, as if that kiss had never happened. Maggie realised that it hadn't really registered with him and that it had just been a result of the general frenzy while the spotlight was on Sorcha and Tom. All fun and games with no particular thought behind it. *Will our relationship ever move forward to something more meaningful?* she wondered as he pulled up outside the cottage. *Or have our experiences during the past thirty years changed us so much we're different people from the Paul and Maggie who said goodbye that day and promised each other to meet again?*

Paul looked at Maggie in the dim light from the dashboard. 'Great evening,' he said.

'Yes, it was,' Maggie replied. 'I'm so happy for Sorcha. She hasn't had it easy.'

'Neither have we,' he said. 'Life never leaves anyone unscathed.'

She turned to face him. 'But has it all changed us so much? Too much to be able to find what we had then, all those years ago?'

'I'm not sure,' he said slowly. 'I'm trying to figure that one out.'

'Me too.'

'You can't turn the clock back,' Paul said as he took both her hands in a tight grip. 'So we have to go forward. I have a week or so before I have to leave. And during that time, I'd like to go on dates with you. See places and things, eat and drink and talk and have fun. Then we'll see where we are after that. What do you say?'

Maggie stared at him and was about to say she wasn't sure, but when he pulled her closer and she looked into those green eyes and breathed in the smell of some expensive soap, her resolve weakened. He was such an attractive man, hard to resist. She wanted to bask in his admiration for a while, feel desired and attractive like she had when she was younger. She just wanted to be happy again. If he wanted to sweep her off her feet, she didn't want to stop him. 'Okay,' she mumbled. 'That sounds great.'

He smiled and kissed her cheek. 'Wonderful. I'll call you. Good night, Maggie.' Then he got out of the car and went to Maggie's side and opened the door for her.

'You're such a gentleman,' she said as she got out.

'That's the way I was brought up.' He looked at her for a moment. 'This hotel thing... Are you going to be very involved with the campaign?'

'I think so,' Maggie replied. 'I want to do what I can to help stop it.'

'Good luck with that,' Paul said with a slight edge to his voice. 'I'd say money will talk very loudly in this case.'

'But there are laws and regulations about the environment.'

'Money can get around that too.'

'Not in Ireland,' Maggie said hotly.

Paul stiffened. 'We'll see.'

'See what?' Maggie asked, confused at his sudden change of mood. 'Do you know anything about this?'

'Not a thing,' he said and laughed. 'Sorry, I think we're in different camps here. But we won't let that affect us, will we?'

'No, of course not,' Maggie said, wondering if that was a question or a command.

'Great. See you, Maggie, I'll be in touch very soon,' Paul said and got into his car. He tooted the horn and drove off while

Maggie stood there with very mixed feelings. What had he meant by that last comment? She had a tiny suspicion that she and Paul had grown up to have very different values. Should she really become more involved with him? But to be wined and dined by this gorgeous man was too lovely to refuse. *Go with the flow*, she told herself. *At least he makes you feel good. What's wrong with that?*

20

The following ten days, Maggie found herself in a whirlwind of activities. Paul kept his word and took her out on a date every evening. After her training session with the biathlon team, she found herself constantly dressing up, washing and styling her hair and putting on make-up or simply making sure she was dressed for every occasion. It was fun and exciting, even if a little tiring, but as she was on holiday she could sleep until ten o'clock, when she met the girls and swam or ran with them before lunch. The afternoons were often busy with meetings at Brian's house with the campaign group against the building project. He didn't have much time to attend himself, but Maggie had offered to keep everything going and to help out with online research and phone calls.

They hadn't got very far, but things were looking hopeful, as Sorcha's son Fintan, who was on a field trip in north Donegal, had managed to establish a contact with someone in the Department of the Environment. One of his fellow students would arrive soon to take samples of plants and study insects and other wildlife that could ensure the area be declared unique – maybe even turn it into a nature reserve. It was the only hope, Mick had said, as the planning office and the county council were not helpful. They only looked at the financial aspect and the job opportunities, so that was a lost cause, he had told them.

Mick's wife, Tara, a well-known photographer, had taken stunning photographs that had been published in all the national newspapers but had soon been forgotten as other urgent news took over. It seemed sometimes to Maggie they were shouting into a void, but Brian urged them to keep going and not to give up. The Tidy Town Association meetings were now nearly all about the campaign, Mad Brendan's memorial bench having sunk to the bottom of the agenda, to Ella's chagrin. Even Darina was oddly quiet and pleasant to Sorcha, which she found unsettling. Darina had suddenly changed from being hostile to friendly and even quite sweet at times.

'I don't know what she's up to,' Sorcha said, over coffee in her shop. 'I think she's hiding something. Why is she being so nice to me all of a sudden? Is she scheming behind our backs and trying to hide it? I find all this sweetness and light scarier than when she was so obviously against me.'

Maggie had to laugh. 'Don't worry. I think all those things I said to her have sunk in.'

'What exactly did you say?' Sorcha asked, looking mystified.

'I just said that she should be happy Tom is marrying someone more mature and that the fact that there will be no small children to look after will give you both more time to look after her.'

'Oh,' Sorcha said. 'So that's it.' She laughed and shook her head. 'Clever of you, I have to admit. But I'm not sure I relish the prospect of looking after her, I have to say. Or have her living with us.'

'I'm sure it won't come to that for a very long time, if at all,' Maggie soothed. 'I'd say Darina is far too independent to want to live with you. You'll just have to have her for Sunday lunch now and then, and maybe invite her to dinner from time to time. Just to make her feel she's part of the family.'

'I hope that's all,' Sorcha said with a worried little sigh. 'But thanks all the same. It's nice that she has been persuaded to accept me. She's even saying she is looking forward to getting to know Fintan. Is that your doing as well?'

'Could be,' Maggie said. 'I floated the idea that he'd be like a grandson to her.'

'I hope Fintan will be able to deal with that,' Sorcha said. 'But I'm sure he will. He's very easy-going.' She finished her coffee, still looking at Maggie. 'But there is something else, though, that Tom and I were wondering about. Darina seems quite positive about the hotel and contradicts us when we talk about how worried we are. She keeps saying it's inevitable and that we should just accept it and get used to the idea. What's that all about, do you think?'

'I don't know. But I'll try to talk to her,' Maggie offered, even though she had no idea what to say to Darina. Then it suddenly occurred to her that this might have been what Paul had been chatting to Darina about, possibly both agreeing that the hotel would be a good thing for Sandy Cove instead of the disaster everyone was afraid of. Darina would have been delighted that someone, even a stranger, was on the same page.

Maggie managed to get Darina on her own one day at The Two Marys' during Darina's usual after-lunch coffee and cake. She sat down at the table without asking for permission.

'Hello, Darina,' she said. 'Do you mind if I join you?'

'Not at all,' Darina said, looking pleased. 'Nice to see you, Maggie. How are things with you and that charming man, Paul? I see you're going out with him quite often.'

'We are,' Maggie replied. 'Having a great time catching up and getting to know each other.'

'So he told me.'

'Oh?' Maggie stared at Darina. 'He did? When?'

'Oh, just the other day,' Darina said, looking coy. 'We are also getting to be friends, you know. Nice man. Very polite and considerate.'

'He is.' Maggie paused. 'You must be busy preparing for Tom's wedding. I hear they're planning to get married in the autumn.'

'Yes, that's right,' Darina said with a bright smile. 'I'm trying to decide what to wear. The mother of the groom is quite an important person.'

'Oh, yes,' Maggie agreed. 'Very important.' She smiled back at Darina, wondering how to change tack. 'A lot of things are going on in the village at the moment. Apart from the wedding, there is also the hotel project. It has to be stopped, I'm sure you agree,' she said casually.

Darina looked away for a moment. Then back at Maggie. 'It's a very complicated issue,' she said after a moment's silence. 'It wouldn't be all bad if it was built, you know. It would mean more jobs, and more visitors will mean a better income for the shops and pubs around here.'

'I suppose,' Maggie said. 'But the negative impact on the environment and this area far outweigh any of those advantages,' she added carefully.

'I don't think it would be that bad,' Darina argued. 'And I, for one, think a nicely designed hotel will look lovely on top of the headland. But we'll see. Nothing has happened yet. No need to worry about it for a long time, is there?'

'I suppose not,' Maggie said, feeling defeated. There was as stubborn look in Darina's eyes she couldn't quite understand. But as she had won the battle of the wedding, she decided to leave the rest alone for a while. Better to keep the peace than start another war. For the moment, anyway.

· · ·

All that receded into the back of Maggie's mind as she sailed out of the house every evening, all done up for yet another date with Paul. He had pulled out all the stops and took Maggie to the best restaurants in the area, all around Killarney, Kenmare and even down to Cork and Beara to do a tour of his 'very own kingdom', as he put it. Maggie had to agree that Beara was beautiful and wild and could nearly compare with the area around Sandy Cove, but not quite, which they often argued about in a good-natured way.

Maggie thoroughly enjoyed Paul's company and during the two weeks they had established a closer bond, even though Maggie often felt he was holding back, especially about his work. She decided to leave that alone for the moment, as she felt he would share more when he was ready, and asked him about his personal life instead. It was nearly time for him to go back to New York, and she felt she needed to know more about him before he left.

'Tell me about your daughter,' she said during the last evening of his stay when they were having dinner at the Park Hotel in Kenmare. She had told Paul all about her children earlier and now felt it was his turn. 'How old is she?'

'Her name is Pauline and she's an architect,' he replied. 'She will be thirty in January, actually, and has just had a baby. My first grandchild,' he said and pulled out his phone. 'It's a little girl called Kathleen. She wanted an Irish name to remind her of her heritage.' He held the phone up. 'Here she is.'

'Oh, lovely,' Maggie said as she looked at the photos of the baby. But she wasn't paying much attention as what he had just said shot through her mind like a burning arrow. *She will be thirty in January?* she thought, suddenly feeling as if the world had stopped turning. She realised in a flash what had happened and why he had stopped writing to her. But maybe she had misunderstood? 'Just a moment,' she said, staring at Paul.

He looked up from the photos. 'Yes?'

'Your daughter is nearly thirty years old? Is that what you said?'

'Yes. In January.' Suddenly, his smile died as he realised what he had just said, and he put the phone on the table. 'Oh.' He took a deep breath, looking down at his hands. 'What a stupid thing to do,' he muttered.

'What?' Maggie asked. 'Stupid that you let that slip? Or that she was already on the way when we were... when you and I were having this... romance?'

He looked at her, his eyes full of pain. 'I didn't know,' he said hoarsely. Maggie met his eyes, taken aback, but as she saw how upset he was, she believed him. 'During that time, when you and I met, I had just broken up with Jane, my girlfriend,' he continued. 'And then I left and went on this tour of Ireland and met you. I didn't know about the pregnancy until just after I left West Point. I was about to move to Chicago when I found out.'

Maggie nodded, reaching out to place a hand on Paul's. 'So then you got married in a hurry and she – Jane – came with you?' Maggie asked.

'No, we got married a little later. Jane stayed behind to have the baby and then she came to Chicago and we got married. I wanted the baby to have my name and for Jane to have the security of being married. We tried to make it work, but it didn't. Because I couldn't forget you,' he said, turning his hand to hold on to Maggie's. 'The marriage was... It didn't mean anything. It was just the decent thing to do.'

'Of course,' Maggie said stiffly, pulling her hand away. Even though she realised it had been hard for him, she couldn't understand why he hadn't told her. 'So that was the real reason that you stopped writing, I suppose.'

'Yes,' he said quietly. 'I couldn't tell you. I thought that would have been a worse blow.'

'Nothing is worse than not knowing,' Maggie stated. She

looked at him for a moment and felt a sudden urge to leave. 'You know, Paul,' she said, 'I think I want to go home.'

He looked surprised. 'What? Go home? But the evening has only started. I booked the spa and then we were supposed to stay the night, and...' He stopped talking as it seemed to dawn on him what she was thinking. 'Is this just because you found out about Jane and the baby?'

'Not just because of that,' Maggie said. 'But a lot of other things I can't explain right now. I understand that you didn't know about your daughter. But you also lied to me when you told me about what had happened after you came back home.'

'I didn't lie,' he protested. 'I just left that bit out.'

'That bit? The tiny little bit of a baby? That's lying by omission. You told me it was because of your problems with your father and your failure at West Point that you stopped writing to me. Why didn't you tell me the truth straight away?'

'I don't know.' He sighed, looking deflated. 'I was blown away by how lovely you looked and what a strong, intelligent woman you had turned into. I wanted you to like me. I wanted to connect with you again and maybe...'

'Maybe – what?' she asked angrily. 'Have a little fling before you went back to the States to pick up your life again? But yes, to answer your question, what you just told me makes me think that I meant less to you than you did to me.'

'But it was thirty years ago,' he exclaimed. 'How can you possibly remember how you felt then? Yeah, we had a lovely romance in a magical place. It was really beautiful. But then I had a life to live. I didn't really think...'

'You didn't mean what you promised me then,' Maggie said, her voice bitter. 'That we'd be together always once we had sorted out our lives and where we were going to live.'

'I meant it at that moment, I guess,' Paul replied, looking suddenly unsure of himself. He tried to take her hand again, but she snatched it away. 'Oh, come on, Maggie, that was then and this is now. We're not the same people. But I have discovered you as an adult woman and I love being with you. You're smart and beautiful and fun and dating has been...'

'What?' she asked. 'Just something to do while you're over here on business? You never even told me what it is you really do.'

'I do so many different things,' he said.

'Like what? I mean, what are you doing over here?'

'We've just started to consider investing in some Irish businesses. We have an office in Killarney that I'm setting up at the moment. Ireland is a great country that is just beginning to attract interest from all over the world. So we're now hiring staff and doing up the office and so on. I have just hired a great person to run the company and I'll be back at the end of the summer to formally open up the new premises. And then I'll be going back and forth between here and Chicago until this company runs itself. We're also planning to launch in Scandinavia and other areas. It could be huge and make us a lot of money.'

'Why didn't you tell me all this before?' Maggie asked.

'Uh, well, I don't want to talk about it until it's up and running. Something I never do, actually.'

'I see. So that's why you were in Ireland? Setting up this office? Not because of me in any way, then?'

'Well, partly. I told you the truth about finding the letters. It did give me a dart of nostalgia and I wanted to meet you again. Just to explain...'

'To tell me a pack of lies, you mean?'

'I told you the truth.'

'But you forgot to mention the little detail of your pregnant girlfriend.'

'I was going to tell you that. I was planning to before we met again. But I lost my nerve.'

'And then what?'

'And then I met you and saw what an attractive woman you've turned into. I didn't expect that. I thought we'd just meet and then say goodbye once I had explained everything to you.'

'But you stayed and we started to get to know each other again,' Maggie filled in. 'That wasn't in your plan, then?'

'Not really. I hadn't thought I would like you so much, or that you would have all the qualities I had been looking for.' He leaned forward with a strange intensity in his green eyes. 'Maggie, you could be a great asset to me. I have discovered during these past two weeks how stylish and fun you are and how good you are with people. I'd like to build on that.'

'How do you mean?' Maggie asked, mystified.

Paul shot her a smile. 'Maggie, we could be such a great team. If we were to be together, we could entertain around here and do some fantastic marketing, simply by being a well-known couple about town.'

Maggie stared at him. 'A couple? You mean, I would be some kind of hostess or something?'

'Oh, no, more than that.' Paul sat back and cleared his throat. 'Okay, I'll tell you what I had in mind. This wasn't supposed to come out until we had become closer, more intimate. But I have been thinking about getting married again, this time to someone who could be my partner in everything, who would work with me and join me in my travels, be my companion and my...' He looked awkward. 'I'm not putting this very well, am I?'

'No, but you've made it all very clear,' Maggie said. 'You're looking for some kind of corporate wife, I suppose.'

He brightened. 'Exactly. I knew you'd understand the concept.'

'The concept?' Maggie said with a touch of anger. 'Oh, yes, I see what's in it for you.'

'And you, too, of course. Both of us,' Paul said, beginning to look unsure. 'You could have a life you always dreamed of. An unlimited expense account. You could buy anything you wanted, clothes, shoes, handbags, well, you know...'

'I've never dreamed of anything like that,' Maggie said flatly. 'Sounds more like a total nightmare, to be honest. I thought you said you've got to know me. In that case, you should know that stuff like that means nothing to me.'

'I thought any woman would love all that.'

'No, they wouldn't. I don't think you have much of a clue about women.' Maggie paused. 'Just one question.'

'Go ahead,' Paul replied, looking flattened by what she had just said.

'Where's the romance?' Maggie asked with sudden passion in her voice. 'The love and affection, the *connection* we had all those years ago? The meeting of souls that I felt then?'

'That will come back with time, I'm sure,' Paul said. 'Won't it?'

'I don't think so. It died that day we said goodbye, I realise now.' Maggie felt tears stinging her eyes as she gathered up her handbag and jacket. 'I don't want to stay here with you tonight. Good luck with it all, Paul. I'm sure you'll do very well, but without me. Thank you for these two weeks. You've been more than generous. But I had no idea it was some kind of test.' She stood up and then turned to walk away without waiting for him to respond.

He caught up with her in the lobby. 'Wait, Maggie,' he said, grabbing her arm. 'Let's say goodbye properly. I don't want you to leave feeling sad. I didn't mean to hurt you and I'm truly sorry if I upset you. And for lying. I know now I should have told you everything from the start.'

She turned and looked at him, noticing a touch of sadness in his eyes. His shoulders were slumped and he looked suddenly a little pathetic. A successful, middle-aged man without a heart. What had happened to that young man with the soulful eyes and the loving spirit? He was gone forever. Maggie suddenly felt a surge of pity, but she also knew there was nothing she could do to help him.

'Goodbye, Paul,' she said and kissed his cheek. 'It was a lot of fun and you gave me back something I had lost. You made me feel pretty and young for a little while.'

He smiled affectionately at her, holding her hand. 'Goodbye, Maggie. Sorry you didn't feel like joining me on my adventure. I just want to say one thing. That guy you like so much is very lucky.'

Maggie blinked. 'What guy?'

'The vet guy. The cousin of a cousin. Brian O'Connor up there in that farmhouse. I've seen the way he looks at you and you at him. Once you sort out your feelings, you'll be very happy, trust me.'

Maggie stared at Paul. 'Oh,' she said, feeling a blush creeping up her face. 'I'm not sure I know what you're talking about.'

'Yes, you do. I think you and Brian have very strong feelings for each other. That was one thing that worried me. So I thought if I could woo you a bit and make you an offer very few women would refuse, you might forget him. But I don't think it would have worked in the long run. I'm not really your type, am I?'

'No,' Maggie said. 'I thought for a second that you were but...'

'I know who your type is.' Paul winked. 'I couldn't lose you to a better man.'

Maggie didn't know what to say. 'I have to go,' she finally blurted out.

'It's a long drive.'

'It's still fairly bright, so I'll be fine.'

'I know you will,' he said. 'Good luck, Maggie. I hope to see you again sometime.'

'Bye,' Maggie whispered and walked out of the hotel to her

car, her knees shaking. She got in and sat there for a while, her mind in a whirl.

What had happened just now had shaken her. Paul's offer of marriage had been strange and oddly cold. And then he had backed down immediately and told her about Brian. As he had said it, she suddenly knew it was true, but she didn't know what to do next or how to deal with it. *Brian,* she thought, *am I falling in love with him? That skinny little boy who used to follow us around?* But that skinny boy had turned into a handsome man, younger than her, yes, but not that much younger. And yes, she had begun to have feelings for him. There was a kind of spark between them every time they met and she had found herself wanting to be in his company. But she had thought it was just some kind of comfort, until now, when Paul had pointed it out to her. He had seen what was there before she knew it herself.

Maggie pulled herself together and put the key into the ignition to start the car. Then her phone pinged with a text message. She picked it up. It was from Brian.

Jessie had her puppies tonight. Two girls, two boys. I'm staying up late so if you're free, come over and take a look. They will steal your heart.

Maggie sent him a text back. *On my way.* Her heart sang as she started the car and drove away, not looking back but forward to the road to Sandy Cove.

21

Maggie arrived at Brian's house an hour later, having driven as fast as she could, anxious to see the new-born puppies, but also wanting to see Brian. She didn't know quite what to say to him, or if she should mention anything about Paul's theory, but it would sort itself out, she said to herself as she drove down the quiet road, across humpback bridges and past little houses and barns and fields with cows, donkeys and horses. She tried to understand why she had held on to the dream of her romance with Paul all these years, why his silence had felt so hurtful. Maybe it was because her relationship with Dermot had never given her the comfort of true love, even in the beginning.

All the sweet memories of the summer with Paul had been an escape, like watching a romantic movie when life was hard. Then, when Dermot left her for someone else and she had come to Sandy Cove, she had thought she could recreate that feeling of being young and carefree.

When she had heard Paul on the radio and then met him again, it had seemed like a dream come true, a second chance to fall in love with someone who truly loved her too. But the adult man she had met had not been the same young man she had known thirty years ago, with whom she had shared all her hopes and dreams of a future together. Despite all this, the past weeks had made her feel lighter, happier and more herself than ever before.

Paul had helped her regain her confidence and independence. Even though he had revealed himself as being someone who was always looking out for himself, she had to feel grateful for helping her to find her old self again. The fact that he had totally misread her and thought he could buy her with money and glamour felt slightly ridiculous, but the wining and dining and dressing up to go to fancy restaurants had been fun for a while, she had to admit. And he had been very astute about Maggie's feelings for Brian, which might be obvious to everyone except her. But now things would be different.

She couldn't wait to tell him how she felt.

The stars came out, one by one, in the darkening sky and when Maggie pulled up outside the old farmhouse, the crescent of a new moon had risen above the chimneys. She got out of the car and breathed in the cool air, laden with the smell of new-mown hay and wild roses. A lone thrush sang somewhere in the tree-tops and she could see the warm light from the kitchen as she rounded the corner to the back of the house.

Brian opened the door and smiled at Maggie. 'I heard the car,' he said softly. 'Come on in. Mother and babies are in front of the stove.'

'Can't wait to see them,' Maggie said as she followed Brian inside. 'I was in Kenmare, so that's why I'm so late.'

He turned his head and glanced at her dress and high heels. 'You look very glamorous. Were you out on a date with Paul?'

'Yes. My last date with him,' Maggie said. 'He's going back to the States tomorrow.'

'Oh, that must make you sad.'

'Not at all. We broke up. Long story,' Maggie began but then spotted the big basket on the floor in front of the stove, where Jessie lay with four tiny black-and-white puppies feeding frantically. 'Oh,' she sighed and sank onto her knees. 'Hello, Jessie. What a clever girl you are.' She stroked Jessie's head, immediately distracted. Jessie licked her hand and wagged her tail before she put her head down and closed her eyes.

'She's tired,' Brian said, crouching down beside Maggie. He picked up a black puppy with a white collar and handed it to Maggie. 'Here. I think this one is for you. She the cutest one of the whole litter.'

'She is,' Maggie said and put the warm, wriggling puppy against her cheek. 'Oh, you are a darling.' Maggie cradled the puppy in her arms and looked at Brian. 'This is so wonderful. Thank you.'

'So you want her then?' he asked.

'Of course I do. I'm going to call her Molly. What do you think?'

'Perfect,' Brian said.

Maggie put the puppy back with the others to feed. 'But she needs to stay with her mum for a while, of course.'

'Yes, for about two months or so,' Brian said.

'So I can have her in August, then? Just before I go back to Dublin?'

'Something like that,' Brian said, getting up. 'How about a cup of tea to celebrate?'

'Oh, but you must be tired.'

'It's only half past ten,' Brian said.

'Yes, but you probably had a very busy day.' Maggie got to her feet. She stood looking at Brian as he switched on the kettle beside the stove.

He turned to look at her. 'So you broke up then, you said?'

'Yes.' Maggie wrung her hands, trying to find the right words. 'We... It never really worked between us.'

'I suppose you had changed too much in the years you were apart,' Brian suggested.

'I think that was part of it,' Maggie agreed, wondering how she could tell Brian that it was also the fact that she had begun to have feelings for *him*. That those feelings had made it impossible for her to have any kind of romance or even flirtation with another man, even if that man was Paul. 'But also because of you,' she said.

'Me?' Brian's eyes softened and he looked as if he was about to say something when he was interrupted by his phone ringing. 'Sorry,' he said, 'I have to take this. Could be something urgent.' He listened intently to the voice at the other end, his expression changing to disbelief as he kept listening. 'What?' he asked, looking at Maggie. 'Is this true?' He listened for a while and then turned his back to her and walked out of the room, still talking. 'I've been doing a bit of research myself,' he said as he walked away.

Maggie shrugged and went back to Jessie and her puppies, kneeling on the floor beside the basket, stroking their soft fur, smiling as they snuffled and whined. She felt so happy and secure in this kitchen, where the stove spread its warmth through the room and everything was as she remembered from her childhood. A safe haven from the cold winds that had blown through her life. But now she had finally landed in a place she felt she could be happy. Maybe she could get a job here and stay on, she thought. Those girls on the biathlon team had said the secondary school in nearby Cahersiveen was looking for a coach for the swimming team. Could be an idea to contact them...

Those happy thoughts were going through her mind when Brian came back into the kitchen. She smiled at him. 'Hope it was nothing too serious,' she said. 'Because I was about to tell you—'

'It was very serious,' Brian interrupted, sinking down on one of the chairs at the table. 'It was about the hotel and that company. I have just found out something... But I don't think this is going to be news to you, of course.'

'What?' Maggie said, alarmed by the cold look in his eyes. She scrambled to her feet. 'Tell me. Who was that on the phone?'

'Darina. She called to ask about the puppies. She said she'd like to have a dog now that Tom is getting married.'

'That's lovely,' Maggie said, confused by the hard glint in his eyes. 'What else did she say?'

'So I said yes to her having one of the puppies, and then she said she had something else to tell me. It was about the hotel project and she insisted I had to know right this minute. So I let her go on.'

'What did she say?' Maggie asked, alarmed. It had to be something bad. 'About the hotel project, I mean?'

'She told me she hadn't really been for or against it in the beginning as she was more interested in the Tidy Town Association and all that. But then she met someone who sweet-talked her into thinking it would be of benefit to the area and if she used her influence with the county council, it would give her huge kudos once the hotel was built and people around here got used to it and started to like it. And, of course, he offered her a large sum of money for her pains.'

'What influence does she have with the county council?' Maggie asked.

'One of her late husband's friends is on the board. They were very close, she said.'

Maggie nodded, anxious to hear the rest. 'I see. Go on. Who was this sweet-talking person?'

Brian shot her an angry look. 'None other than your former boyfriend. Paul O'Sullivan.'

Maggie blinked. 'Paul? Are you serious? Why would he do that?' She suddenly had a premonition of what he was about to say as the image of Paul being so chatty and charming to everyone popped into her mind. And he had been especially nice to Darina, which had puzzled her at the time. And then, of course, all his talk about his Irish company...

'For a very good reason,' Brian said. 'Which I'm sure you're aware of.'

'No, I'm not,' Maggie protested as she met Brian's eyes that were suddenly full of anger and suspicion.

'So you have no idea why he would do that?' Brian asked, looking intently at Maggie.

Maggie bristled. 'Of course not. But I have a feeling you're going to tell me he's involved with this hotel project in some way.'

'In every way,' Brian said. 'It's about Hy Brasil. Guess who owns it?'

'Who?' Maggie asked as it dawned on her what Brian was going to say next. 'You mean...?' She sank down on a chair opposite him.

'Oh, yes,' Brian said, holding up his phone. 'I did a quick research after Darina hung up . And this is what I found. Hy Brasil is owned by a large investment and property development company in Chicago called O'Sullivan Beare & Company. Guess who's the CEO?'

'Paul?' Maggie whispered, feeling cold waves of shock wash over her. Of course. Everything suddenly fell into place. She should have known this and seen the signs, but she had only been thinking of herself and her feelings and didn't notice the obvious. Paul had been busy plotting and scheming to try to insinuate himself into the village with the people who might help him get the hotel built. 'Are you sure?' she asked, even though she knew.

Brian nodded, his mouth in a thin line. 'Yes, of course. And the architect who is designing the hotel is called Pauline O'Sullivan.'

'Oh, God. That's his daughter,' Maggie said, her hand to her mouth, feeling nearly sick. 'What an utter shit he turned out to be.'

'Just one of those money-grabbing slieveens who think they can buy everybody,' Brian said in a scathing tone. 'But he couldn't buy Darina. She was tempted, she said, but then she felt so guilty she couldn't sleep. The more she heard about how bad it would be, the guiltier she felt. So she told Paul she wouldn't help him and he went back home in a huff. This was shortly before your last date with him this evening, by the way.'

'Oh,' Maggie said. 'But how on earth did you manage to find out who was behind Hy Brasil? We have been trying for weeks to figure out who runs it.'

'I started at the other end, after talking to my cousin's cousin in Beara. They told me about his businesses in Chicago, so I started to look at that end. I had got very close but not managed to discover who it was. Then just now, after my conversation with Darina, I did another search. Didn't take me long to find it.' Brian glared at Maggie. 'But you must have known.'

'No,' Maggie said stiffly. 'I had no idea at all.'

'But you went out with the guy nearly every night for weeks. Surely he told you what he was doing?'

'No, he didn't. Just in general terms and I didn't want to push him.'

'Not even tonight when you had that date in the posh hotel?' Brian asked incredulously.

'No, he just said something about his new company, but not what they were doing in Ireland. Not in detail, anyway.'

'And this didn't make you want to find out what he was up to?'

'I tried but he managed to change the subject. I thought he was just superstitious and didn't want to talk about it until he was ready.'

'So you just went along on the fancy dates and never asked any questions?'

Maggie stood up. 'No. And now I want you to stop accusing me and looking at me that way. I haven't done anything wrong. And might I remind you that it was because of you I managed to meet Paul. I thought he was the same young man I knew thirty years ago, but he had changed. I suppose we all do, for better or worse. I'm not the same person I was then either.' Maggie suddenly laughed. 'Sorcha and I talked about what Paul would be like before we met again. She thought he might be bald with a huge beer belly and that I'd run a mile when I saw him. But he was this handsome mature man with the same green eyes and gorgeous smile. Only he was ugly on the inside instead. And that was difficult to see at first.'

'Maybe we need a little space after this,' he said. 'I do anyway.'

Maggie felt cold all over. 'But I... We... I mean, I thought...' She leaned across the table and put a hand on his arm. 'Please, Brian,' she pleaded. 'You can't possibly believe that I knew all this and never told you? That I worked hard on the campaign knowing Paul was behind it, and then went out on these fancy dates...'

Brian looked thoughtfully back at her. 'I'm not sure what I believe or how I feel, to be honest. I need to think about this.'

Maggie withdrew her hand, feeling a wave of sadness. She got up from the chair. 'If you're the kind of person who'd believe this about me, then yes, I think we do need a break. Or whatever it would be for something that didn't quite take off,' she added. 'I came here tonight to tell you how I feel about you. But now I'm not even sure myself.'

Brian sighed and rubbed his face. 'I just want to go to bed now.'

'Good idea,' Maggie said, suddenly feeling sorry for him. This news had upset and confused him after what had probably been a long day with work and then Jessie's puppies. 'I'm going home now. We're both tired and upset. And angry,' she added with a flash of fury at Paul. 'Not with you, but with him,' she said with feeling. Not only had he been deceiving her, he had also managed to ruin her relationship with Brian. Possibly forever.

'Yeah. Me too,' he muttered. He looked up at her. 'Are you leaving?'

'Yes. Bye,' she whispered, before she walked out of the kitchen and closed the door behind her. She didn't cry until she had started the car, but then the tears rolled down her cheeks all the way home.

She pulled up outside the cottage, got out of the car and walked to the front door where she paused and looked up at the stars. 'Why is life so complicated?' she asked into the darkness. 'Why am I never allowed to be truly happy?' Then she opened the door and went inside, wondering if she would ever be able to get back that feeling of having landed in a place she could call home.

22

After a restless night, Maggie got up early the following morning for the training session with the biathlon team. She felt it would cheer her up to exercise, and the girls were such a lovely bunch. She had been planning to go to Brian's house to meet the campaign team who were mapping out a strategy to organise protests to various departments and government bodies. But after her row with him the night before, she didn't quite know what to do. He had said he needed some space so she assumed he wouldn't want to see her. But then she decided to go anyway, if only to explain to the team that she had had no idea that Paul was behind the hotel project.

She knew Brian wouldn't be there during the day, and she could leave before he came home. The others in the team might not believe her, but she had to at least try to persuade them that she had nothing to do with Paul's work and that she had been completely in the dark about what he had been doing. Hopefully, they'd believe her. She wanted to keep working with them and help out with the campaign as there was so much to do. While some of them did research into the flora and fauna of the area, some also did their best to look for more information about the firm who was going to build the hotel if the planning permission was granted. But now they didn't have to spend time trying to find out any more.

She arrived at the farmhouse just after lunch, finding Ella, Sorcha, Maggie's mother's old friend Catriona and two members of the Tidy Town committee in the kitchen with their laptops and piles of notes on the table.

'Hi, Maggie,' Ella said. 'We're doing some detective work here, trying to find out about that company.'

'And Brian won't be back for a while,' Maggie said, just to be sure, glancing at the basket with Jessie and the puppies.

'No. He's at the surgery,' Sorcha said. 'And then he has a few calls before teatime. So we're puppy-sitting and working at the same time.'

'So he didn't say anything? About me, I mean?'

'No,' Sorcha replied. 'He was gone when we arrived. What was he supposed to say about you?'

'I'll tell you in a minute,' Maggie said, feeling calmer. She sat down and put her bag with her iPad on the table. 'I have something to tell you. About the company and who's behind it.'

'Oh great,' Ella said. 'Maybe you've got further than we have. We're not sure who is actually running this company,' she continued. 'Hy Brasil only has a small office in Killarney with two staff who seem to be sworn to secrecy. We can only find the plans for the grounds and the building, which have to be on the county council website. The Hy Brasil people keep saying they will announce the details and date of construction once the permission has been granted. So what was it you were going to tell us?'

'I'm not sure how to start,' Maggie said, a nervous knot forming in her stomach. 'But I know who's behind all this. The person who runs that company, I mean.'

'Who?' Sorcha said as they all stared at Maggie.

'Paul,' Maggie said, her voice hoarse.

'Your Paul?' Ella asked.

'He's not mine, but yes. The man I've been dating,' Maggie said.

There was a stunned silence while they all stared at her in shock. 'What do you mean?' Ella asked.

'Paul is behind Hy Brasil, which is part of a company called O'Sullivan Beare that's based in Chicago. Paul is the CEO.' Maggie drew breath, feeling miserable as she spelled it all out to them.

Sorcha's jaw dropped. 'What? You mean...'

Maggie nodded. 'Yes,' she said miserably. 'He is the one who's planning to wreck this village with that huge hotel complex. That's mainly why he was here and not to meet up with me at all. That was just an afterthought, something fun to do in his spare time.' She paused, wondering if she should tell them about the offer he had made her, but decided against it.

'Did you know about this?' Ella asked.

'No,' Maggie protested. 'Of course I didn't. I wouldn't have gone on those dates with him and then been working with you on the campaign at the same time. That makes it feel as if you think I'm some kind of spy.' Maggie blinked back tears as she looked at the team. 'I would never do that. Not in a million years.'

Sorcha got up and put her arms around Maggie. 'Of course you wouldn't. I know you couldn't do something like that.'

Maggie hugged Sorcha back. 'Thank you. I'm glad you believe me.'

'I do too,' Ella said. She looked around the table. 'We all do. Don't we?'

They all nodded and Catriona got up. 'Why don't we take a break and have a cup of tea?' she suggested. 'Maggie looks as if she could do with a cup, and so do I.'

Maggie smiled. 'Thank you, Catriona. A cup of tea would

be heavenly.' She sighed deeply and looked at the others. 'I hope I can still work with you on the campaign?'

'Of course you can,' Ella said. 'We need all hands on deck. Even more now that we know what we're up against. A big American company with lots of money.'

'I just talked to someone at the county council,' Sorcha cut in. 'She said it looks like they're very much for the building of the hotel. Job opportunities, economic boost for this remote rural area, blah, blah.' She closed her laptop. 'Looks like we're losing this fight.'

'We can't give up,' Ella said, picking up her phone. 'That botanist student friend of Fintan's has just arrived, I heard. He's gone up to the headland to do some digging around and will let us know if he finds anything. And I'm going to contact An Taisce to see if they can do something.'

'An Taisce?' Maggie asked. 'You mean the National Trust of Ireland? I thought they only dealt with heritage and buildings and such.'

'No, they also deal with the environment and biodiversity. A kind of watchdog in that area, actually. Should have thought of that earlier.'

'But what can they do?'

'They could do a lot,' Ella replied. 'If they find that the area is worth protecting, they could get onto the EU Commission and get this stopped.'

'That's a brilliant idea!' Maggie clapped Ella on the back. 'You clever thing.'

'It only just came to me,' Ella said. 'I was clutching at straws, I suppose, but you never know.' She got up from the table. 'I'd better go. I promised to meet Rory for a late lunch at The Two Marys'. Will you be okay here on your own for a bit?'

'Of course.' Maggie laughed and pointed at the basket where Jessie's puppies were whining and snuffling and crawling around, wrestling with each other. 'I'll babysit while Jessie is having a break outside. But I'll leave before Brian comes home. I don't want to get in his way.'

'Why?' Ella asked. 'I thought you and Brian... So fabulous that you found each other at last.'

'How did you know?' Maggie said, blushing. Then she sighed. 'Yeah, well, it hasn't worked out the way you think. He seems to believe I knew what Paul was up to, so nothing happened except a few angry words.'

'What?' Ella exclaimed. 'The stupid eejit. How could he possibly think you knew and didn't tell anyone? That makes me really cross with him.'

'Maybe he's jealous?' Sorcha suggested. 'That could make him mess things up in his head. I know what a crush he had on you when you were young, Maggie. And I think that crush came back when you arrived to spend the summer here. And then you seemed to be falling for Paul and went out on all these dates looking like a million bucks.'

'But I told Brian that Paul and I broke up when I came to see the puppies last night,' Maggie protested. 'And I'm sure he knew I was going to tell him how I felt about him, but then he was in the middle of researching the company and found out who ran it just as I was going to tell him. It happened so fast, I didn't have time to think. We had a bit of a row and then I left.'

They were interrupted by frantic barking outside and then Brian entered with Jessie and Bella in tow, both jumping up at him. 'What a welcoming committee,' he said. 'Hi, Ella. Are you staying for lunch?'

'No, I'm off,' Ella said. 'You two need some space, I think. Bye, Brian, we've done some great work this morning and we think there's a glimmer of hope. I'll be in touch, Maggie.' Ella waved and disappeared out the door.

'Me, too,' Sorcha said as everyone rose from the table and gathered up their things. 'We'll leave our notes here and pick up again tomorrow. We might have some good news by then. See you, Brian.'

Everyone else said their goodbyes, leaving Maggie and Brian looking awkwardly at each other.

'What was that all about?' Brian asked and put a paper bag on the table.

'Ella thinks we have to play the environmental card,' Maggie replied. 'She's getting An Taisce on the case.'

'Could work,' Brian agreed. 'I brought lunch from The Wild Atlantic Gourmet. Spring rolls with crab. There's enough there for two.'

'I thought you wanted a break from me,' Maggie said, still standing at the table.

He looked blankly at her. 'I did. But then...' He sat down suddenly. 'Let's talk. I was being stupid last night and didn't think it all through properly.'

'Okay,' Maggie said and fetched two plates from the cupboard over the sink along with two glasses and a jug of water. Then she sat down opposite him. 'There. Lunch and talking.'

'Lunch first. I'm starving,' Brian said and took a spring roll out of the bag. 'Help yourself.'

They ate in silence for a while, avoiding each other's eyes, until Brian finished his last bite, took a sip of water and wiped his mouth on a paper napkin. 'Right,' he said. 'Now we can talk.'

'About what?' Maggie asked, wanting him to speak first before she said something that would ruin this moment. Their relationship seemed suddenly so fragile that even one false note could wreck everything.

'Us,' he said. 'You must know how I feel about you.'

'I'm not sure,' she said. 'I thought I did, but after last night...'

'I was jealous,' he said. 'I had this image of you and him together and I saw red. I didn't know what had happened between you during those dates.'

'Nothing at all,' Maggie declared. 'We just had dinner and went on outings and stuff like that. He took me to posh restaurants and we had lobster and champagne and all kinds of fancy food, which I now realise was a way to seduce me into accepting an offer. But I won't go into that right now. We talked a lot but nothing really important was said. He told me a lot of things about himself but never asked about me. Then last night... he told me something that made me realise what kind of person he is.'

'But you were going to spend the night with him? Wasn't that the plan?'

'No,' Maggie said. 'That was never the plan. Not for me anyway.'

'Are you sure?'

'Of course I'm sure!' she said hotly. 'I had a fleeting attraction for him, but that was all. I would never have gone that far. Something stopped me from liking him that much.'

'What was that?'

'He wasn't you,' Maggie said softly. 'I couldn't help comparing him to you when we were together and he always lost. Do you know what I'm saying?'

'I think so,' Brian said. 'Maggie, I'm not very good at expressing my feelings, but I want you to know that I'm in love with you and have been since you walked into my practice that day at the beginning of the summer. It blew my mind to see you again after all these years. And then we became friends and you seemed so happy here with me and the dogs. That made me love you even more. But I never dreamed you would ever feel the same.'

Maggie sighed, tears welling up in her eyes. 'Oh, Brian, I do. Of course I do. When you said last night you needed a break and I thought you thought... well, you know. It broke my heart.'

'I'm sorry. I didn't really mean what I said. I was very tired.

And you were upset after breaking up with Paul, I suppose. Even if you weren't in love with him.'

'I was, but not because of us breaking up,' Maggie said. 'He asked me to...' She stopped. 'I'll tell you about that later. I was so shocked when you told me he was the head of that company,' she continued. 'And you seemed to believe I knew, which upset me a lot because of how I feel and how you...' Maggie laughed. 'I'm not doing a good job explaining, am I?'

'You're doing a crap job,' Brian said, with a grin. Then he rose and pulled Maggie up from her chair, wrapping his arms around her. 'Are you trying to say that you're... I mean, that we could...'

'That's exactly what I'm saying,' Maggie replied, hugging him close. 'Brian,' she mumbled into his chest. 'I feel the same for you. I love you and your dogs and the house and everything about you.'

Brian's eyes lit up and he hugged Maggie tighter. 'Oh,' he said. 'That's...'

'Isn't it?' Maggie said softly as she touched his face and their lips met in a first, shy kiss. And then they pulled apart and smiled at each other and then kissed again, for real this time, long and tender, while the old clock on the wall ticked, the kettle boiled and the puppies snuffled and sniffed and whined and Maggie's heart felt as if it was going to burst with happiness.

This is it, she thought as she relaxed in Brian's arms and looked into his brown eyes. *This is what was supposed to happen. This is the karma that brought me here, to this man who is so right for me.*

Later, sitting on the sofa in the large living room, they talked. Maggie told Brian all about her final date with Paul and what he had suggested.

'Holy Mother,' Brian exclaimed. 'What a weirdo.'

'He said he thought we'd learn to love each other in time,' Maggie said. 'But that's not how it works. You don't *learn* to love anyone, you just do, whatever happens or whether it's right or wrong or convenient.'

Brian kissed her hair. 'Yes, that's so true. I didn't plan to fall for you. I had forgotten about that old crush but then here you were, thirty years later and just as lovely as before. Maybe even lovelier.'

'And you had grown into this handsome hunk.'

'Ah sure, that was just accidental.' Brian put his arm around Maggie. 'Can't understand how yer man could say those things to you. How he didn't fall in love with you all over again.'

'His business is his first love, I suppose,' Maggie said, putting her head on his shoulder, cradling her cup of tea.

She looked around the room where a whole wall was taken up with a large bookcase crammed with books. A mahogany chest of drawers beside the fireplace held a multitude of framed photographs and the faded Donegal rug covered the wooden floor. The sofa where they were sitting stood beside the window where she could still glimpse the overgrown garden through the French windows. This house was a little run-down and scruffy but with a warm, beating heart she had always felt when she came here as a child. Brian was on his own here now, but his love of animals and people kept the flame burning and the homely feeling going. It needed a little love, and some spit and polish, but it was still such a lovely house to come back to. 'I love this room and the whole house,' she said. 'It's unique.'

'It's a mess,' Brian said with a laugh. 'It needs a lot of work. I do have plans but I haven't had time to do anything about them yet.' He looked down at her. 'What about your plans? What happens now?'

'I want to have the rest of the summer with no plans,' Maggie replied. 'A summer with you. Then, who knows? Can we just *be*, do you think? For now? Enjoy this... us, Jessie's babies and work on the campaign? It's only the end of June. I have another two months' holidays.'

'Sounds good to me,' Brian said. 'I could take on a locum and have some time off, too.'

'That would be great.' Maggie paused. 'Tell me,' she said. 'Why did you help me find Paul? I remember you said that it was important for me and for you too.'

'I thought it would get it out of the way. I wanted to see if the two of you would fall for each other again and then I could give up all hope and close that chapter, before I got in too deep. Like ripping off a plaster or something.' He shook his head. 'Sounds really silly, I suppose.'

'No, I understand what you mean.'

'I also thought that it might make you happy to see him again. You looked so sad and hurt when you came here at the beginning of June. I wanted to see you smile again, no matter who you were with. And I thought you looked a lot more cheerful when you started seeing him.'

'Paul made me feel good about myself, I'll give him that,' Maggie admitted. 'He made me feel pretty.'

'You are pretty. I hope I make you feel that, too.'

'Oh, even better than that,' Maggie said and kissed Brian's cheek. 'Paul made me feel beautiful. But *you* make me feel loved. That's much more important.'

They stayed there for a while, chatting, until nearly dinnertime and they both realised they were hungry again. 'I don't suppose you have any food?' Maggie asked.

'No lobster, I'm afraid,' Brian replied, getting up. 'But I could do sausages and chips, if that would be okay. I might even have a tin of baked beans somewhere.'

'Sounds like a feast,' Maggie said and jumped up. 'Come on, I'll help you.'

They went back into the kitchen, where Jessie and the

puppies had gone to sleep and Bella had wandered in and settled on the floor beside them. The black cat slunk in between their legs and jumped up on the fireside chair while Brian rummaged in the fridge and Maggie found a big cast-iron frying pan in a cupboard. Then they fried sausages, cooked chips in the oven and warmed the baked beans, eating the meal at the kitchen table, talking about old times and new and simply enjoying being together.

Maggie smiled at Brian and felt a surge of joy as he smiled lovingly back at her. Sausages and baked beans had never tasted so good. Could life be more perfect?

23

The following morning, as thick fog enveloped the bay, and the training session on the beach was cancelled, Maggie decided to tidy up and prepare the guest room for Orla's visit the following week. If Brian found a locum, they would be going away for the weekend, which she was looking forward to. Then Orla would arrive on Monday and would stay ten days.

Maggie had a whole list of things for them to do, which also included Brian. She couldn't wait for them to meet. She was sure Orla would take to Brian very quickly. It felt important to introduce Brian to her children and that way make him part of her life even more. And her parents would be so happy for her when they heard they were together. This could mean a great way to reunite with her whole family eventually. But what would happen to their relationship when – or if – she went back to Dublin? That little 'if' had just popped into Maggie's head as the thought of leaving Sandy Cove made her feel very sad. But how could she stay? She loved her job and the school in Dublin where she was teaching – and those young people who had become so dear to her. But they would leave school next year only to be replaced by others who she had yet to meet. It suddenly didn't seem so important to go back. If she could find a job in this area...

That job as swimming coach in Cahersiveen the girls had mentioned might be a possibility. Maggie decided to send her CV to the school, even though they would be closed for the summer holidays. That way her application could be the first one they got, she thought hopefully while she made up the bed in the front bedroom, the one her parents had slept in. And now Orla would sleep here and wake up to the sun shining on the mountains.

Her thoughts were interrupted by the doorbell and she glanced out the window and saw Brian's SUV parked outside. What was he doing here this early? She ran down the stairs as fast as she could to find out.

'Hi,' Maggie panted, flinging the door open. 'What's up?'

Brian didn't reply but stood on the doorstep looking at her, grinning. 'I just had a call that will make you very happy,' he said.

'Oh?' Maggie stepped aside. 'A call? From whom?'

'Sorcha. Fintan just called her with some news.'

'Good or bad?' Maggie asked. 'Come in and tell me about it.'

'I just told you. It's very good news,' Brian said, his face breaking into a smile as he followed Maggie into the kitchen. 'Fintan's friend – the botanist who was up at the headland doing some digging – thinks he has found something that will help. In fact, it could solve the whole problem.'

'Found what?' Maggie turned around. 'Tell me!' she exclaimed. 'I know it has to be something amazing, the way you look.'

'Hang on,' Brian said, taking his phone from his pocket. 'I'm waiting for a text message.' His phone pinged. 'Aha!' he said and picked it up. 'Here it is. *The* Vertigo angustior *narrow-mouthed whorl snail*,' he read out loud.

'Huh?' Maggie said, staring at him. 'What's that?'

'A very rare snail that is close to extinction. It appears that it lives up there in the boggy area of the headland. If that area is drained, the snail will die out and the species will be lost forever. Fintan is going to send a report to An Taisce and they will go to the commission in Brussels. It's all about the ecosystem and biodiversity.' He looked triumphantly at Maggie. 'It'll be a while before all this is over, but we'll win this in the end and the hotel project will be scrapped. How about that, then?'

'That is the best news I've had for a very long time,' Maggie said, hugging Brian. 'Sandy Cove is saved. Hooray!'

'The best news I had was when I heard Paul O'Sullivan had left,' Brian said, kissing Maggie loudly on the cheek. 'But this is a close second.'

Maggie smiled. 'One has nothing to do with the other, but I'm flattered.'

'Anything to make you happy.'

'Can we name one of the puppies Angustior after the snail?' Maggie asked.

'A bit of a mouthful, but why not? And here is another bit of news, talking about puppies. Darina's coming to my house tomorrow to pick one of them.'

'Do you want me to help with that?' Maggie asked.

'No, that's not necessary. She said she'll come early tomorrow morning. I'll deal with her.'

'Rather you than me,' Maggie said. 'I find her a bit tricky. You never know what she's going to say next.'

'Neither does she,' Brian said, laughing. 'I have a feeling she just says whatever comes into her head and then she's surprised at how people react. But you just have to take her the way she is.'

'Hmm. That's not always easy. But I suppose now that she's

changed her mind about the hotel project, we'll have to be nice to her.'

'Until she stirs up trouble somewhere else,' Brian said.

'I know.' Maggie smiled at him. She loved his easy-going ways and how he was so accepting and forgiving. But in his job he must meet all kinds of people and have to deal with a lot of strange situations. She thanked her lucky stars yet again that they had found each other.

'How about the weekend?' she asked. 'Have you found someone to replace you?'

'As a matter of fact, I have,' he replied. 'I spoke to a nice woman this morning. Grace Coffey. Just qualified and looking for a job. She's coming down on Thursday and if I hire her, we can go away for the weekend. How about some hiking on Mount Brandon? And then we can stay at a B&B in Castlegregory and have dinner at one of the little fish restaurants out on the Maharees. Walk on the beach in the evening, see the sunset. How about that?'

'Does this mean I'll be spending the night with you?' she asked.

'It could,' he said, looking suddenly a little awkward. 'If you feel we're ready.'

'Do you?' she asked, turning her back to him to make tea at the stove.

He touched her shoulder. 'I do. But if you don't feel...'

She twirled around to face him. 'I couldn't think of anything nicer,' she whispered.

Brian looked at her for a moment. He took a deep breath. 'I love you, Maggie,' he declared. 'I don't think I've actually said those words to you before. I said I was in love with you and then we've kind of danced around it for the past few days.'

'I know.' Maggie stood rooted to the spot, the teapot in her hand. 'It's lovely to hear you say it.'

'I couldn't stop myself.' He looked at her for a moment. 'What about you?'

'I feel very much the same,' Maggie said. 'I think I even told you a few times.'

'I know, but I wasn't sure.' He paused. 'Because you never said anything about what you're going to do when the summer's over. If you're going back to Dublin, then that makes me think this is just another summer romance to you.'

'Oh, God,' Maggie said, alarmed. 'Of course. I never thought of that. I should have said...'

'Said what? That you're going back to Dublin at the end of August?'

'No,' Maggie protested. 'I should have told you that I'm sending off my CV to the secondary school in Cahersiveen. They're looking for a swimming coach. And then I thought I'd look around for other fitness-related jobs.'

Brian's face brightened. 'Are you sure?'

'Of course I'm sure,' Maggie nearly shouted. 'I love this village. It has made me so happy to be here and to be part of the community. I want to stay here for good. With you. I'll let my house in Dublin and send my notice to the school there. That's my plan.' She drew breath and looked at him. 'Please, Brian, will you trust me? And believe in yourself too. You're the only, the most ideal man for me,' she ended.

His whole heart was in his smile as he looked at her. 'You're amazing.'

'I know,' Maggie said, laughing. 'I just want to say one thing before you go.'

Brian's phone pinged. He glanced at it, frowning. 'Sorry. I'm afraid I have to be off. A sick calf up the mountain road. I don't even have time for that tea you're trying to make. I'll call you later, Mags.'

He was gone before she had a chance to reply. Maggie put

the teapot on the stove and ran after him. 'Hang on, I haven't finished,' she shouted as he was about to get into his car.

He turned around. 'What?'

She came closer. 'I love you too,' she whispered in his ear.

'You do?' Brian looked deep into her eyes and then he wrapped his arms around her so tight she nearly stopped breathing. 'Well, that's the best news I've had for a long time.'

'You must have known.'

'I hoped you did.'

'Shut up and kiss me,' she ordered.

'Right here? In public? Where anyone could see us?' he asked, glancing over his shoulder at Saskia and Lydia, who had just appeared around the corner.

'Yes,' Maggie said. 'I want everyone to know.'

'We do already,' Lydia called. 'Go on, you fool. Kiss her!'

And then he did, long and hard, while Saskia and Lydia whooped and clapped.

Maggie pulled out of Brian's embrace and beamed at them. 'You know what? *This* is what was meant to happen. How stupid I was not to see it. Susie said it was karma that led me here and I thought it was so I would meet Paul again and we'd fall in love. But it was Brian I was meant to meet and fall for. It took me a while to get that, but now I do.'

'Karma wins again,' Ella said. 'Oh,' she sighed, 'I love happy endings.'

'Not an ending,' Brian corrected, his arm around Maggie. 'But a happy beginning.'

EPILOGUE

Mad Brendan's memorial bench was inaugurated on a cold crisp day in October. The sky seemed bluer than ever and the ocean lay like a mirror across the bay. Maggie, dressed in a down jacket and jeans, walked hand-in-hand with Brian to the incline at the end of the main street, where Brendan used to sit, watching the world go by and chat to anyone who sat down beside him. His worldly wisdom was well known, but also his sense of humour and acerbic comments on politics and people in general.

A compromise had been reached and the colour of the bench decided. The seat was bright green, but the back was painted a light blue with a motif of seagulls and wildflowers surrounding the plaque that said:

In fond memory of Brendan O'Shea, a philosopher and political analyst second to none. Missed but never forgotten.

Peace had been declared in the Tidy Town Association after the news that the planning application of the hotel had been turned down. The area was now a nature reserve as not only the rare snail had been found, but also a number of protected plants, including a very rare orchid, unique to Kerry. After that, everyone breathed a sigh of relief and nobody was in a mood to pick up the fight about the bench. During a good-humoured meeting everyone agreed to the compromise, even if it meant that the colours would clash. But now that Maggie saw the bench all newly painted, she realised that the green and the light blue went quite well together.

'Green like the grass and blue like the sky, just as in real life,' she said to Brian as they stood with the others and admired the bench.

'Looks really nice,' he agreed. 'And Ella's designs are beautiful.'

Mick O'Dwyer had been given the task of cutting the ribbon – green and gold, the colours of Kerry – and his speech, as he held the scissors, brought a tear to everyone's eye.

'I am honoured to inaugurate this fine bench in memory of one of Sandy Cove's best,' he said. 'Brendan was a real character and a true blue, standing up for what was right and never shirking from his duty when, as a young man, he worked with the mountain rescue team and helped support the oldest and most vulnerable around here. When he was too old and frail to work for the community, he would sit here and chat to tourists, enjoying telling them tall tales and making them laugh. I used to sit down with him often, as did many of you, just to have a good old chinwag and get his take on everything that was going on. He had an eerie talent for predicting what was going to happen and was the best storyteller known to man.

'I will sit here now and then and chat to him like before, as I know he is looking down from the heavens and smiling at us. I'm sure there is a star up there in the sky that shines especially bright on a winter's night when we're all struggling with what-ever life throws at us. Brendan will never be truly gone from this village. His spirit lives on in all of us who were lucky enough to meet him. So, I now declare this bench open and available to all. Please sit here now and then and look out at the ocean and think of Brendan and all he did for us.'

Mick cut the ribbon and everyone clapped, some surreptitiously wiping their eyes. Then there were drinks to celebrate 'everything', as Nuala put it as she announced the first drink was on the house. So a huge crowd gathered at the Harbour Pub and it turned into a party that lasted until late in the evening, even though it was the middle of the week.

'But hey,' Sorcha said as they stood at the bar, 'it's not every day that we get to inaugurate a bench, shed a tear for old Brendan and watch my future mother-in-law having turned as soft and mellow as a marshmallow. What happened to make her so sweet all of a sudden? She has even offered to pay Fintan's university fees until he graduates.'

'Oh, I think she has realised that with you, she's getting a family,' Maggie said. 'And maybe she has changed her ways since the whole hotel project collapsed. She was initially for it but then changed her mind when she thought about how it would damage the environment.'

Sorcha shot Maggie a suspicious glance. 'Did someone talk to her about me?'

Maggie shrugged. 'Maybe someone did. But why knock it? It's a win-win for you and Tom, isn't it?'

'Of course. And you still being here is even more of a win-win for me,' Sorcha said. 'Just looking at Brian's happy face makes me smile every day. I hope you don't regret quitting your job.'

'Not at all,' Maggie replied, looking lovingly at Brian. 'I know I'm here for good, so it made no sense to take leave of absence. And I love my new job in Cahersiveen. I think it was the fact that the local team won the biathlon at the end of August that swung it for me.'

'And you're going to run keep fit classes at the Wellness Centre, I hear,' Sorcha said.

'Who told you?' Maggie asked. 'We haven't worked out the schedules yet.'

'Oh, we saw you go in there to talk to Cormac,' Sorcha replied. 'And then Helen O'Dwyer said something about new fitness classes starting up soon, so I put two and two together.'

'She'll be torturing you all three times a week,' Brian filled in. 'But you know what she's like. Can't sit still for a minute.'

'It keeps me out of trouble,' Maggie replied. 'Otherwise I'd be torturing you.'

'Whatever makes you happy,' he said, squeezing her hand.

'*You* do,' Maggie said, feeling the usual dart of happiness as Brian smiled at her. She was so at home and at peace here in this village, with this man.

The rest of the summer had been wonderful with Orla arriving and staying in the cottage for a little over a week. They had explored the area and Maggie had shown Orla all her favourite places and told her all about her childhood summers with her family. Orla had liked Brian instantly and they all spent many fun evenings together at the old farmhouse. Maggie had taken on the task of redoing the rose garden and planted herbs in a plot near the kitchen. And when Orla left, Maggie moved into Brian's farmhouse, even though she had nearly a month left on the lease of the cottage. But it made no sense to live separately as they wanted to be together as much as they could. Jason did, however, find someone to rent the house for a few weeks so all was well.

Maggie sent a letter of resignation to the school in Dublin and put her house up for rent through an agency. She didn't want to burn all her bridges, and decided to keep the house for her children should they want to move back to Dublin. In any case, it felt good to keep the property as an asset and extra financial security. The rent gave her a small income, which was fine for now, as her salary on both her new jobs would keep her finances afloat. At the moment, she was too busy to contemplate getting a full-time job as the house and garden and the dogs took up a lot of her time. They were doing up both the kitchen and living room and Maggie did some of the painting and decorating herself, which she found hugely enjoyable. Brian's mother had been around and they had spent some happy hours together planning the repairs and redecorations, 'Auntie Mo' having her own ideas about how the house should be spruced up.

Paul had not been in touch after that last date and, as far as she knew, he hadn't come back to Ireland, although Maggie had heard on the grapevine that the office in Killarney was now up and running and that they had started building a hotel complex on the other side of Waterville. 'Rather there than here,' she had said to Brian, feeling relieved she didn't have to have anything to do with Paul anymore.

'Great craic, wasn't it?' Brian said as they arrived home in his battered SUV.

'Fabulous,' Maggie agreed. 'I love impromptu parties like that.' She opened the door, ready to get out, but Brian put his hand on hers.

'Let's have another party soon,' he said. 'Something fun and different.'

She turned to look at him, his face illuminated by the headlights. 'What kind of party?' she asked. 'Can we talk about that when we get inside?' she added with a shiver. 'It's freezing. And the dogs are barking like mad inside. They must have heard us arrive.'

'Never mind the dogs,' Brian said. 'We'll go inside in a minute. I want to say something to you.'

'What?' Maggie said, laughing. 'You look strange. What is it?'

'I want us to get married,' he said.

Maggie stared at him in surprise. 'You do?'

'Yes,' he said. 'I know you're not that hung up on marriage vows, but I am. I want us to be a real couple, a "Mr and Mrs" kind of couple, not this modern rubbish of you being my "partner" and all that. I want to have a wedding with all the "until death do us part" stuff in a church with our families and our mothers crying and then a fantastic party where everyone gets drunk and disorderly and the whole village sends us off on our honeymoon having tied old boots and tins to the car.' He drew breath. 'But maybe that's not something you'd like. If that's the case, we'll forget what I said and carry on—'

Maggie silenced him with a kiss. 'Be quiet for a moment, will you. Give me a chance to reply.'

'Okay. So reply, then,' Brian urged. 'What do you want to do?'

'I want what you want,' she said. 'All of it. I know I'm probably too old to be a bride and I never thought marriage was that important. But what you said makes me feel so incredibly happy. And you made it sound so beautiful. So yes, let's do that. Let's be a boring old Mr and Mrs and let's have a church wedding with all the trimmings and the mammies crying and the party and the honeymoon. Nothing would make me happier. But...'

'But what?'

'I don't want to be engaged. I just want a fabulous wedding, but not before Sorcha and Tom are married at the end of this month. Can we do it at Christmas time, do you think? Then we could go to some winter wonderland for our honeymoon, like Austria, which I've heard is stunning at that time of year.'

'I'll go wherever you want,' Brian declared, kissing Maggie.

'Right now we need to go inside,' Maggie protested. 'Just listen to the racket in there. Those dogs are so spoiled.'

'Okay,' Brian said and reluctantly let go of Maggie. 'I

thought snogging in the car would be so romantic. Let's go inside and spoil those dogs some more, then.'

Maggie laughed. 'You're such an old softie,' she said as she got out of the car. She started to walk to the front door and then stopped for a moment to look up at the starry sky, where the glittering band of the Milky Way was clearly visible. It was so cold her breath came out in a plume of steam as she spoke. 'He's up there,' she said. 'Brendan, I mean, looking down at us and smiling.'

Brian put his arms around her from behind and followed her gaze. 'I'd say he's happy to see us together like this.' He let her go and started to open the door. 'But now we have to go inside and get warm. How about a mug of cocoa in front of the fire before bed?'

'Sounds heavenly,' Maggie said.

And then they stepped inside to the light and warmth of the old house, where the dogs greeted them as if they had been gone for weeks rather than a few hours. Maggie picked up Molly the puppy, who started to frantically lick her face. Maggie smiled at Brian. 'I can't wait to be your missus. Then I'll feel truly at home.'

'But this house is already your home,' Brian said as he helped her take off her jacket.

'No,' Maggie said. 'Home for me is where *you* are, wherever you might be.'

Brian smiled. 'I feel the same.'

Then they spent the rest of the evening in front of the fire in the living room, sitting on the old sofa drinking cocoa, the dogs at their feet.

Maggie looked at the flickering flames and cast her mind back to all that had happened since she returned to Sandy Cove, and then further back, to her relationship with Dermot. She began to realise that she had held on to the memories of her romance with Paul for far too long. It had been the real reason she hadn't wanted to marry Dermot, as deep down, she had somehow hoped Paul would come back and they would reignite the flames of their young love. It had been a foolish dream that could never have been realised. But Paul had led her to Brian, who she knew was the love of her life. She wanted to marry him and never leave his side. During this journey, she had come to realise that love was not about the past, but the present.

It's not about who I was, she thought, *but who I am right now, right here, with the right man.* She put her head on Brian's shoulder and closed her eyes. Her dream of true love had finally been realised, in a much better way than she could ever have imagined.

A LETTER FROM SUSANNE

Thank you for reading *The Lost Promise of Ireland*, which I so enjoyed writing. If you want to keep up to date with my latest releases, just sign up at the link below. Your email address will never be shared and you can unsubscribe any time.

www.bookouture.com/susanne-oleary

I hope the book swept you along to the beautiful south-west of Ireland that I love so much. While I wrote this story, the pandemic was still with us, but there was a light at the end of the tunnel, and now life is slowly going back to something close to normal. But perhaps we will have a new normal from now on? In any case, I hope reading my book cheered you up, wherever you are in the world.

I would really appreciate it if you could write a review as I love feedback from readers. Your take on my story is always so interesting – and even surprising sometimes. Your comments might also help other people discover my books. Long or short, a review is always helpful.

I also love hearing from my readers – you can get in touch on my Facebook page, through Twitter, or my website.

See you soon again in Sandy Cove!

Susanne

www.susanne-oleary.co.uk

facebook.com/authoroleary

twitter.com/susl

instagram.com/susanne.olearyauthor

ACKNOWLEDGEMENTS

As always huge thanks to my editor, Jennifer Hunt, for her never-waning support and hard work to make my books shine. Also all at Bookouture – always such a delight to work with.

My husband, Denis, deserves an extra enormous hug and thanks for all he does for me, and all my family and friends who are there for me and let me talk about my writing without yawning or even the slightest eye-roll. With all these wonderful people in my life, I feel incredibly lucky.

Last but not by any means least, I want to thank my readers for your kind messages and comments. You are the reason I keep writing and your enthusiasm is my best inspiration.

THANK YOU!

Made in the USA
Las Vegas, NV
09 September 2023

77330169R00142